SUSAN LUTE

The Little Tea Room on River Road

A Wally Creek Novel

Contents

Preface

Sometimes, love doesn't go according to plan.

Sage Dawson loves her job as a cruise director or did. When her current guy (Shipmate, Gordan Simen) turns out to have feet of clay, a broken heart takes her back to Wally Creek and the comfort of her grandparents' loving support. What she gets instead is the house she grew up in as they take off for a new life in Arizona, four seventy-something tenants who have a plan of their own for her future, and Luke Marshell, a sleek, polished, uncompromising businessman who, for some reason she can't fathom, is convinced she's after his great-uncle's retirement fund.

Under other circumstances, Luke would be any girl's dream guy, but not Sage's. The man is an uncompromising workaholic and not user-friendly. The only thing worse than getting surprised by a sneaker wave on the way into the dock is standing by doing nothing while her heart makes another disastrous mistake.

Chapter One

"Goodbye room," Sage Dawson said out loud, snapping a picture with her beloved camera of the opened suitcase and boxes on the narrow bed. Grams had given her the Rebel when she turned twenty-one. "Hopefully, when we see each other again, I'll be an engaged woman."

Her grandparents were like that. They loved to mark her milestones with memories that stayed forever. Hence the camera. Over the years since then, she'd used it as instructed and taken photos of all the places she'd visited. But there was one thing they couldn't give her. She squealed inside, bouncing lightly on her tiptoes. *That* she would take care of herself. Okay, yes, in today's fast-paced, modern world, she admitted it was a little old-fashioned to look at romance and love like a Hallmark movie. Some might even say it was naive. Not Sage.

Holding out her left hand, she imaged a shiny, diamond engagement ring on her finger as she spun in a circle in the close quarters. The ring didn't have to be big. It just had to promise that the one who put it on her finger and his love would be there forever. And that passion would light her way until she was an old lady. Her heart would still beat in anticipation on that faraway day, as it did now, for the man sitting next to her on the porch swing of the house where they'd raised their children. The same man would sweep her off her feet every day they were together, aging side by side.

Gordan Simen, her fellow shipmate, and explorer was that man. He didn't blame her for not being a good cook. He appreciated her love of plants and gardening when she had the chance—even though for now, that garden had to thrive in community plots or in colorful ceramic pots wherever the Emerald Star docked. And he seemed to appreciate her willingness to go on any adventure with him at the drop of a hat.

The best news yet? With the Emerald Star in port to get a quick facelift, it was the perfect time to take that long-delayed trip home to introduce her man to her grandparents and her favorite place in the whole world—a little town in the foothills of the Cascade mountains, Wally Creek. Why she hadn't taken him there yet was still a bit of a mystery, but she was about to rectify that little omission.

Stopping in the middle of the cabin, she swallowed back the nerves threatening to capsize her hope. Being afraid wasn't an option, hadn't been since the day Grams and Grandpa had taken her and Jack home to live with them. They would love Gordan as much as she did. As much as they loved her. She was certain that would be the case.

Taking a quick look around to make sure she hadn't forgotten anything, she closed the suitcase, zipped up her laptop case, and sealed the boxes. Gordan loved *her* . . . Sage Dawson. He'd even gone so far as to hint he wanted to merge their separate lives into one. Just last week, over an impromptu dinner at their last port of call, he'd taken her hand, and looking deep into her eyes, had said her persistent optimism and adventurous spirit were just two of the things that attracted him. He hadn't used that all-important L word, but the smile on his handsome face had been enough to make her feel wrapped in the one thing she wanted more than anything else. Her own special love connection.

In her world that meant a lot. Most men found her merely unrealistic and odd. Her mom, up until the day her parents died, had been a woman who only saw the very best in life and her daughter. No one but Grams and Grandpa understood that following in her mother's footsteps, seeing as much of the world as she could, and looking on the bright side as thoroughly as Amelia Dawson did, was how Sage kept the memories of her parents alive. It was thrilling that Gordan saw that in her too.

A grand passion like her parents had, and her Grams and Grandpa still had, wasn't too much to ask, was it? Yes, she knew it was a big step, introducing Gordan to her grandparents. A step she kept telling herself she'd waited to embark on because she wanted to make sure he would stick like glue through the tough times. Not that they'd had any disastrous situations to work through yet, but he hadn't made a fuss when she'd asked him to go with her to Wally Creek, where he knew he'd meet her grandparents. That was a very good sign.

"Here we go," she whispered and crossed her fingers.

Rubbing the sterling necklace Gordan had given her at the

start of their last cruise to Mazatlan—a delicate faerie in flight he'd said reminded him of his girl—Sage raced up the stairs to the main deck, making sure her hair was still in place. Gordan got that line between his brows, his only fault really, when the heavy strands sprung loose like a baby kangaroo freed from its mama's pouch. The tight bun at the back of her head should keep the thick ropes under control until the last of the passengers were waved off the ship.

Tugging her blazer into place over well-rounded hips, she took her spot on the opposite side of the gangway from Gordan. Catching his eye, she smiled. He didn't smile back but she wasn't surprised. He didn't like being distracted from his on-board duties.

Sage dragged her gaze away from her potential fiance. This part of the job she loved. The last goodbye as the Emerald Star's guests exited the ship with the best memories and a reason to book their next cruise, it was great. A job well done, if anyone asked her.

Mrs. Henders gave her a big scented hug. An octogenarian who barely reached Sage's chin, she'd transformed, with a little help from Sage and her staff, from one of the quietest, shy passengers to come on board in a long time, morphing like a butterfly into the life of the party. And she'd made new friends who all promised to stay in touch with Fran when they got home.

"Thank you so much, dear. You made this cruise the most fun I've had since before I lost my sweet Albert."

Sage hugged the older lady back. "So you'll come again soon?"

"You can count on it." Fran edged back and turned her head from side to side. "What do you think of my new hair?"

"I love it." She eyed the older woman with a smile. "That color—" a beautiful shade of rose pink over stunning silver white, "—is perfect for you."

Fran blushed and patted her short bob. "I had it done last night. I hope it's not too bold."

"Not a bit. Your granddaughter will love it." Sage lifted her camera. "Do you mind if I snap some pictures?"

Normally she left people out of her photos, but Fran, with her cheeks a lighter shade of pink than her hair, was so dang cute.

"Of course, you can." After Sage snapped the picture, Fran looked down and searched in her purse. "That reminds me. I made something for you."

"You didn't have to do that." Sage took several more pictures.

"I know, but I wanted to give you something as a thank you for making this trip so special." Fran held out a peach-colored square of tissue. "It's for your camera strap."

Sage unwrapped the fragile paper to find blue and green glass beads dangling on a thin wire. "Fran, it's beautiful. Thank you so much."

"You're welcome. I'd better go. Goodbye, dear." Fran's eyes twinkled as she waved her fingers at Gordan. "You kids these days aren't in a hurry to get married, but when I come back next year, I hope to hear that you and your handsome young man have set a wedding date."

"That makes two of us," Sage said with a quick laugh. Her heart squeezed as she imagined Gordan waiting for her on the upper deck where they'd agreed to meet when all the passengers were gone.

Clutching Fran's gift, she stepped aside, watching as the older woman made her careful way down the gangplank.

When she got to the end, a man dressed in a dark suit took her elbow to help her navigate the last step onto the dock. Impressed by his gentle manner as he threaded Fran's arm through his, Sage attached the dangle to her camera strap. After one last look at the two, she fervently hoped the older woman would make it back to the Emerald Star the next summer.

Heading for her and Gordan's pre-arranged meeting place, once she got there, Sage didn't have to wait. A brisk breeze played with her hair, and as she'd predicted, playfully pulled wisps free. He leaned on the rail. Seagulls squawked happily as they soared above his head in the baby-blue sky.

Fran was right. Gordan Simen was an exceptionally good-looking man. Slender and tall in his cruise staff uniform. Hair as dark as night. Eyes the color of rich chocolate. Some women had a thing for dark chocolate. Sage was one of them.

"Are you ready to go?" she asked, not working all that hard to keep her excitement under wraps. "We need to pick up my car before the lot closes."

"Actually—" Gordan hesitated. Finally, stuffing his hands in his pants pockets, he blurted, "—I'm not going with you."

It took a disconcerting minute for the words to penetrate her eagerness to get on the road. Was he kidding?

She searched the dark eyes focused on her face. "I don't understand. I thought—"

"I know. I'm sorry. You've been planning this trip for a while. I should have said something sooner."

He didn't sound all that sorry, just defensive, which was Gordan's way of placing blame elsewhere when he'd changed his mind about something. Another small, very small, tick not in his favor.

"You want to delay our trip?" Confusion morphed into cutting disappointment that spread through Sage's chest like wildfire. She couldn't breathe. "Has something happened to your mom?"

Gordan was an only child and very close to his mother. It was one of the many things she loved about him. It showed he could be counted on, even when life battered them with rough waves.

"No, she's fine. I'm sorry," he said again. "I'm just not ready to meet your family. That's a pretty big step." The charming eyes that usually laughed at her crazy ideas shuttered. "I got a call this morning from one of my college buddies. You've met Will. Anyway, a spot opened up on that Yellowstone River white water rafting trip he's going on."

Gordan had mentioned the trip when it was being planned, but all Sage heard was he didn't want to meet her family. How had she gotten on the wrong boat? "The rafting trip? How long will it last?"

"A week."

A sick sense that something bad was about to happen made her voice squeak. "And you'll meet me in Wally Creek after you return from the trip?"

"No."

"I see." But she didn't. The pit of her stomach churned. Hand on the rail to steady herself, she stepped away from the man she'd been so sure moments ago was The One. "Are you saying . . . " Hand shaking, she gestured back and forth between them. "This isn't going to work? *We're* not going to work?"

"We don't want the same things, Sage. You want a promise. A lifetime commitment."

"Of course, I do," she exclaimed, catching herself before the words turned into an incoherent shout.

Gordan gently took her hands. "I can't give you that. I love life on the Emerald Star. I love the spontaneity of passengers coming and going, and how a new group shows up at the beginning of each cruise. I love the different towns we dock in, the bars, the markets, meeting people who like exploring as much as I do."

She jerked her hands free and said with firm conviction, "I love those things too."

"You say that now, but deep inside, you don't." He shook his head, pity pushing at one corner of his mouth. "Look. I like you. A lot. But you have all these dreams in your head, and I'm not ready for a lifetime relationship or to be tied down in a small town that has no nightlife. Maybe that'll happen someday, but it's not what I want right now."

He was wrong. She loved life on the Emerald Star! She wasn't looking to 'tie him down' in a town where each day blended into the next. Wally Creek could be loads of fun. And what she wanted was just what she and Gordan had. It didn't matter where they had their grand romance, just that they had one. Could he blame her for thinking now was a good time to take their adventure to her hometown and include her Grams and Grandpa?

Gordan stepped back, the look in the eyes she'd thought so yummy, not at all focused on the future that had been her dream for a long time. Apparently, he could and did.

"The truth is, I don't want to live in a house with a mortgage, work a dull nine-to-five job, or be a father. Not for the foreseeable future, anyway."

You don't want me.

That's what he was really saying. For him, they didn't have that special passion. There would be no ring or grand adventure. Not with Gordan. Not today. Not ever.

Raising her chin, Sage fought the tears that burned her eyes. She would not cry. She wouldn't!

"Maybe I don't want permanent, either," she said with as much determined resolve as she could put into her voice. It was a lie, but at this point, who cared?

Gordan shrugged before taking another step away. "I have to go."

His unexpected about-face crumbled Sage. Hysterical laughter bubbled up in her throat, but the only sound able to get past the boulder lodged there was a snarky snort.

The sound of happy departing travelers fizzled.

Enough. She grabbed the necklace around her neck and yanked hard enough to break the thin chain. Thrusting the symbol of their relationship gone bad over the rail, she dangled the little faerie over the water.

Gordan lunged for the rail. "What are you doing?"

"Getting rid of a lie."

And pretending I don't want to push you into the water along with your stupid necklace.

"Come on, Sage. You don't want to do this."

"No, no. I really do." Quite the softball player in high school, she wound up and threw the necklace out over the water as far as she could. She finally lost sight of the sparkle of silver as it started its downward arc.

"That necklace cost a lot of money." Gordan's mouth, the mouth she'd enjoyed kissing so much, opened and closed like a confused fish. He shook his head. "I can't believe you did that."

"Believe it," she said in a strangled huff.

Leaning over the rail to see if there was any chance at all she'd missed her mark—not that she cared—the only thing she found was the man who'd met Fran. He still had a hand on the older woman's arm but was also pulling a cart that contained her luggage. At that exact moment, he looked up, then shielded his eyes from the bright sun over Sage's shoulder. She thought he frowned but she couldn't be sure. Anyway, who gave a flying fig?

She aimed a brittle smile at the stranger. When he dropped his hand, she still couldn't see his face, nor did she intend to hang around long enough to imagine his expression changing from curiosity into something more cringe-worthy. Pity. That was the last thing she needed.

She turned back to her now ex-boyfriend, but Gordan hadn't waited to say goodbye. Words stuck in her throat as she was treated to his retreating back. Her shoulders slumped. How could she have been so clueless? Curling her fingers into her palms, she dug her nails in until they became as numb as her heart.

~ * ~

After taking Gabi's grandmother to her condo and depositing her luggage in the bedroom, Luke Marshell drove straight to his place to get ready for Dara's gala. He looked in the bathroom mirror as he tied his bow tie, but couldn't stop seeing the glint of sunlight that bounced off something shiny, as whatever it was sailed through the air, a high fly down center field, after being thrown from the Emerald Star.

He hadn't seen where the object landed, and when he looked up, he'd only gotten a brief glimpse of an arm extended over the rail and fingers splayed wide open. The man who leaned over the rail, watched the bright object—jewelry perhaps?—arc into the sun, his posture stiff with horror.

A woman, her face surrounded by a fluff of dark hair and backlit by the sun behind her, briefly leaned over the rail next to the enraged dude. She retreated too fast for Luke to see her face, but he got the distinct impression she wasn't as horrified as the man to see the trinket disappear.

That was exactly why he'd put off getting into a committed relationship. While he grew the business, it wasn't easy to devote time to a girlfriend or to compromise with anyone other than his business partner. MR Investments was way more important than figuring out the demands of keeping a relationship on an even keel.

At some point that would change. Once he didn't have to spend so much time on the business, there would be plenty of time to devote to finding the perfect woman, court her, get married, have children with her, and then settle down with his new family on Mercer Island. He would have to get a bigger house, but that wouldn't be a problem. Mercer Island was the best place to raise kids. And houses did occasionally come up for sale. The schools were exceptional, and community-friendly. Having a home close to Seattle where he could be hands-on with MR Investments, while also close enough to an international airport, was an absolute must for his overseas expansion plans.

There was just one problem with that plan. Luke pulled on the sides of the black bow tie.

Business was where he excelled most. Relationships not so much. Except for the few that were important, like his Uncle Charlie, Gabi, Dara, and Fran, and occasionally, when they weren't in Coober Pedy, Australia, or somewhere in Europe teaching students, his parents. He hadn't met a woman yet who made the state of his heart more important than growing MR Investments.

Fortunately for him, he had plenty of time to eventually organize the rest of his life the way he wanted it to be. For the present though, that left him to focus all his energy on the here and now, which included acquiring Portman Technologies as a client. He was okay with that. With this small circle he called family, he didn't need anyone else.

An hour later, with his business partner, Gabi Rendal at his side, Luke strolled into the Glass Works Gallery on Pioneer Square in Old Town Seattle. He tugged on the sleeves of his suit jacket. "Do you see Portman anywhere?"

The social atmosphere of Dara's first big show had seemed the perfect place to introduce himself and his company to the CEO of Portman Technologies, but in hindsight, he wasn't so sure. Today was Dara's day, not his. Still, it was better than getting nowhere by going through Portman's admin assistant, which he'd already tried. Three times.

Luke scanned the gallery for the owner of the newest information tech company to take Seattle and the rest of the world by storm. "If we can convince Portman to come on board, you know what a deal with his company could do for us?"

"Which is why as soon as I heard he was coming to Seattle I sent him and his daughter an invitation to Dara's exhibit." Gabi slanted him a look. *Go easy, buddy.* "With Dara's permission, of course."

He and Gabi had gone to college together where on their very first day they'd become instant friends. Four years later, they'd graduated and started MR Investments with nothing to their names but their wits and an empty office.

Gabi was impressive in a green sheath that fell gracefully to her calves. No one would guess she was the best investment attorney in the business. Spiked heels elevated her to his chin. Brown, shiny curls flirted with her shoulders. There had been a moment back in college when he found himself interested, but it hadn't taken him long to realize she had her eye on a cute little pixie getting her art degree.

He looked around the gallery floor until he found Dara standing next to a display pedestal. She was discussing one of her best pieces—a stunning blue hummingbird in full flight—with a gentleman who leaned in to study the delicate flow of blown glass.

Gabi's eyes lit up. "There's Dara." She patted him on the shoulder. "Circulate. Have fun. And talk to the ladies. You never know."

"Whatever you say, partner."

She shot him one of her trademark don't-mess-with-me looks that had Luke raising his brows with a grin. Her lips twitched, but she was more interested in her wife than playing their familiar game of tit-for-tat.

That was his problem. He might have secret visions of someday having a wife and family, but at the moment, he didn't have time for 'you never know'.

Gabi crossed the gallery floor as she wound through the crowd and casually draped an arm across Dara Kane's shoulders. Dara owned Kane Glass Studio in Pearl Park near Central District right next door to her and Gabi's duplex.

Dara herself was as compelling as her art. Instead of her usual long thick gloves and protective heavy cotton pants, tonight she wore a slim-fitting cobalt pantsuit. Her black hair hung straight, like a waterfall down her back. On one wrist she wore her favorite bracelet with her and Gabi's names etched on a flat glass bead in Japanese Kanji.

Dara's exhibit spread like a crystal brick road across the main floor of the gallery. Blown, sculpted, and cast glass in the most astonishing colors showcased her passion in bowls, goblets, vases, and ornaments. Rightfully deserved, the gallery was saturated with hushed admiration as art lovers and collectors alike wandered through her stunning creations. His favorite was the snowy white owl she'd given him for his last birthday.

When the gentleman moved away, Luke joined Gabi and Dara. With a spurt of envy at the couple's closeness, he leaned in to place a brotherly kiss on Dara's cheek. "Looks like your show is a huge success, Princess."

Her dark eyes gleamed back at him. "Exciting, isn't it?"

"Very. Congratulations." He took her hand and gently urged her to circulate the room with him.

"Isn't that Mr. Portman over there?" Dara nodded at a tall, elegant, middle-aged man, with a young woman on his arm. They stood just inside the gallery entrance.

Luke and Gabi answered at the same time. "That's him."

They grinned at each other. That's why they made such a good team. Their minds traveled along the same wavelength.

Luke drew the ladies through the crowd. When they got close enough, Gabi held out her hand. "Mr. Portman. We're so glad you could make it."

They shook hands. Portman turned to the young woman next to him. "This is my daughter, Eliza."

After introductions, and with a nod of encouragement in Luke's direction, Dara took Eliza off on a personal tour of her show.

"This is very impressive," Portman said, slowly heading in the opposite direction around the room from the one his daughter and Dara had taken.

"Dara has an exceptional eye for bringing out the exquisite beauty of glass," Gabi agreed.

Anxious to pitch MR Investments to Portman, but waiting for the right moment, Luke hung back. He would only get one chance at this.

"I assume you invited me here to discuss business?" Portman asked, proving there was a good reason why the man had a reputation as an astute businessman.

"You've got this," Gabi mouthed when Portman got distracted with another of Dara's pieces.

Luke squared his shoulders. "We did, but we also hoped you'd enjoy Dara's show. She's an extraordinary artist."

Portman circled a majestic lion cast in amber glass that had caught his eye, taking in every angle of the stunning piece.

"While you're in town, perhaps we can set up another time to meet."

The older man's assessing gaze shifted to Luke. "I have to tell you, Mr. Marshell, I already have an investment firm I trust."

"Luke, please." He stepped into the opportunity Portman offered. "I know we can do better. I'd love to have more time to talk to you about my ideas."

It took a long, nerve-racking minute for Portman to agree. "I'll be in Seattle at my daughter's for the next three weeks. Have your assistant call my office to schedule a meeting."

"I'll do that. Thank you, sir." Luke pulled a business card from his pocket. He handed it to Portman.

"It won't be easy to change my mind," Portman warned.

Luke loved a challenge. He nodded. "I understand."

"Let me show you my favorite piece," Gabi inserted smoothly, as she cast Luke a satisfied smile. She led the way to a vase shaped like a graceful calla lily. Milky rose glass poured like a fall of water into crystal clear glass.

Portman circled the impressive vase. "This has to go home with me. I have the perfect place to display it in my London house."

Gabi laughed in delight. "I'm glad you love it. It's one of Dara's best pieces. The gentleman in the black suit over by that display case will help you with your purchase."

As Portman walked away, Luke pulled Gabi aside. "I think I'll head out." He looked around and found Dara and Eliza in a lively discussion over a stunning fluted red bowl. "How about I take you and Dara for a celebratory dinner after the show?"

Gabi's gaze followed him. The gentle smile he'd grown accustomed to seeing when she looked at her wife softened his partner's eyes. "She's worked hard for this success. I'm sure she'd love to celebrate."

They'd both worked hard. When he'd met Gabi in college, she and her grandmother were living on next to nothing in a rundown studio apartment. Gabi was smart and determined to graduate with her law degree. He'd tutored her in chemistry. She'd shown him, a lonely freshman who had retreated so far into himself that he had no clue how to find his way out, how to emerge from his self-isolation. It didn't take long for her to become the sister he'd always wanted.

Now he had a chance to open doors for her and Fran. And Dara too. Not that any of the ladies would ask. Gabi wouldn't hesitate to punch him in the arm hard enough to hurt him for thinking he was responsible for their future happiness. They weren't his only motivation for taking the company global, but they had been one of the seeds of his ambition in that regard.

"Did you know Fran has pink hair now?" He asked. Gabi's grandmother had a good time on her cruise.

"She sent me a picture." Gabi grinned. "She looks adorable."

"That's what I told her. Give me a call when you're done here. I'll meet you at Hayden's."

Gabi nodded but was already on her way across the gallery toward the love of her life. Dara and Gabi were lucky. Not everyone was. Like that guy on the Emerald Star. And Uncle Charlie. And him. They'd all crashed and burned in the love department.

Still, that small niggle of envy at Dara and Gabi's happiness struck a strident chord in his chest. Luke quickly muted the lonely sound. Except, there was something about the woman on that ship, her hair curling wildly in every direction, the bright sun highlighting the ends in teasing gold and amber—

Forget it, bub.

Love, the kind that sent a guy's heart soaring into the cosmos and back, took just as much time to nourish as molding his business. Someday, perhaps it would be his turn to get lucky. Just not with a sexy, angry stranger, whose face he couldn't see. A stranger he was sure he would never get the opportunity to meet.

Chapter Two

The drive to Wally Creek—all three hours and eleven minutes of it—was long and lonely. With a raging headache promising to erupt, Sage pulled into her grandparents' driveway on River Road well after dinner time. She turned off the engine and just sat there.

There would be no surprise for Grams and Grandpa. Or pursuing a wonderful life with someone she loved to distraction. She straightened her shoulders. All that was left was to look to the future just like she had after her breakup with her high school sweetheart, Danny Heartwell. With a name like Heartwell, you'd think he would follow his heart anywhere his girlfriend wanted to go. No, not so.

When she'd taken a summer job at Yellowstone Park after high school graduation, the first of many journeys she'd hoped they would make together, he decided to move to Georgia instead. And that was that.

Just like Danny, Gordan had left her to make his own future.

As exciting as her job was, and despite how much she loved it, over the last few months, she'd started to want more than living the life of a cruise director whose sole relationships were the shiploads of passengers who were entrusted into her care. She hadn't intended to give up her position on the Emerald Star. She was just tired of being alone, at least in her private life. Now, she wasn't certain she could go back.

Gordan had been perfect, she'd thought, easy-going and fun to be with. He loved the audacious cruise line life as much as she did. Seemed to enjoy spending time with her, the same as she loved being with the man of her dreams.

But, he didn't love her, did he? Not enough.

Love couldn't possibly be worth all this heartache. What it did though, was drop her off right where she was on the day she'd lost her parents. Heartbroken. Alone. Turning to her grandparents for solace like she had most of her life since.

It was obvious she wasn't the kind of woman guys saw as a lifetime partner. Instead, only appealing enough for a temporary, ordinary relationship. A tear finally found its way down her cheek, Sage banged the steering wheel with the palm of her hand. She hated settling for ordinary.

Give it a rest, girl. All you have to do from now on is remember . . . men are off the menu.

What really sucked was she didn't know if she was madder at Gordan for giving up on them before they had a chance to see what they could become together, or madder at herself for being foolish enough to lay her heart at the clay feet of the wrong guy?

Returning to Wally Creek towing a monumentally failed relationship behind her was not the way she had wanted to return home. Worse than that, everything of value she cared about was in the boxes in the trunk of her car. A picture of her and Jack with Grams and Grandpa when they were teenagers. Flowery pillows she'd picked up in Panama City that had made her laugh when she'd seen them in that quaint little shop. A statue of Tonatiuh, the Aztec God of the sun that usually lounged on her cabin desk next to her laptop. And the printer for her photos.

There wasn't a single unforgettable picture of her and Gordan, arms ardently wrapped around each other, in the box. That should have been a clue.

Grabbing her camera and the colorful, teal knapsack that passed for her purse, she whispered defiantly, "Breaking up with Gordan Simen isn't the end of the world, kiddo."

She wasn't the first woman to get dumped at the last minute. Nor would she be the last. Two or three weeks in Grams and Grandpa's company would ease the pain. It was another sign that she'd put her heart in the wrong hands.

After her visit with her grandparents, she'd go back to the Emerald Star. Only it would be under her own terms, her head held high, and if she ran into Gordan, which she would, she'd ignore the quitter. He'd just be background noise from her past. That was all.

Putting on her game face, she marched up to Grams and Grandpa's front door, glad to see nothing had changed. It was exactly as she remembered.

Thank goodness some things remained the same. Small strips of grass lined the walkway cutting between two small flower beds. Overflowing orange daisies bloomed. The same covered porch ran the length of the front of the white house. Three stories tall, counting the attic and not the basement, tall windows with green shutters balanced its charming appeal.

This was home. Her brother might want to be anywhere other than Wally Creek, but the small river town they'd moved to when she was in the eighth grade was the retreat Sage's hurting heart needed just now.

She took a deep breath. Who was she fooling? Even without her breakup with Gordan, Wally Creek would always be the place where her heart was happiest, and where she wanted someday to settle down and raise her family. How sad was it that she hadn't realized that was still her dream before her ex unceremoniously left her choking in his tsunami?

Sage knocked on the door. The next minute she was snugly wrapped in her grandfather's strong embrace. Grams squealed behind him. "Oh, my word! You're here! And just in time."

With a big grin, Grandpa let her go and she was engulfed in the vanilla scent that always came with Grams' hugs. Yup. She was definitely home.

She swallowed the lump in her throat. Man, she'd missed them. Too much had gotten in the way of returning to see them regularly. Her job on the Emerald Star. Gordan. Her stupid pride. Only wanting to come back when she could show the most important people in her life she'd found that special love, just like they'd found theirs so many years ago. Staying away for such silly reasons was never going to happen again.

Pulling back to study her grandmother's face, Sage didn't miss the splash of shine in the brown eyes that matched her own. "Just in time for what?'

"I'll get your bags." Her grandfather kissed her on the temple. "You're still driving the Sunbeam?"

She gave him the key and glanced back at the turquoise sports car. "Of course, I am. You gave that car to me for my sixteenth birthday. I'm going to keep it forever."

Before her grandfather could do more than grin at her fierce response, Grams linked arms and pulled Sage into the house where they ended up in the kitchen. "You didn't bring your young man with you?"

She didn't want to talk about Gordan's desertion, but what was the point in hiding the truth? He wasn't going to change his mind and miraculously show up in Wally Creek. Besides, she'd never lied to the woman who was more mother than grandmother. "He broke up with me, Grams."

Her grandmother's welcoming smile flattened into a straight line. "I'm so sorry. I know you liked that boy. Clearly, he had no idea he had the best girl in the whole world."

Sage hugged Grams tight. The waterworks tried to start up again but she wouldn't let it happen. "You're the best." Blinking the tears away, she silently pulled up her big girl panties and admitted. "I love him, but it turns out he doesn't want the same things I do."

Grams gently patted Sage's cheek. "It's normal to hurt when you lose someone you love. I know it might not make you feel better, but that old adage is true. Where one door closes another opens."

Sage wrestled back from her sense of failure. She even managed a wobbly smile. Doors opening and closing aside, she wasn't about to spend the next three weeks feeling sorry for herself or weeping on Grams' shoulders. "I'm just glad to spend the next few weeks with you and Grandpa before I have to go back to the Emerald Star."

Grams' brows drew together.

Grandpa poked his head into the kitchen on his way upstairs. "I'll put your things in your old room."

"I can do that Grandpa."

"Nope. I've got it."

Grams opened the fridge and reached in to shift things around. "Have you eaten? I think I have enough ingredients to make an omelet."

"That sounds great." Sage leaned on a stool at the breakfast bar. Fatigue rolled over her. "I'll help."

Grams hooted, "No you won't. You drove all the way from Seattle without stopping, didn't you?"

"I can do the dishes, then," she bargained. "When I stopped for gas, I got a power bar and some cashews at the mini-mart."

"You can't call that real food," Grams insisted, bringing eggs, milk, and shredded cheese to the counter. "I have your favorite tea. You'll feel much better with a hot cup of Oolong and home-cooked food in your belly."

"Thanks, Grams." Sage sighed. She *would* feel better. Nothing eased her troubles like being in her grandmother's kitchen. She leaned forward on the bar and propped her chin in the palm of her hand to do a little probing of her own. Grams had never been good at keeping secrets. "So, what's going on?"

Pulling a bowl from an overhead cupboard, Grams avoided eye contact. "Your grandfather has something he wants to tell you."

"After you're done eating." Grandpa stood in the doorway, his arms crossed over his chest. He leaned against the jam.

Grams raised her eyebrows at her husband. He grinned and shrugged. They were so dang cute together. That oneness was exactly what she couldn't seem to find, no matter how hard she looked. But thanks to Gordan, she knew what to do now. No more searching for some elusive man who wasn't waiting to be found.

"I'll hold you to that."

The eggs and milk Grams whisked together went into the omelet pan heating on the older model stove. When she finished her meal, Sage did the dishes as promised while she told stories of her most memorable passengers. When she finished, she followed her grandparents to the living room, taking her tea with her.

The main room of the house was her grandparents' favorite place. Rounding the corner into the cozy space, she saw why and couldn't help smiling when she found them sitting side by side on the couch near the fireplace—a dark blue sofa that had been around for as long as Sage could remember. They talked quietly, holding hands.

Photographs of their lives decorated the mantle. Pictures of Grams and Grandpa. She and Jack, with Grams and Grandpa, when their grandparents had first taken them in after the climbing accident that took their parents' lives. The four of them in front of the River Road house after they'd moved to Wally Creek. A picture of Sage when she'd first gotten her job as the Emerald Star's cruise director.

Getting comfortable in one of the matching tufted chairs on the opposite side of the maple coffee table, Sage cradled her warm cup.

Grandpa spoke before she could start to quiz them. "Your grandmother told me about your fella leaving you. Don't you worry. That boy wasn't right for you."

Sage sipped her tea before asking, "How do you know?"

"I just do," he reassured her with a gentle smile. "He was foolish enough to let you go."

"That's nice of you to say, Grandpa, but I thought he was the one. He ticked off all the boxes I was looking for in a lifelong partner."

"Falling in love isn't about ticking off boxes," he said, the words shrouded in quiet conviction. "Someday, you'll find a man who may tick off only the most important boxes, but he'll be perfect for you, and he'll be the love and passion of your life."

Her grandfather was the sweetest man, but Sage no longer believed she would find that guy. Even if he was out there, she wasn't willing any longer to go on a fruitless hunt. Her questing days were over. She had a life to live and other adventures to go on, even if they were by herself. And she wasn't about to waste years pretending there was a superhero on an equally fruitless search to find her.

Gordan was proof that this happy-ever-after thing wasn't as easy as her grandparents, or the memory of her parents, made it look. Still, she had to ask. "How do you suggest I go about finding this wonderful guy?"

As soon as the words were out of her mouth, she wished she'd bit her tongue instead.

Grandpa laughed. "That's a Grams' question."

Since she couldn't take the words back, Sage pulled her legs onto the chair, crossed them, and hugged a yellow paisley pillow to her middle. "Grams?"

More times than she could remember, she'd sat in this very chair, waiting with bated breath for her Grams' sage advice. It was one of those memories she would always hold close to her heart . . . family who was there whether she needed their opinion or not.

Grams leaned into Grandpa's shoulder as if there was no place she'd rather be. He sandwiched her hands between his.

"You've heard the story of how your grandpa and I met?"

"No, I don't believe I have," Sage said tongue-in-cheek, giving her best interpretation of a serious young girl, sitting on the edge of her seat, waiting to hear the best story.

Of course, she'd heard the story. A hundred times over again. It was the love story that spurred her own dreams for the perfect romance.

"Cute, young lady." Grams' fake scold couldn't hold her frown in place for long. "It bears repeating one more time."

"You met Grandpa at the beginning of your sophomore year of college. You were about to register for classes—"

"That's right. We both wanted to take Professor Riposa's Philosophy of the Ages class. Everyone did, but seats were limited. The professor insisted on small classes. I was looking at my course booklet instead of where I was going and bumped right into John."

"It was the other way around." Grandpa laughed. "I was so determined to get into Professor R's class I wasn't paying attention to where I was going. I'm the one who bumped into you, my love. You almost dropped your books, but I saved the day by taking hold of your arm before they fell to the ground."

"You did. And I looked into those sweet blue eyes—"

"We've been together ever since," they said together, then laughed.

Sage shook her head and asked, "So you're suggesting I go to college so I can bump into a cool guy?"

"It couldn't hurt." The dimple deepened in Grams' cheek. "But whatever you do or don't do, love *will* find you, Sage. You just wait and see."

"I'm not so sure about that." But it didn't matter. All she could think about was getting over Gordan. The girl inside, who'd put all her hopes and dreams in the wrong basket, wasn't about to get fooled like that again. "So, tell me about this surprise you mentioned."

"We're—" Grandpa started.

As usual, Grams finished. "—moving to San Antonio."

Sage straightened. "What? When?"

"You got back just in time. After we finish packing a few last-minute things, we'll be on the road bright and early tomorrow morning. At least we don't need to have Charlie empty the fridge." Grandpa wrapped his arm around Grams' shoulders. He snuggled her close.

"But why didn't you tell me you were planning to move?"

"We didn't want you to talk us out of it," Grams said softly. "You're not the only one who can go on an adventure."

"Who will take care of your house?" *I just got home.* "Did you sell it?" She leaned forward, arms on her knees. That would be, Sage didn't know, disastrous. And sad. And, none of her business, since it was their house.

"That's the surprise." Grams scooted to the edge of the couch. "The house is yours. It's all paid for, and we've already put the title in your name."

"But—" She sounded like a parrot who only knew one word. "What will I do with it? I don't live in Wally Creek."

Grams stood and circled the coffee table to kiss Sage's forehead. "You can do whatever you want, sweet girl. Keep it. Sell it. It's up to you."

"I don't understand." She was dumbfounded. Had she been so taken with Gordan, the fink, that she'd missed the whole conversation that had led up to their decision to move? "What are you going to do in San Antonio?"

"Grandpa and I have done well for ourselves over the years

with the cafe, but it's gotten to be too much work. We sold the business for a tidy profit to a nice young lady with a little boy." Grams tugged Sage to her feet and steered her toward the stairs that led to the second-story bedrooms. "The winters here make our bones cranky. We're tired of climbing stairs. And yes, we should have told you sooner, but we weren't sure we could make the move until we sold the cafe."

She tugged her grandmother to a stop. "How did I not know any of this?"

"The decision happened very fast. Rickie made an offer for the cafe out of the blue. The next thing we knew, we'd signed the papers." Grandpa placed a hand on Sage's shoulder. "We decided to give you the house so you'll have options. You won't always want to work for the cruise lines. The deed is upstairs in my desk drawer. Your desk now."

"But I love my job, Grandpa."

Grams cupped Sage's cheek. "Do you? Or is the Emerald Star just a placeholder until you come up with something that suits you better?"

Sage held her breath. She hoped that wasn't true.

Grandpa squeezed her shoulder. "Get a good night's sleep. Everything will look brighter in the morning."

Sage didn't think so but was too tired to argue or try to sort all the changes out before she went to bed. What she did know was that a good night's sleep wasn't in the cards. She watched her grandparents slowly climb the stairs. Grandpa protectively followed behind Grams, his hand on her waist.

They were leaving in the morning, and the house where she'd spent most of her teenage years all of a sudden felt big and empty and too much to handle for a single, thirty-two-year-old woman whose only immediate plan was to try and forget about a two-bit heart-breaker.

~ * ~

By the time Luke left Dara's show and crawled behind the wheel of his silver Camaro, it was late enough in the afternoon, he reconsidered spending some well-earned quiet time with his current book selection. Participating as a silent member of his uncle Charlie's Sunnybrook Book Club had its perks. The cozy mystery waiting on the chair-side table at his house held his attention more than most of the book club's picks. And the best thing was it gave him the opportunity, not that he needed the nudge, to stay in touch with his favorite elderly uncle. Great-uncle really, but Luke never felt the distance in their ages. Charlie was too spry. It took a lot to keep up with the old man.

Being a member of the book club also gave him a good excuse to take the time he wouldn't otherwise indulge in to break from the stacks of work on his desk that required his attention. Reading a chapter while he waited for Gabi's text, then quickly calling Charlie to discuss the book was tempting. Very tempting.

On the other hand, to get to the office, a turn right rather than left after crossing the bridge onto Mercer Island was all it would take.

When he was a kid, he'd heard a lot of stories about the time Charlie had spent in Paris at the Sorbonne University working on his postgraduate degree and how he would love to go back sometime and explore some of his old haunts. His uncle hadn't talked about it so much after he retired and moved to Wally Creek, but Luke had not forgotten.

It would be great to give the older man a chance to spend six months or more in France reliving the good old days. And he wouldn't mind accompanying Charlie. To experience the city through his uncle's eyes before he himself settled down would be extraordinary. Too bad now wasn't the right time.

That's where Portman Industries came into play. London was not that far from Paris. And if he could convince Portman that MR was everything his tech business needed, then the plan was workable.

With a heavy sigh, business won. He'd give Charlie a call in the next day or two, once he was sure he'd finalized the perfect pitch for Edward. He turned right after crossing the bridge and parked near his office. Settling in at his desk he went over his plan one more time. He was deep into it when his phone alerted him to an incoming text.

"Where are you?" It was Gabi.

"At the office."

Before he could text back to tell her he was hungry and that he'd meet her in fifteen minutes, she sent a second message. "Be right there."

Luke shut down his computer just as she walked through his office door. "I could have met you at Haydens," he said before he noticed that Gabi was alone. "Where's Dara?"

Gabi dropped into the chair usually reserved for clients on the other side of his desk. "Eliza commissioned a special piece for her home. Dara went straight to her studio. I couldn't stop her."

That was a very Dara Kane thing to do. Luke grinned. He wasn't beyond pulling the same stunt himself, pointed out by the fact that he was at the office late into the evening tonight, instead of at his house taking a load off while he waited for his partner and her wife to show up.

"So, are we going to celebrate without her?"

Gabi snorted. "Are you surprised?"

"Not really."

Gabi folded her hands across her lap. "That was good work today. Pat yourself on the back for a job well done. You should go see Charlie next weekend as planned."

He hadn't told his uncle yet that he planned to visit and while there, hoped to get in a day of trout fishing with the older man. He'd wanted to surprise Charlie, who shared his love of a day on the Wally River, then a fish fry for dinner.

Now that Portman was in play, that changed things. "I'll have to postpone the trip. I want to get the Portman presentation polished first."

"Okay, while you and Dara are eyebrows deep in work, I think I'll head home and indulge in a long soak in the tub." Gabi rose and walked to the door. "Just F.Y.I., Edward doesn't like being fought over like a prized piece of real estate."

"I promise, next time I talk to him, I'll have all my manners and charm in place."

Another snort was accompanied by a sassy finger wave. His office door closed softly behind Gabi.

Luke wandered over to the window. From the office's third-story vantage point, he had a clear view of the skyline on this end of Mercer Island, but he didn't see the splash of city lights as they started to twinkle like a promise in the blue skies turning to dusk. His mind was elsewhere.

Gabi was right. Sometimes he went after what he wanted with too much single-mindedness. He was aware his business style intimated folks. But he didn't want to leave anything to chance with Portman. Like all those years ago, after Charlie's wedding that never happened, and his own brush with almost marrying the wrong woman shortly after starting the company. The near miss hadn't impressed his parents, either.

Back then, he'd been young, and foolish, and he'd taken chances they never would have sanctioned. But he thought he was crazy in love, and because of that, he'd put his fledgling company, the one thing he'd done that had at least elicited his parents' interest, in jeopardy. From the vantage point of more experience and hopefully, some maturity, when he looked back on the whole episode, he recognized careless puppy love. He was more cautious now, determined to take his time making sure all the puzzle pieces fit nicely before he took any more unnecessary risks.

After his aborted wedding ceremony, Charlie stayed a bachelor, putting all his focus on his students and teaching career. Following in his uncle's more responsible footsteps, MR Investments and Luke's few employees had become his family. It was only more recently that he felt like something important was missing.

More lights blinked on. The scene at the Emerald Star flashed through his mind again, reminding him that though they might have elements in common, managing a growing business was not the same thing as managing a relationship.

He didn't like not seeing Charlie next weekend, but it couldn't be helped. When they went to France, there would be plenty of time to discuss books and spend some time walking along the Seine River talking about the one who got away . . . not that there had been many of those in his case.

Returning to his desk, he put the fiery woman from the Emerald Star out of his mind and went over his presentation one more time.

Chapter Three

The next morning, after a night spent in a useless attempt to follow her grandfather's advice, Sage finally stopped kicking around her blankets and got up. Her grandparents were already in the kitchen. Coffee was made. Bacon and eggs sizzled on the stove. Their excitement to get on the road was sadly palpable.

Fatigued from her sleepless night and from the fact that no matter how she looked at it, she couldn't find a valid reason that would change her grandparents' minds about going to Arizona. Just like they hadn't been able to change her mind when she was so determined to work for a cruise line that took her away to show her the world.

Could she blame them? Not really. So she claimed a spot at the breakfast bar. Grams filled a plate and brought it over with a steaming cup of tea, Earl Gray, this time. "Now that you're single again, I wish we had time to introduce you to Luke."

"Grams—" Unfortunately, she couldn't turn off her curiosity. "Who's Luke?"

Grandpa sat next to Sage. "He's Charlie's great-nephew. He's an investment analyst and lives in Seattle. A steady, successful, very nice young man."

"Kind, and good looking too," Grams interjected. "You would like him."

Grams always thought Sage would like all the guys. That Luke was related to Charlie was icing on the cake.

Charlie Brennan was her grandfather's best friend. Had been since the day he moved to Wally Creek after retiring. By that time, she'd already left home to find out what was going on out there in the world.

"Very funny, you two." Suddenly, not all that hungry, she nibbled on her bacon. "He sounds like another city boy. Not my type. Besides, I've given up looking for a steady guy. Or even a not-so-steady one."

"You can't mean that," Grams gently scolded.

"I do, Grams."

Her grandmother leaned against the bar, on the other side from Sage. "Well, in my estimation, what's been missing from your boyfriends is commitment."

Sage had thought Gordan was committed enough. She definitely would have been there for him, no matter what. "You're probably right, but that's a moot point now."

"We'll see," Grams' eyes twinkled with a spark that always indicated she had some kind of mischief up her sleeve. "I'm sure you'll meet Luke sooner or later."

"The steady guy?" Sage teased. "When did you say you guys were leaving?"

"Okay—" Grams laughed. "We'll let you find a man in your

own way. But you know, in the old days, arranged marriages were the way things were done."

"Haha. No, thank you."

An arranged marriage to a stranger? She couldn't even make a relationship work with a guy when they were on the same ship. Trying to make it work with one she hadn't met before the nuptials would be an absolute nightmare.

"Speaking of Charlie," Grandpa carried his empty plate to the sink, rinsed it off, and put it in the dishwasher. "He's going to stop by later today to ask for a favor."

Sage polished off her scrambled eggs. She had a soft spot for Charlie because he made her laugh. Every time she was in town he'd come up with some new scheme to keep her in Wally Creek. It'd become a kind of contest between them to see who won. Wally Creek or the Emerald Star and wherever her next port of call was. So far, she was the winner. "What kind of favor?"

"Has something to do with a fire at Sunnybrook Senior Living where some of the Sunnybrook Book Club members live. I'll let him tell you all about it." Her grandfather looked around, and patted his pockets. His gaze landed on the suitcases stacked by the front door. "Well, looks like it's time to get going."

Sage already missed them, but she would not show it. Not after all they'd done for her since her parents had died. Pasting a smile on her face, she walked them out to their Suburban. The car was packed to the brim with the things they wanted to take.

"Have fun getting reacquainted with the town. You'll be surprised by how much it's changed and how much it's remained the same. You might decide to stay," Grams said, hugging Sage tight.

Grandpa put the last of their luggage in the back seat. While Grams got in the car, he folded Sage close and whispered, "Take care, Granddaughter. Something special is waiting for you just around the corner. I'm sure of it."

Just because it was her grandfather making the wish, Sage crossed her mental fingers that he was right, then walked him to the driver's side door. "Let me know when you arrive in San Antonio."

"Grams will text." Grandpa gave her one last squeeze, then climbed behind the wheel. "I'm not fond of that texting."

The Suburban pulled away from the curb, taking her grandparents off on an adventure of their own. Grams' arm waved out the window until they turned onto the road that would take them south to the land of the Grand Canyon and red rock formations.

Wandering back into the house, she absently ended up in front of the fireplace. The photos stared back at her. No matter how much her grandparents encouraged her to, she didn't see how she could keep the house. For one thing, it was too big for a single person. Without Gordan. Without them. Taking up residence made absolutely no sense.

And even if she decided to keep the place, what in the world would she do with it? This house was made for a big family, which thanks to Gordan the deserter, wasn't in her future. At least not her near future. Besides, her rainy day fund wasn't nearly large enough to pay monthly expenses on a house of this size. Especially while she was away at sea.

A cheerful knock in a familiar bouncing rhythm spun Sage around. Relieved to have some company who would take her mind off her endless circling, she went to open the door.

"Charlie. You just missed Grams and Grandpa. They've already left." She backed into the living room. "Come in. Can I get you a cup of tea?"

"That would be nice, thank you." Her grandpa's best friend—hair gray, round glasses perched jauntily on his nose—was dressed for summer comfort in a short-sleeved, cambric shirt and well-worn denim pants. He followed her into the kitchen. "Actually, I had a nice chat with your grandparents and said my goodbyes yesterday. I came by to see you, young lady."

Sage filled the silver kettle that always sat on the stove with water and turned on the burner. "Grandpa told me you have a favor to ask?"

Leaning against the counter next to her, his hands clasped in front of him, Charlie's gaze settled on her face. "I'm sure you're aware that there are six of us who belong to the Sunnybrook Book Club. We meet every Wednesday night. Of course, now that John and Vanessa have moved, we'll have to do that virtual thing. There's just one small hiccup."

"What kind of hiccup?" She knew about the book club, and sometimes even read one of their monthly picks, but she wasn't an active member.

While she waited for the water to boil and for Charlie to clarify, sunlight streamed through the kitchen window warming the sunny, pale-green room. Sage pulled two cups from the cupboard above her and dangled a tea bag in each one.

"There was a fire in Sunnybrook's kitchen that spread toward the independent wing. Thank goodness no one was hurt, but there's a lot of smoke and water damage. It will take a while for the repairs to be completed. In the meantime—"

"That's awful." The kettle whistled, the sound similar to a

far-off train whistle. Sage poured steaming water into the waiting cups, then handed one to Charlie. They took seats in the living room.

"Bette, Lily, and Verne are at my place. I only have two bedrooms. It's pretty crowded."

Sage was starting to see where this was going. In its early heyday, Grams and Grandpa's home had been a well-known boarding house. There were six bedrooms and two bathrooms upstairs. Five of the bedrooms were empty. Very empty.

"I'd love to help, Charlie, but I have to sell the house. There's no way around it. I don't make enough money to keep it going when I'll only be here for a few days every four or five months." She took a sip of tea as she sorted through possible options. "I guess I could shut down the utilities when I'm gone." She shook her head. "There's the taxes. Upkeep of the landscape. Just those two are expenses I can't afford."

"We won't be here for long. Only long enough for the repairs to be done at Sunnybrook." Charlie put his cup on the coffee table. "You'd be doing us a huge favor. In return, if you go back to work," His blue eyes lit up. "We could help you out by paying rent. We'll be here to take care of the maintenance. And we'll keep an eye on the place while you're gone. It would be a win-win for all of us."

If she went back to work? Sage almost spit out her tea. "No, you will not pay rent. That's just wrong."

"Of course, we will." The corners of Charlie's mouth quirked up. "We'd insist. And you can't say no, because we're much older than you are and will get our way. It's one of the privileges of being considered part of the 'aging population.'"

Charlie wasn't wrong. That still didn't make it right to take money from the elderly. He was like her second grandfather.

How could she say, no to that sweet face?

Just like this. "I'm sorry, but I can't rent rooms to you."

He didn't even blink, just said, his smile growing bigger, "You don't mean that, young lady."

She was fighting a losing battle. Sage hesitated. Just for a second. Long enough to come to the conclusion that maybe having the four book club members in the house might not be such a bad idea. She'd never thought about being a landlord. That was one of those career choices she'd never taken the opportunity to pursue. Not that the possibility had ever presented itself. She considered it now and still wasn't excited to take on the job.

Her brother, Jack, on the other hand, if she could talk to him about it, would probably think installing renters was a smart idea. Passive income, he'd call it. He always had been the more practical one. And he and Charlie might have a point. Having someone in the house to keep an eye on things while making enough extra income to fund the house and its needs *was* smart.

And tempting. "How long are you thinking of staying?"

"A month? Maybe two? However long it takes for the rooms at Sunnybrook to be fixed." Charlie pushed his glasses up the bridge of his nose and smiled his big grin. "What do you think? We'd be good housemates. I promise. You won't even know we're here."

"I doubt that," Sage said, finally giving in. She laughed. "But I can't think of a good reason not to have you and the rest of the book club here. Especially since they need a place. But only temporarily. It'll give me time to decide what to do with the house."

There was one added benefit. She wouldn't be in this big,

empty house all by herself for the three weeks before she had to go back to the Emerald Star.

"The book club, eh?" Behind his glasses, Charlie's blue eyes sparked with humor. "Maybe you should start a business. Then you could stay in Wally Creek for as long as you like. Lots of young folks work from home these days."

"I'm not much of a businesswoman." Sage shrugged, then smiled back. It really would be nice to have a full house. "I do like that I can lend you guys a hand. When do you want to move in?"

"With all your experience with taking care of tourists, I bet you could come up with a small business that catered to customers looking for a good time." Charlie's cell rang. Pulling it out of his pocket, his whole face lit up. "If you'll excuse me, I need to take this. It's my nephew, Luke."

Before stepping outside onto the front porch, he sent her a quickly veiled, calculating look. "Don't worry. Everything will be alright. And I would love for you to meet Luke. I think you two would hit it right off. He started his business right out of college with practically nothing. I'm sure he'd have some good advice for your little startup."

What startup? What was the older man talking about? She knew that look. As long as she'd known him, Charlie had never been all that good at hiding what was on his mind, whether it was good, bad, or when he was up to no good.

Since there was no business idea, and she didn't want to hit it off with a stranger, even if that person was the highly acclaimed Luke, an introduction with the famous, or more likely infamous, man was exactly what she didn't want.

With a wink, Charlie left the front door open. Sage shook her head. His persistence must come with his age. When her grandparents got an idea in their heads, there was no stopping them, either. Their sudden move to Arizona and gifting her the house were prime examples.

She wandered to the kitchen to give Charlie privacy and to have a little scream inside her head. Why did her favorite people think she needed a man in her life? Why was she even questioning that? Because just a day ago, she'd thought the same thing. And look how wrong she'd been. They were all wrong. And honestly, miscalculating with Gordan wasn't a mistake she was eager to repeat. Ever.

A few minutes later, Charlie stuck his head in the kitchen. He cast her his trademark grin. "Is this afternoon too soon? Say four?"

And there she had it. She was back to reality. "Sure. Of course. That sounds fine."

"Don't worry about dinner. Verne will cook."

"Verne?"

"Yeah. You won't be able to stop him. He used to be a chef in the Navy and thinks he owns any kitchen he steps into."

Charlie waved as he left.

Hanging around in Wally Creek wouldn't be so bad. She could give Charlie and his friends a temporary place to stay. Make sure they were comfortable. Even have some fun with the older folks, her favorite generation. Together, the five of them could have their own mini three-week adventure. What happened after that would just happen.

And since Gordan, the wimp, was out of the picture, a break from foolish dreams was just what she needed.

So the decision was made. There would be no romance. Not with some elusive perfect guy who didn't exist. Not even the arranged marriage Grams had teased her about would become part of her new lease on life. It would be her, Charlie, and the book club, a troop of Alexandre Dumas' Musketeers, who would have some fun while they kicked up the dust together.

With that daring image in her mind, she took the stairs to the second floor. With the book club here, her life would be much easier. And she wouldn't be half of a couple trying to make compromises that the other half didn't feel any obligation to make.

Upstairs, she made up the bed in what used to be Grams and Grandpa's old room at the front of the house. She smacked pillows into place on the bed she never thought in a million years she'd be sleeping in, unpacked her bags, and shoved the boxes she'd brought with her onto the closet shelf.

With fresh June air coming in the windows to perk up her spirits, she aired out the other rooms, changed the linens, and dusted and vacuumed all the area rugs. When she was done, both bathrooms were sparkling clean and stacked with fresh towels.

Landlord duties might not be such a hardship after all. She glanced at the time on the bedside clock. If she was quick, she had enough time before her housemates arrived to open a bank account and get a safe deposit box where she could keep her legal documents.

Locating the deed to the house in her grandfather's desk as he said she would, she slipped the document inside her purse, and decided, while she was out and about, she'd stop in and see Em. Her best friend from high school had owned The Oak Hotel, a boutique bed and breakfast for several years now. Em would have more than enough tips to share about being a landlord, even a temporary one.

Her bank business quickly completed, Sage parked in front

of The Oak. A silver, vintage Camaro pulled in beside her Sunbeam. She had a thing for old cars, especially the model parking next to Annabelle. The Camaro was a sweet ride and a rare sight in Wally Creek, except during the classic car show that came annually to town. Not just anyone could afford such a beautiful ride.

A tall, dark, and okay, up close and personal, gorgeous city slicker emerged from the car. Sage would bet anything, from his starched, polished clothes he wasn't from Wally Creek. He'd left his suit jacket draped over the front passenger seat. His sleeves were rolled to his elbows. The button-down shirt and flawless slacks gave him an air of appealing confidence.

He was what every small-town girl thought successful city dudes looked like, but Sage didn't hold that against him.

If she hadn't just been dumped by Gordan, the defector, she might appreciate how the Camaro owner's dark hair curled in waves around his ears and down the back of his neck. She might have let herself fall headfirst into eyes the color of a clear Pacific northwest summer sky when they flicked in her direction, then lingered on her face, but she resisted. If she were in a reckless mood, she might even have introduced herself. Maybe flirt a little with the man who, like his car, was a little too sleek and shiny to be super comfortable. He couldn't possibly live in her small country hometown. He was definitely an out-of-towner.

Just in time, she stopped her lips from curling into a hospitable smile, broadcasting a message—*let me be the first to welcome you to Wally Creek.*

Do not trust this, this . . . top-shelf specimen. Don't forget— burnt fingers and all that.

Like Gordan, the . . . okay, this man was probably all bubbles and no substance.

"Nice car." The deep, inviting rumble in the stranger's voice stopped Sage from paying attention to her own sternly given advice. Especially when he didn't stop there. "How old is she?"

"My car?" Sage pulled her failing defenses firmly back into place. "Old enough. How do you know she's a she?"

He came closer. "Because she's a beauty. A Sunbeam, right? 1956 or '57?" he guessed, his interested gaze locked on her face.

Breathe, girl. Breathe.

Given what he was driving, of course, the guy knew his classic cars. An unexpected attraction washed over her skin. Sage took a step back as he rounded the back of the Sunbeam. He ran a hand gently over the turquoise finish.

Hadn't she learned her lesson with Gordan Whatshisname? Her ex had made her pulse skip, but even thinking he was her passion, she couldn't recall a single time when she'd been left breathless or flooded with a desire to indiscriminately throw herself into his arms.

Now that she'd had time to think about it, Gordan was . . . comfortable. And until he'd left her standing alone on the Emerald Star's deck, she'd thought they fit together like two halves of well-traveled shoes. She'd thought that was a good thing, but apparently, it wasn't.

"Annabelle is a '57 Sunbeam Alpine," she blurted, then wished she hadn't.

"You named a classic British car, Annabelle?" The slow swipe of his fingers across the classic's shiny surface scattered every coherent thought Sage could bring to bear. Goosebumps rose on her arms.

Before the mad pump of her pulse could make her do

something crazy or worse, stupid, she took another step back. Suddenly, her heel hit the curb. Arms windmilling as she tried and failed to catch her balance, she knew she was going down.

Just before she landed on hard pavement, strong arms wrapped around Sage. Twisting in mid-air, the man, who seconds ago had been ogling her Sunbeam, landed on the sidewalk, on his back, between her and the pavement. Her chest was squished against his, her imagination spiraled through impossible intimate scenarios. It only took half a second for her to recognize more than their chest matched up, all the way down to his toes.

She sucked in a deep breath and regretted it the second her chest pushed against his firm body. One brow raised, the spark in his eyes brightened with a lethal interest he didn't attempt to hide. When Sage took another breath, she was swamped by his scent of warm man mixed with an earthy summer day.

Sage Dawson! Less drooling and more action, please. Now!

She tried to move off the poor man but there was her knee, and his um— "I'm so sorry. Are you hurt?"

People who claimed love at first sight was a thing, needed a good stiff drink. *Lust* at first sight, on the other hand, was probably just a side effect of her recent rejection. The air around Sage went still. The sound of slow, local traffic dimmed.

"No harm done." His eyes turned a deep color of the sky, and lazy like a good chocolate martini.

Sage paused, elbows straight, the upper half of her body angled off his. "Have we met before?"

"I don't think so." He stared at her. "I would remember if we had." His gaze shifted to the space she'd created between them. "Maybe we should introduce ourselves." His voice graveled out before he cleared his throat. "I'm Luke Marshell. It's nice to meet you—?"

He aimed a smile at her that curled her toes. Supposedly, a girl could fall for a stranger straight out of the gate. She wasn't usually one of them.

"Sage Dawson." Realizing they were still locked together, she started to move. "Wait. Are you related to . . .?"

She didn't get a chance to finish. Before she knew what was happening, firm hands gripped her waist and lifted Sage from her prone position. He dropped her unceremoniously on her feet like a sack of potatoes that had suddenly gotten too heavy. If she hadn't been embarrassed earlier, she was now.

Reaching out to her rescuer to steady herself, this time it was Luke Marshell who was the one putting as much distance between them as he could. The smile that had knocked her socks off was nonexistent, the interest pointed in her direction earlier put on ice.

"You should watch where you're going," he said, his earlier earnest perusal gone. "If you're okay, I've got some business to take care of."

With that terse announcement, he left her standing there and headed into The Oak Hotel. Hopefully, her mouth wasn't hanging open.

"I'm fine . . ." Sage trailed off. For the second time in the space of two days, she was staring at the back of a man who couldn't get away from her fast enough.

Luke Marshell disappeared into Em's bed and breakfast without so much as a backward glance. So, not so charming after all. What was wrong with him? Her? Was her good-guy radar completely shot?

Sage lost it. It was unreasonable. She knew it, but couldn't stop herself, even if she wanted to. The guy walking away was about to find out he was not dealing with a flimsy rowboat that couldn't stand up to foul weather.

Shoulders back, chin up, she marched in after Marshell, scooting between the tall double doors as they closed behind Mr. No-manners-big-city-boy.

~ * ~

What was Charlie up to? Instructing him to cash in a significant amount of his stocks to create a small business grant for someone Luke had never met or even heard of before he'd talked to his uncle earlier that morning. It made no sense.

He couldn't just stand by and let anyone take advantage of his closest relative's kind heart. Dropping everything and giving Gabi explicit instructions regarding the Portman deal, he'd made the three-hour plus some minutes drive to Wally Creek in a lot less time than his GPS had said he would.

His appointment with Edward Portman was ten days away. That gave him time to check out what the heck was going on with his uncle, and without Charlie cluing into how concerned he was. At least not right away, anyway.

And then he met her. Or rather caught her.

From the thunk of sneakers following close behind, he had only a few seconds to decide what his next move would be before the beautiful owner of the classic car parked alongside his Camaro caught up. If he was a betting man, which he wasn't, he would wager money, not his Uncle Charlie's, that the sound came from the black and white Converse-style shoes he'd noticed Sage Dawson wearing when he'd bluntly plunked her on her feet.

At this point, he didn't need a public scene. He would never have guessed the lady making his pulse climb like a Yellowstone geyser was *the* Sage Dawson he'd come to investigate. How likely was that?

Walking away hadn't been his best move. His only excuse was that he hadn't been prepared to come face to face with the woman chasing his uncle's money until after he talked to Charlie. And he hadn't expected her to be a beautiful *young* woman who could sidetrack him from his mission if he let her. What he'd expected to find was a woman who was on the far side of fifty or sixty looking for well-padded pockets to make her life comfortable in her retirement years.

He lengthened his stride to get to the check-in desk before Ms. Dawson caught up to him and gave him a piece of her mind. If he ignored her, he might get lucky and she'd go away. No harm. No foul. At least not until he was ready to confront her on his terms. He usually wasn't that lucky.

"Can I help you?" The lady at the front desk was all professional in her dark jacket over a crisp white shirt.

Blonde hair, every strand in place, and finely drawn brows over tawny-colored eyes that looked at him with an intelligence he could appreciate, and normally would under any other circumstances, called out for a second look. He didn't often take the opportunity. But she had the appearance of someone who knew how to do business. And who might, in a polite manner he'd moments ago lacked, be willing to help ward off the dark-haired, brown-eyed scrapper he'd rescued from scraping her bum as she toppled backward over the curb. The same woman who stomped up behind him, her footsteps echoing a determination to storm up and rain all over his hasty retreat.

She'd been adorable and so warm, and a perfect fit, lying stretched out on top of his suddenly wide-awake body. It'd been a long time, longer than Luke cared to admit since his senses had gotten so worked up at the sight of a woman wearing a flowery dress that led his gaze on a lively exploration from soft, rounded shoulders, down a full figure with a dip at the waist and generous hips. Legs had peeked out from the flowing material as it flipped up in the light breeze. The sight had taken his breath away. He'd almost been too distracted to save the beauty from bodily injury.

Luke corralled his whirling thoughts. It wasn't likely that there were two Sage Dawsons in Wally Creek, so there was no point giving in to temptation before he figured out what was going on. "I have a reservation."

"Your name, sir?"

Gabi's ongoing advice for him to have fun and talk to the ladies he met hadn't worked out the way his partner intended. Yes, he'd flirted with Ms. Dawson but only a little. When he wanted to, he could score a seven or eight out of ten on Gabi's get-out-there-and-expose-yourself-to-the-possibilities meter, but mostly, it was just too dang complex. Like now.

"Luke Marshell," he said firmly, determined to unravel this knot, but only after he got to his room and took some time to regroup.

The footsteps behind him stopped. A throat cleared delicately. "Excuse me."

Luke pretended not to hear. It was cowardly on his part, he admitted, but he needed space to catch his breath.

"Very good, Mr. Marshell. All I need is a credit card." He focused on the desk clerk's request. She was very efficient and wasted no time, another thing he appreciated. Her name tag identified her as Emerson. He'd have to leave a good review on the hotel's web page.

A foot started tapping at his back. "Excuse me."

He took the key card and receipt from Emerson and listened carefully to her instructions so he could find his room. Unfortunately, his usual ability to concentrate on the project at hand and block out everything else was failing. If he could just put Sage Dawson off long enough to escape to his room.

Inhaling a breath, he stuck a smile on his face and turned to the insistent woman. He raised his brow at the finger poised mid-air on the way to poking him in the shoulder. Dawson immediately dropped her hand.

Wow. He could use that look of stubborn purpose pressing her lips together and the light of battle sparking in dark eyes working for him at MR Investments, not aimed at him while she took advantage of a sweet old man.

The desk clerk squealed. Her all-business manner suddenly gone, she whipped around the check-in counter and threw her arms around Dawson. "You're here! How long have you been in Wally Creek?"

The reason for his need to drop everything and come to this tiny, spit of a town to sort out his uncle's crazy scheme, cast him a quick hard stare.

This isn't over.

Then she closed him out and returned Emerson's exuberant hug with the same excitement. "I got in yesterday."

It'd only taken the woman two days to talk Charlie out of a big chunk of his retirement? Luke frowned. She was craftier under that pretty face than he'd thought.

Emerson leaned back. "And you didn't call me?"

Was Emerson involved too? Had he somehow—lucky him— managed to get a room right in the middle of the crisis Charlie had landed himself in?

"There's a lot going on."

No kidding.

Sage linked arms with the desk clerk. "Do you have time to talk?"

"Absolutely." Emerson waved over a younger version of herself coming out of what appeared to be a small dining room. The teenager carried a pitcher of water laced with sliced lemons. "Allie will watch the front desk."

Luke backed toward the stairs that supposedly would take him up to his room.

Glancing over her shoulder at him, Emerson smiled. "If you need anything, Mr. Marshell, call the front desk. Allie will help you."

Allie nodded as she poured the water into a tall, elegant dispenser on a sideboard near the stairs.

Unexpectedly bothered by how quickly Sage had set him and his beef with her aside, not that she knew she was the vortex of his problem, Luke stopped and watched the two head toward the dining room. If he could just be a fly on the wall during their conversation, he might learn a thing or two he needed to know.

"Did you hear my grandparents moved to Arizona?" Sage asked Emerson.

"Sure. They've been talking about it for a while."

"Why didn't I know they wanted to move?" Their voices faded as they sat at a table near a window on the far side of the room.

Was that why she was willing to take Charlie's money? Because her family wasn't here to help with her situation, whatever that was?

About to turn and take the stairs to his room, he hesitated.

Shoulders slumping, Dawson looked a little lost. Sudden sympathy built in his chest for the woman.

Luke frowned. He was here for one reason and one reason only. Protect Charlie and his retirement investments at all costs and without raising his uncle's hackles.

Breaking free of the unexpected affinity, he took the stairs to the third floor and his room at the end of the hall. It was a charming room that looked more like his master bedroom in Seattle than a hotel suite. When he'd checked, The Oak Hotel had top ratings. He could see why. The room was clean and inviting. One window looked out over a side street, while a larger one faced the front of the hotel where he'd parked. The elaborate large star of greens and blues that spread across the quilt covering a roomy queen bed and matching pillowcases was stunningly cheerful.

The room called to him to take a nap after the long drive from Seattle. He had no time for that. He tossed the key card on the desk and opened the window sash of the front-facing window before he settled in the cushy blue chair near the bed. Legs stretched out on the matching ottoman, he stared tiredly at the thin veil of curtains as they fluttered slightly in the breath of fresh air.

He had to unravel this grant thing before Charlie realized what he was up to. Easy peasy, right? Should be, but it was better that Charlie didn't get wind that his nephew and financial advisor hadn't gotten started on setting up the grant as ordered. His uncle was a stubborn guy. Once he set his mind on a thing, Luke had yet to see him deviate from that decision.

When he was a boy, his mother's uncle had always been there for his lonely great-nephew. Now it was Luke's turn to have

Charlie's back. He'd do whatever it took to protect the kind, decent, and yes, genuinely nice guy. If it meant becoming casually acquainted with Sage Dawson to get her to back off, he'd make the sacrifice.

Unfortunately, on their first meeting, he'd managed to raise Ms. Dawson's hackles. Big time and unintentionally, sort of, but still. Gabi would read him the riot act for the misstep when she found out. Orchestrating an acquaintance with the lady was one thing. He had no intention of letting an unaccountable attraction linger.

Dropping his feet to the floor, he went to the window. The traffic below was slow and meandering. He'd always been surprised that Charlie had settled in this small town. During his career as a university professor, he'd lived in all kinds of metropolitan cities. His last stint was in Portland, not a super-small city by any means, where he'd retired from the history department of the University of Portland.

The scene outside the window was too quiet for Luke's tastes. He couldn't wait to settle this grant thing and get back to the bustling comfort of Seattle. A movement down below caught his eye. Dawson crossed the street with Emerson. They parted ways at the opposite corner, Emerson going one way, while the lady who was at the epicenter of his problem went the other, then disappeared into what looked like a bookstore on the same block.

Now was as good a time as any to take advantage of the opportunity to approach Sage Dawson in a public place where she probably wouldn't want anyone seeing her come apart at the seams. Though earlier, self-control didn't seem to be one of her stronger skills.

Grabbing the key card, Luke dashed down the stairs to catch

up with the lady who, by her response when he'd protected her from her fall, didn't seem like she would be interested in an older man. But she had to be. Why else would Charlie suddenly instruct his nephew to use his retirement stocks to set up a secret business grant for a woman he knew nothing about?

Chapter Four

Luna's Books could have been transported straight from Charing Cross Road in London. The first time they'd dropped him off to spend the summer with Charlie, he and his parents had met his uncle at the surprising shop filled to the brim with books that could take a young child on adventures he'd only dreamed about. At the time, Charlie was teaching at Oxford University. For Luke, it had all been a new, exciting world where he didn't feel left on the sidelines anymore.

Luna's large windows displayed stacks and stacks of books. Taking up the storefront, they instantly took Luke back to that day. Luna's Books was painted in fading gold, scrolling letters on the center picture window. Like the London bookshop, a green awning that mimicked fish-scale siding hung over the windows and the barn-red door.

He pushed through the door. A bell chimed over his head as he looked for Sage Dawson. Luke couldn't help himself.

His business mind checked off the boxes he considered most important for the success of every thriving business. There were plenty of shoppers—book lovers no doubt—some carrying books clutched close to their chests, others spread along the bookshelves, still searching. Floor-to-ceiling shelves lined both sides of the sizable space. Brick walls peeked through evenly lined books. Cushy seating areas were scattered around the main floor, half-filled with small groups of two or three customers chatting or reading.

The bookstore made good money, which made him wonder what the owner had invested in her or his future. Remembering why he'd come into the place in the first place, he straightened and checked all the first-floor nooks and crannies. He didn't find Dawson.

At the back of the store he climbed a wide staircase leading up to the second floor, each step labeled with the names of famous authors, hand-painted on the step-fronts. Off the top landing, there were empty cubicles where a book enthusiast could easily spend all day researching or typing away on their latest masterpiece. Business-wise, it was a very smart addition. Luke would love to have a place like this to retreat to at his local bookstore on Mercer Island.

A short hallway opened into a room occupied by scattered tables and chairs, and more shoppers. Cushy seating lounged strategically around a colorful area rug in the middle of the room. The entire space was cozily lit by sunlight streaming through a bank of windows on the far wall. Shelved books were everywhere. It was a reader's paradise.

He wished he could spend more time exploring, but there was Dawson, sitting on the large, overstuffed couch, while a stack of books leaned against her lap. She was completely engrossed in the one she was reading. Light coming from the window behind her turned Dawson's hair a shimmering dark auburn. She was almost too pretty to be a scam artist. Not that he knew what a scammer should look like. He just had a gut feeling. And his gut was telling him he might have jumped to the wrong conclusion, thinking she was up to no good.

That didn't let him off the hook as far as his uncle was concerned. He still had to do his due diligence, because Charlie hadn't changed his mind about cashing in a good share of his retirement. Luke frowned. For a second, she kind of looked like—

Nah. He hadn't seen the woman's face and Wally Creek was a long way from the Seattle docks. The skirt of her dress hugged her calves, bringing back the memory of their encounter of the best kind. Earlier, when he'd broken her fall, all he could think about was how well they fit together, shoulders to toes. And when she went still— He hadn't been alone in the recognition that something other than sorting out a difficult situation was going on. From the spark lighting up her brown eyes, she'd felt the splash of sudden awareness too.

Not about to be taken in by a pretty face or a flicker of attraction, he quickly returned to the reason he'd come to Wally Creek. Charlie deserved his best efforts, except, in her summer dress, thick hair falling past her shoulders as she explored the book's pages, his gut chimed in again. Could she really be someone who would happily take advantage of a man three times her age?

It seemed like it. Unfortunately, sorting out this mystery wouldn't be as simple as he originally thought when he'd started up his Camaro to make the drive down to Wally Creek.

Stuffing his hands in his pants pockets, Luke wandered

around the room trying not to look like he was on a mission. Not an easy task since his gaze kept returning to the lady on the couch. He was in the fantasy section when he got close enough to glance casually her way as if he hadn't planned to run into her all along.

At the same moment, she looked up. It was perfect timing. He put on his most charming face. "Nice to see you again." Okay, that sounded not so charming, especially after how he'd behaved earlier. He tried again. "Do you mind if I join you?"

"Why?" She snapped the book closed and stared at him. The look she gave him silently challenged him to explain himself.

First, he had to come up with a believable excuse without telling her the real reason he'd plopped her on her feet and then walked away as fast as he could. Looking back on the whole episode, he really couldn't blame the lady if she wasn't ready to cut him some slack.

"I want to apologize." As an olive branch, that at least was the truth.

The guarded look in her dark eyes eased a little. She put the book on the stack beside her. Leaning back, she sighed softly. "I'm the one who should apologize. I didn't thank you for saving me from a very embarrassing fall."

"No need for an apology. I'm happy I was there to help." Also the truth. He couldn't have arranged a better first meeting. It just would have been better, if he hadn't been so surprised to find out the lady who had his pulse racing was also the same woman who had his uncle making changes to his financial accounts.

"Okay, well, thanks, just the same."

Luke winced at her unsure tone. *Way to impress the lady, dude.*

He sat next to her and picked up the stack of books. They were all about the art of drinking tea. "You have a passion for tea?"

"Yes." She didn't add anything more, just sat for a long silent moment watching him.

Luke mentally laced his fingers together and cracked his knuckles. When it came to uncovering whether a business was a good or bad investment, he wasn't known for his astute snooping skills for nothing. The same abilities should apply to uncovering the real person under a mask meant to hide the truth.

He put the books down. "I'm a coffee drinker myself. I would love to buy you a cup of coffee. Or tea, if you'd prefer."

Her eyes narrowed. "Why? You don't even like me."

Yup. The Lady was a hard nut to crack. She crossed her ankles and settled more comfortably into the couch. Her hesitation and the soft rustle of her dress against those distracting legs made it hard to concentrate on his mission.

When he was a kid and his parents were taking teaching jobs all around the world or running off to Australia, Charlie was his rock. The least he could do was repay the favor by keeping his mind on the game. "I'm hoping you'll give me a second chance."

The moment she decided in his favor, her chocolate eyes went even darker. Luke didn't welcome the sigh inside his chest that had him wanting to linger longer in Wally Creek than he'd planned. Getting tangled up in the wrong kind of intrigue would not accomplish his goal.

"I have to pay for these books." The still-guarded look she gave him was a good indication that while Dawson was prepared to let him buy her a cup of her favorite pastime, that didn't mean she was ready to open the door to a new friendship and let him in.

"All of them?" When she nodded, Luke collected the books, stood, and waited for her to join him. "Who makes the best tea in town?"

She finally smiled, a genuine smile that turned up the corners of her lips. Success. "That would be Emerson Finn."

"The lady behind the check-in desk at The Oak Hotel?"

Sage nodded. "The hotel is her baby."

"How long have you been friends?" He followed her downstairs to the cashier.

"Since eighth grade."

She made short work of paying for the books. Taking the cloth book bag that had sturdy handles and Luna's Books logo on the front from Dawson, he had one last question. For now. "How about having lunch with your tea?"

She didn't answer right away, but he wasn't about to let her change her mind, either. Hearing Gabi's voice in his head, he coaxed. "You can tell me about Wally Creek and I'll give you some fun facts about Seattle." He winked. Okay, that was taking things a bit far, but he continued nonetheless. "You might even want to move to the Emerald City."

Which realistically, would solve his problem. As long as she didn't take Charlie's money before she moved.

"I don't think so," she said, ignoring his small flirtation as she led the way out of the bookstore.

He didn't like going against his uncle's wishes, but he couldn't bring himself to give Gabi the go-ahead to draw up the grant papers without being certain Sage Dawson was as innocent as she looked.

By the time they were seated in the dining room of The

Oak, he had his priorities straightened out. And even though, against his better judgment, he was beginning to like the lady with the spunky attitude who loved classic cars and pouring through books at her local bookstore, it wasn't enough to make Luke change his mind. At the moment. He only had a few days to uncover the truth. He had to use the time wisely and not squander it by going all soft on the woman sitting on the other side of the table.

"You're from Seattle?" she asked politely, pulling her hair to one side. "What brought you to Wally Creek? Are you visiting family?"

His fingers suddenly itched to test the softness of the cascading locks. "Maybe I'm here to check out the town to see if it's a good place to start a business." That sounded plausible.

"Are you? What kind of business?"

Or not. She was a smart cookie, which meant he would have to be craftier and stick to as much of the truth as he could.

"I'm here to visit my uncle," he said and left it at that.

"Of course you are," she muttered, making his radar ping.

"Pardon me?"

"Nothing."

"Are you sure? I'm not hard to talk to." Questioning always went better when the person asking the questions got the someone he wanted information from was truthful about what was on her mind.

She glued her gaze to the menu. "Really. Nothing."

Luke arched his brows. Had he unintentionally alerted Sage that he was on to her shenanigans? Before he could explore the subject more with her, Emerson showed up at his elbow. "What can I get for you two?"

She looked up from the menu, but not at him. "I'll have a

Reuben."

"Same," he said to hurry this part along.

A slight frown formed between her brows. Emerson gave him a serious once over. "Fries or a salad?"

"Fries and a cola, thank you." Had Dawson told her friend about this weird thing with his uncle?

"Salad with ranch dressing for me, Em. And iced tea." Sage finished ordering.

Emerson nodded and headed for a door that Luke presumed led to the kitchen. His lunch companion leaned back, hiding her hands in her lap. "Did Charlie call you?"

Straight to the point. Luke liked that. They could get this whole debacle straightened out before they finished their Reuben's. "Yes, he did."

"I was afraid of that. I'm so sorry."

You should be, lady. "Glad to hear it."

It wasn't exactly the reaction he'd been expecting. He'd been expecting a woman all blustery and full of excuses, but Sage looked so earnest. Her apology made his job easier. He wouldn't have to make that call to Gabi after all.

Delicate brows drew together. Luke rushed in to clarify. "My uncle means well, Sage. His heart is in the right place—"

"Mr. Marshell—"

"Luke."

"Okay, Luke." She slowly unfolded her napkin and placed it in her lap. "I just want to make my situation clear."

"I'm listening." He leaned forward on his forearms. This was going to be good.

"I'm not looking for a boyfriend, no matter what Charlie told you. I just got out of a relationship, and no matter how much my grandparents and your uncle think we'd make a good match, right now I'm not ready to jump into another one."

He straightened. "You think I'm here to ask you out on a date?"

"Aren't you?" she squeaked.

"No! We don't even know each other." Luke clarified for the woman staring at him like he was a crazy man. "I'm not looking for a girlfriend."

Even if Gabi thought he should get himself one, Sage wouldn't be his first choice. She was too, by her own admission, unavailable.

"Good." Grabbing her glass, she gulped the water down before plunking the glass on the table. "My mistake."

What could he say to that? Fortunately, Emerson and Allie brought their food and drinks, giving him a chance to withdraw from the crazy conversation with his pride semi-intact. Wait until he told Gabi about this little fiasco. Meeting Sage Dawson had so far not been what his partner would call 'fun'.

What if her 'I'm not looking for a boyfriend' had been a clever ploy to distract him from the reason he'd come to Wally Creek? Well, it worked.

Emerson placed her Ruben in front of the woman whose cheeks were still splashed with pink. "Sage told me you saved her from a bad fall."

"I didn't exactly put it that way," his lunch, not a date, said lowly. Sage pointed a warning stare at her friend.

Luke couldn't help himself and said with a straight face, "I'm always happy to help a damsel in distress."

"How long are you planning to stay in town?" Humor lit up Emerson's expression as she leaned a hip against one of the empty chairs.

"I'm not sure." That part at least was true. "Maybe a day to two?"

Long enough to hunt his uncle down and talk his older relative out of giving away so much of his retirement. Then, he'd straighten Charlie out about this dating Sage thing, and make sure there was nothing else the older man needed before he went back to Seattle to make his presentation to Edward Portman. It was a tight turnaround but doable.

Emerson's gaze shifted over his shoulder. "I'd better get back to work. See you two later."

After she left to take care of other customers in the rapidly filling dining room, he turned his attention to his meal and the woman sitting opposite him.

"This is not a date," he said to make certain there was no confusion.

Picking up half of her sandwich, Sage said firmly. "I agree."

It was none of his business, but that didn't stop him from being curious. "So, what happened to the last guy?"

She stalled but finally answered. "He thought going white-water rafting was more important than the plans we'd made to see my grandparents."

She shrugged, returned the sandwich to the plate, and dropped her napkin on the table as she slumped back in her seat. A beam of light from the window highlighted her from behind. Luke suddenly realized why the lady felt so familiar. It wasn't because he was attracted to her, it was because— "So you tossed his ring into the water?"

"Necklace," She said with a huff of breath. Her gaze latched onto his. "How did you know?"

He could make up a story and say it was a good guess, or tell her the truth, which couldn't be worse than telling her about his suspicions.

Neither choice was a good one. And he was pretty sure she wouldn't believe he was a good guesser. "I was there."

"Just my luck." Pinking up more, she dropped her face in her hands, then peeked at him through her fingers. "That was you with Fran?"

"Fran is my business partner's granny. Gabi and Dara had an appointment they couldn't change, so I volunteered to pick up Fran." Sympathy got the best of Luke. "The jerk shouldn't have broken up with you in a public place like that."

She dropped her hands. "Hence the jerk's necklace ending up in a watery grave."

"Good for you. I think he deserved that." Luke raised a hand in a high five. The small sting of their palms automatically coming together sent a zinger up his arm.

She'd stood up for herself. That he could appreciate. Until her courageous self-confidence involved Charlie.

She finally laughed. A laugh as soft and soothing as the chimes in his mother's garden in Coober Pedy. "Thank you, kind sir."

And just like that Luke didn't mind playing Prince Charming to her damsel in distress. But before he got in any deeper, Luke made himself step away from the bewitching woman. It wasn't his job to help Sage find her smile. It was his job to find out more about the lady and what or who had given Charlie the idea of setting up a business grant for her in the first place.

"Tell me about your job," he said, a little too briskly, but maybe he'd find an angle there.

Her good humor disappeared. "I'm the cruise director on the Emerald Star."

How in the world had she gone from entertaining cruise line passengers and with infrequent visits home—from what he could figure out—to being matched up by her elderly family members and friends to a complete stranger? Yeah, he hadn't missed that little nugget.

"And you like being a cruise director?" While he waited for her answer, he dug into his sandwich. The Ruben was good. Better than the tale Sage was spinning.

"I love it. There's lots of variety. And the passengers are great."

Then why was Charlie giving her a grant? If it wasn't for his uncle's gag order, Luke would ask. "I'll bet you can't wait to get back."

When silence elongated from her side of the table, he looked up from his half-eaten sandwich. Sage had barely made it through half of a half.

A frown deepened between her brows. "I do love it, but I don't know."

"The stupid dude works on the ship too," he guessed, returning his unfinished Reuben to the plate. Here was his angle.

"It's not just Gordan. I love shipboard life." She looked up from her sandwich. "But I sort of inherited a house."

Luke cocked his head. "How does a person 'sort of' inherit a house?"

"My grandparents put my name on the deed. They said they wanted to give me a chance to explore my options."

Luke could read between the lines. They wanted Sage to have stability. He got the sentiment. Having a home planted a person's roots, which was why he'd bought the house on Mercer Island.

"When I'm working, I'm gone for months at a time." She rubbed her temples. "What am I supposed to do with the place while I'm gone?"

The real question was what was his uncle getting himself into? Luke prided himself on being able to read people. MR Investments would never have grown as much as it had if he couldn't. Sage Dawson was clearly a woman who found herself at a crossroads. Did she want to get off the boat? Had Charlie already told her he'd give her the money, making Luke's job that much more complicated?

There had to be another scenario where she could keep the house and not take Charlie's retirement money. "Won't your grandparents take care of it for you?"

"No," she said but didn't elaborate.

"You didn't grow up in Wally Creek, I take it," he persisted. Maybe the Emerald Star was her home, not Wally Creek. If all he had to do was encourage her to go back home to the cruise liner, that would be a simple solution.

"We lived in Portland before moving here."

"We?"

"My grandparents, my brother, and I." She picked up her sandwich. "Do you always ask this many questions when you ask a girl to have lunch and tea?"

Busted. "Blame that on my interest in investment opportunities. I have to ask a lot of questions before deciding if a company is worth investing time in." He shrugged, hoping she wasn't getting suspicious again. "Unfortunately, that means my conversational skills need some improvement."

Without talking to Charlie first, that was about as close to the truth as he could get. Polishing off his sandwich, he wiped his hands on his napkin.

Life, like the uncomfortable situation he currently found himself in, could be messy. Trying to discover where to stand between his uncle's instructions and a woman who half baffled and half intrigued him wasn't as easy as it should have been. No matter how he squared the numbers, Sage Dawson just didn't make sense.

He sat back, quickly searching for something that resembled normal conversation. "How about your parents? Don't they want the house?"

She motioned Allie over and handed the girl her plate. "Can you box this up to go?"

"Sure."

After putting her small backpack in her lap—so lunch and his gentle interrogation were over—Sage said softly, "My parents died in a mountain climbing accident when I was seven."

The punch of her loss hit Luke's gut. "I'm sorry. That must have been tough."

Her fingers curled into her napkin before her mouth formed into a determined smile. "It was a long time ago. After that Grams and Grandpa moved us to Wally Creek. We've been here ever since, until—"

"Until?" Without thinking, he reached across the table to hold her in place. He stilled her fingers and felt her disquiet reach his chest.

"Grams and Grandpa's last day in Wally Creek was yesterday," she said evenly.

There was something about Sage that insisted she wasn't the grasping woman he thought her to be. He just couldn't figure out where the disconnect was between that woman and the one putting on a brave face at the loss of her parents. If she was a bad person, his bad girl radar was having a hard time coming to that conclusion. If she was innocent in all this, and Charlie was just up to his misguided good deeds, his good girl radar was off kilter too.

His heart would ache for any child who lost their parents at such a tender age, but especially the woman staring at their linked hands. He might not have the warmest relationship with his own parents, but at least they were still with him. And he could see them whenever he wanted, as long as he had time for the hours-long flight to Australia, where they'd finally settled after all their years of moving around.

When Allie brought her take-home box, Sage pulled her hand free. She took out her wallet. Luke stopped her with a shake of his head. "I've got this."

"Are you sure?"

"Pretty sure," he smiled. "I asked you to lunch, remember?"

"I have to go." She grabbed her boxed food and took off. Stopping just before she left the dining room, she glanced in his direction before moving on.

Lunch hadn't been a total loss. He'd learned a lot more than he expected.

Chapter Five

B ack at the house, Sage finished getting the upstairs ready for her new housemates, but couldn't turn her mind off and just revel in the promised company Charlie and his friends would bring when they moved in later that afternoon.

Luke Marshell was not what she expected. Sure he was good-looking in a glossy magazine cover kind of way, with all that thick, curly, dark hair, intense blue eyes, and long dark lashes to match that hid what he was thinking.

She liked her men more transparent and had thought Gordan fit that description. He'd certainly had her fooled. She hadn't seen their breakup coming.

At least Luke wasn't pretending to be someone he wasn't. He was nothing if not the opposite of transparent. He didn't say so, and maybe that was the issue, but she got the distinct impression there was something he was hiding. Look at all the questions he'd asked. Not one of them was, *hey girl, want to go on a date?*

He'd treated her to a meal, which he was quick to assure her wasn't a date, but not once did he disclose anything personal about himself, except that he was business partners with Fran's granddaughter. That was quite a coincidence. What a small world.

Even after she'd told him about acquiring the house and her grandparent's move and her job on the Emerald Star— why had she babbled on like that? Still, he said nothing about himself. She was pretty sure that was a warning, in and of itself.

Luke Marshell, a big-city business guy, was not the usual man of adventure she was typically attracted to. Not that she would call what she was feeling when he was around attraction. It was more like . . . huh, she'd have to think about that.

Watch your step, girl. The guy is trouble.

He exuded confidence and wore it like an expensive suit he'd had especially made. Sage wished she had even a little bit of that self-assurance. Especially, after practically telling him her life story and then, stalling out at the touch of his hand and the flash of awareness that finally stopped her blathering tongue. Maybe she should be grateful for that.

Or not. He could keep his confidence and shiny business suit. What she wanted to know was, without a doubt or hesitation, what *she* wanted her future to look like. That future didn't include a man who didn't appear to have room in his life for fun. Not that he'd come right out and said that. And anyway, maybe being all business and no play was what Luke considered fun.

What was she thinking? It was no business of hers how Charlie's nephew lived his life. Like a stunning book cover, what lay underneath—a man dressed to impress his business associates, and by extension the world—was not her cup of tea. Still, the rolled-up sleeves showing off manly hair on his arms had been a nice touch.

Sage mentally gave herself a swift kick. She'd trusted Gordan. No matter how sexy the guy's arms and the rest of him were, she would not put herself in that position again. Not soon, anyway.

A dramatic sigh escaped just as voices filtered through the open window of her new bedroom. Saved by the bell, er . . . Charlie. And bless the man, he'd brought her new tenants as additional distractions. Sage moved closer to the half-open window to get a glimpse of her new lodgers, but from this angle overlooking the front of the house, all she could see was the top of the porch roof.

"What a lovely home," said a female voice that reminded Sage of the deep, firm vocals of Dorothy Spornak on The Golden Girls. When she couldn't sleep at night, reruns of her favorite show were her go-to for settling her restless mind.

A more chirpy voice added, "The gardens could use some more color, don't you think, Bette? Maybe some petunias and pansies?"

Fighting an upward twitch of her lips, Sage raised a brow. Grams had always been a minimalist when it came to gardening. And actually, she wasn't much better. Except for familiar gardens, she helped with when she stopped in southern ports, the only flowers she knew what to do with were the ones that required a vase when she brought them home from the grocery or small potted plants that were easily replaceable when they faded.

"Wait until you see the kitchen, Verne. You'll love it." That was Charlie.

"I'll be the judge of that," Verne, she presumed, grouched.

The expected knock on the front door had her dashing downstairs, curious to meet the book club friends. Especially Verne, who Charlie was so certain would take over her kitchen. Sage almost laughed. She wouldn't fight the older gentleman on the takeover. She'd be grateful. A good cup of tea she could handle, but cooking meals wasn't her thing. She knew how. It was just that she was more of a finger-food person. And when she wasn't on the Emerald Star with its banquet of foods, if she wanted something more substantial, like lasagna or homemade pot pies, that was what restaurants or the market deli were for.

She opened the door. "Hey, Charlie."

"Hi. Sage, let me introduce you to the Sunnybrook Book Club." Staying in serious mode wasn't one of Charlie's superpowers. The corners of his eyes crinkled. His whole face folded into a smile as he introduced the first lady. "This is Bette Lanley. Bette is the best seamstress in Wally Creek. And she likes to read cozy mysteries."

"Don't be silly, Charlie," Bette said firmly. Looking at Sage, she insisted. "I don't sew very much these days."

This lady really could have been Dorothy. She had the same short white hair with just a hint of curl, arched brows, and dark, serious eyes. She was tall and sleek, dressed in tailored pants and a flowing, rose-colored tunic top.

Charlie shook his head. "It's a shame you don't. It was only a few years back that you sold the clothes you made to that little shop on Birch Street. Maddie's, wasn't it?"

Bette's brows lifted. "You're losing your mind, Charlie Brennan. That was a long time ago."

"Still, such a special talent shouldn't be wasted," he insisted, earning a frown from Bette for his stubborn refusal to take his words back.

Smiling at the two bickering friends, Sage took the hand Bette offered. "It's nice to meet you, Bette."

Bette turned her back to Charlie. "You have a lovely home."

"Thank you." Almost immediately, Sage wished it *could* be her permanent home. But she'd already had this argument with herself and come to the conclusion it wasn't possible.

"It's very sweet of you to invite us to stay." The lady standing beside Bette surprised Sage with a quick hug. "I'm Lily Crane. My favorite books are cozy romances. And I'm a painter. Have been since I took my first art class in kindergarten."

Lily was the exact opposite of Bette. Her flowing knee-length, orange and yellow print dress took Sage back to the seventies. Not that she was alive then to wear the bohemian clothes herself, of course. She'd seen pictures. And the style had been trying to make a comeback for several years. Wild, white ringlets curled down Lily's back falling as freely as her dress. Pale blue eyes, holding the experience of a lifetime and finding the whole experience a good workout, studied Sage's face.

"I'm glad to have you. Come in." Sage moved aside so the newcomers could enter the house.

Lily practically glided over the threshold. "It's pretty crowded at Charlie's place, and there isn't enough room to paint."

"There are plenty of places to paint here. The back garden is in full bloom, and upstairs there's an extra bedroom with extraordinary light at the end of the hall. It would be a great place to set up an easel.

"Sage, this old codger is Verne Winsten. Ignore his gruff exterior. He's a former Navy man," Charlie said as if that explained Verne's sour expression.

Sage lifted her brows. So this was 'the chef'. Maybe if he knew she wasn't territorial about her cooking area, he would be relieved. "Charlie warned me you'll want to take over the kitchen. Don't let me stop you. I'm not that fond of cooking."

She expected him to smile at her admission. A soft grunt came from the big-as-a-bear man, but that was all. The fact that he didn't smile made Sage want to loosen him up, the same as she might a grumpy passenger who'd never been on a cruise before boarding the Emerald Star. Verne definitely offered a fun challenge.

Someone else to focus on was a good thing. Also having the four older folks staying with her would push her conversation with you-know-who far into the background.

"What do you like to read, Mr. Winsten?"

Verne frowned and it looked like he wouldn't respond, but then the storm in his gray gaze seemed to reluctantly disperse. "Thrillers. Dan Brown, Gillian Flynn, Clive Cussler. That kind of thing. What do you read, Ms. Dawson?"

"Sage, please." She pursed her lips, giving his question some thought. "I don't know if I have a favorite, and I don't get much time to read. When I do, I like historical novels." A nod was all she got, but it was enough. A beginning. "Welcome to my home, Mr. Winsten . . . Verne."

"Thank you, Ms. Dawson."

So, he was going to play hard to get. *Bring it on, Mr. W.*

Keeping her laughter to herself, Sage put on her best hostess face. She figured it wasn't much different than being a cruise director on the Emerald Star. "Let me show you to your rooms."

It was hard to subdue the bounce in her step. And unfortunate that she'd never been very good at keeping her enthusiasm under wraps. With Charlie and the book club staying with her, remaining in Wally Creek without her grandparents, even for three short weeks, was looking like it wouldn't be so bad after all.

Upstairs, Lily checked out each room, finally choosing the yellow room with its abundance of sunlight streaming across the floor. The beams brightened wide wood planks and splashed across the multicolored quilted bedspread. A gentle breeze moved the gauzy curtains slightly.

The other three took the first rooms they walked into. The blue room across from Lily for Verne. The green room for Charlie. And for Bette, the peach room, which was closest to Sage, and as far from Charlie's room as she could get.

Interesting. If something was brewing between the two, it probably wouldn't amount to anything.

Catching up with Charlie, Sage let him know, "While you're all getting settled in, I'll head down to the kitchen and make tea."

"Coffee for me," he said. They all followed her downstairs and then went outside to bring in their things.

In the kitchen, happy for something to do other than wondering what she should do next, and if she was being honest, also happy not to be reliving over and over the moment Luke had become a cushion that kept her from taking that painful fall, Sage found a variety of teas but no coffee.

Leaving a note on the counter by a coffee press she'd located in the back of the pantry, she made a quick run to the Birch Street Market. For the first time since returning to Wally

Creek, with the baby-boy blue sky overhead, and a white butterfly dancing in the air in front of her windshield as she drove up the main street running through town, it felt good to be home.

She'd been to a lot of beautiful places during her time on the Emerald Star, but really, she was beginning to think Wally Creek, with its small-town streets and charming buildings that could have come right out of a historical book on the region, was quickly becoming the most beautiful place she'd ever been. She only wished she'd brought her camera so she could take pictures of the huge, colorful flower baskets hanging at every corner between River Road and the market.

Her favorite Hawaiian blend only took moments to find. And while she was there, she couldn't pass up snagging cinnamon rolls from the small bakery.

On the drive back to the house, stopped at the only light in town, she wondered about Verne. What was his story? Had he been born crotchety or acquired the attitude from a hard-lived life?

The light turned green.

Back at the house, she walked into a kitchen smelling an awful lot like the Mexican restaurant she liked to frequent when the Emerald Star docked in San Diego. Verne was at the counter by the stove, surrounded by tortillas, a bowl of refried beans, and shredded cheese. Taco meat sizzled in an open pan. The former Navy guy knew his way around a kitchen.

Sage emptied her grocery bag on the breakfast bar, then leaned around Verne to take a deep breath. "Smells wonderful. What are you making?"

"Taco stacks. It's my own recipe." He frowned at the pastries she'd brought home. "Next time you want cinnamon rolls, leave me a note. I'll make them."

Sage ignored his grumpiness. It turned out that unhappy passengers were her favorite to untangle. "Can I help with anything?"

He continued to stir the taco meat. "You said you're not much of a cook."

"True. But I make a mean salad." Salads of all kinds were her specialty.

Verne shrugged as he began to place the taco ingredients in layers in nearby baking pans. "I guess you can slice lettuce into shreds, then dice the tomatoes. They're in the fridge."

"Yes, Chef." Sage couldn't help teasing. She was beginning to like the cranky old guy. "Right away, Chef."

His grunt came with a muttered, "Saucy girl."

She smothered a grin and made a mental mark on an invisible chalkboard. First point to the home team.

From the fridge, she grabbed the lettuce, tomatoes, and carrots to shred, and an onion while she was there. By the time the others came down for dinner, the dining room table was set. The taco dish and her salad were on the table. Tea and coffee makings were set up on the sideboard. And lastly, Sage had added the bouquet of bright, cheerful flowers she'd picked up at the store to celebrate their first meal together.

"Smells wonderful, Verne," Lily said, taking a seat.

Charlie poured himself a cup of coffee before sitting at the table. Sage fixed a cup of tea and took it with her to sit across from Bette. Did Charlie know Luke was in town? Should she be the one to tell him? Seemed like Charlie and Luke's relationship was sketchy, but that was none of her business.

When she looked up from covering a portion of Verne's taco dish with a scoop of salad, she suddenly realized the room had gone very quiet. All four of her new roomies were staring at her.

She laid down her fork. "What?"

"I know we said this earlier, but we just want to make sure you understand how much we appreciate you taking us in," Charlie said.

"It's no problem, guys. Really. My grandparents would want you to stay. Besides, there's more than enough room here."

Charlie studied her with a rare, serious look. "This isn't your grandparent's house anymore. It's yours. John and Vanessa told me about their plan to give you the house."

The house was hers.

Sage took a deep breath. So it was, but ownership didn't change the fact that she couldn't keep it.

Lily sipped her tea. "Well, I for one, would love to stay longer than a month or two. You have such a wonderful place. It feels like home. I would be willing to pay rent."

The rest of the book club nodded, murmuring their agreement.

Luke's assumption that she couldn't wait to get back to the Emerald Star was incorrect. With everything that had happened, she wasn't sure she wanted to go back. In the back of her mind, she'd been thinking about that for a while.

Grams and Grandpa had wanted to give her options. Unfortunately, she still had to be realistic. Unless she came up with a brilliant plan that would lower the house bills, none of them, including herself, could stay beyond a month or two. That was as far as her savings would go.

"I am not charging you guys rent." Leaning on her forearms, she said gently, "I wish we could stay here forever, but I don't have enough funds to keep the house going for more than a couple of months, tops. Eventually, I have to go back to work."

In what seemed to be his usual way, Verne scowled. Bette pressed her lips into a straight line as she added a fork full of shredded lettuce to her wedge of taco stack. Lily looked hopeful. Sage wished she could be too.

Charlie put his napkin beside his plate. "Then, we should talk money,"

"I'm not taking your money," Sage repeated firmly. She put her fork down beside her plate. They weren't hearing her. There was no way in the world—

"But if you rent the rooms to us you can take all the time you need to decide if you want to go back to the Emerald Star or not," Charlie insisted followed by a chorus of agreement from the others. "Besides, to stay at Sunnybrook, Bette, Verne, and Lily pay way more than you'll charge, and it's not near as cozy as your home."

For the first time since meeting him, Verne's grouchiness faded as he said softly, "We don't want to go back to Sunnybrook. If you let us stay and pay our way, you'd be doing us a huge favor. That way, everyone wins."

The sound of his chair scraping the floor as Verne pushed his seat back crumpled Sage's defenses. He disappeared into the kitchen.

Still, she tried to get them to see reason. "I can appreciate that. Honestly, I do, guys. But it doesn't feel right to take your money."

"But, you can," they all said in one form or another.

Even Verne, who'd come back from the kitchen with her cinnamon rolls on a plate, said, "That's the beauty of it. You get time to think about your future. We get to live in this big, beautiful house. And I get to cook in that kitchen."

What would Luke think of his uncle insisting on moving in with her? She had a feeling it wouldn't take long to find out he didn't like it.

She couldn't keep fighting them, so finally Sage gave in. She named a low enough room rate she could live with and not feel like she was taking advantage of seniors wanting to make a house their home. She hoped.

They all quickly agreed.

"Now that's settled, let's get down to business. Since this is our usual book club night," Charlie rubbed his hands together. "Verne, it's your turn to pick our next book club selection."

Sage shook her head. Leave it to Charlie to move on full steam ahead.

"Isn't it Lily's turn?" Verne asked in a low voice, looking suddenly tired.

"Nope," Lily and Charlie said together.

"Bette?"

Bette's fork, loaded with a small bite of her meal, stopped midway to her mouth. "Oh for Pete's sake, Verne. Pick something already."

After a fairly long silence where he glared at the rest of them, he named a Dan Brown title Sage didn't recognize. Dan Brown was a favorite of many of her passengers.

"Good choice. Now, on to other important matters." He looked directly at Sage. "One thing you can do to stay in Wally Creek is open your own business." Charlie switched his gaze to his friends and asked, "Remember how John and Vanessa used to talk about opening a tea room after they closed the cafe? Whatever happened to that idea?"

Sage sat up straight, instantly suspicious at the shrewd twinkle in his eyes. She knew exactly what he was referring to.

The dream of opening a tea room had started with her mom, and after she died, Grams had kept it alive. But after a while, they talked about it less and less until by the time Sage left home after graduating high school, and eventually landed the job on the Emerald Star, she'd put her mother's dream away in her mental treasure box, only to be brought out, like now, when someone brought up the tea room, or she was missing her mom like crazy.

"They said they were done working long hours. And I presume they caught the Arizona bug," Bette said with a graceful shrug.

"Why haven't you all caught the same bug?" Sage asked, mostly to distract Charlie from wherever he was going by bringing up her mother's dream.

"I don't know about everyone else, but Wally Creek is my home. I don't want to live anywhere else." Lily finished her tea and then stacked her dishes.

"Same here. I moved around a lot when I was in the Navy," Verne wiped his mouth with his napkin. "After I retired, it took a while to find a place that I liked and where I could settle. Then I came to Wally Creek. Anyway, that ended my traveling days."

Sage gathered up her dishes and carried them to the kitchen. The others followed with their stacks, putting them on the counter by the sink.

Charlie put his dishes on top of Sage's. "I have an idea."

Uh oh.

He cast her a challenging look. "*You* should open the tea room."

Instantly tossed back to the last time her mother had talked about the tea room she'd dreamed of opening for so long, Sage was stunned into silence. It was the morning of the accident. Wishing she hadn't been in such a hurry to go rock climbing that day, that she'd spent just a little more time sipping tea—hers was decaf—and dreaming with her mom, she finally found the strength to say, "I can't."

"Why not? I think it's the perfect solution." Charlie's gaze sharpened with that look she'd come to know meant she was on the wrong side of one of his arguments.

And this one was just the beginning. The man could be like a dog with a bone when he got his mind set on something. The tea room had always been her mom's dream, not hers. Better to nip this in the bud before she couldn't say no.

"I have no idea how to run a business," She reminded Charlie, then counted off on her fingers. "Secondly, there's not enough money in my savings to keep the house going, much less open a business too."

Oddly disappointed her finances couldn't handle both—in the recesses of her mind, she'd sometimes secretly thought . . . maybe . . . someday—

But then a remnant of her brother's pragmatism took over and she shrugged. Life was what it was. "I'm sorry. It's just not possible."

Charlie, however, wasn't convinced by her argument. "There has to be a way. You have plenty of experience making travelers happy so they'll come back for another cruise. You could easily do the same thing here and give regular customers an experience that will bring them back to a sweet little shop where they can take a moment out of their busy day to have a soothing cup of tea. Bette has experience running a business. She can be your mentor." He glanced at Bette.

"I'd be happy to help," Bette said, smiling at the crazy man.

His enthusiasm having gotten a boost, Charlie continued, "As far as the money goes— Well, as they say, build it and they will come."

For no reason at all, Sage wondered what Luke, the big-shot businessman from Seattle would think about his uncle's idea. The same thing as Jack, no doubt. Her brother, a former military man, ran his own highly respected search and rescue team all over the world.

He'd be the first to tell her, *Be smart, Sage. Think this through.*

The only problem with that advice was her heart. Every memory she had of her mom insisted that she consider Charlie's impossible idea as a way to keep those memories fresh. But how would she get started, much less see a project of that magnitude through to the end? It wasn't like she had unlimited time or funds.

It didn't help that her encounters with Luke Marshell lingered in her mind, with his fancy business clothes and sharp, assessing look in stunning blue eyes that appeared to take everything in. Jack would like the man. They were two peas in a pod. Knowing two such take-charge men was enough to make Sage momentarily rethink her opposition.

"Okay, let's just say I was on board with opening the tea room, which I'm not even considering, just playing devil's advocate. Where would I put a tea shop in Wally Creek?"

Lily brought the remaining dishes in from the dining room. After setting them on the counter, she grabbed the broom and dustpan from the pantry. "There's that empty building on Birch Street, right across from John and Vanessa's old cafe. It doesn't need much fixing up."

Verne silently put the leftovers away.

"That's too big. The tea room should be warm and cozy, not

some high-end place that would do better in Portland than a small town like Wally Creek. You should open the tea room right here."

Turn her grandparent's house into a business? Not going to happen. "This is a home, Charlie, not a commercial building."

"That's the thing. John told me once that this property is zoned commercial and residential. All the properties along this stretch of River Road are." Charlie paused, one finger tapping his cheek as he outlined a plan on the fly. "You could convert the main floor into the tea room and keep the upstairs for our private area. The spare room could even be made into an upstairs living room."

Even though she could live without Charlie butting into her business, Sage had to admit she was a little intrigued by his suggestion. The idea was outrageous, wasn't it?

Still— She leaned toward him across the breakfast bar. "A project that big would take permits, a project manager, a lot of work, and I'll say again, funds I don't have."

Charlie rubbed his chin with thick knuckled fingers. "We could all chip in—"

"Oh no you can't," she said firmly. "It's bad enough you're paying rent."

In any case, if she was going to do this thing, she wanted to do it under her own steam, not by taking money from her elderly friends.

"You could get a small business grant," Bette suggested. "I looked into it once. You have to jump through a bunch of hoops, but the result would be completely worth it."

"I was already thinking the same thing, Bette." Charlie circumvented the bar. "I'm glad you thought of it too."

At the twinkle in his expressive gaze, Sage tilted her head, watching skeptically as everyone, including Charlie, started talking all at once.

"We'll help." Lily reached for Sage's hand, looking at the others. "Won't we?"

Charlie and Bette nodded. "Yes! Of course, we will." And then Verne's gruff, "You bet."

"Bette will help with the business details and sew our uniforms. She's so good with a sewing machine. Charlie can oversee the remodel. He's very good at organizing people. That comes from having to herd students all those years. Verne can develop the menu and do his chef thing." Lily finally took a breath, her gaze landing on Sage's face. It was hard not to grin back at the excited woman. "I'll come up with a theme for the tea room."

Lily leaned against Sage's shoulder. "You could call the tea room, Tea at the River's Edge."

"Or Tail's End Tea Room," Bette suggested, putting water in the kettle and turning on the burner. "You know, to honor Oregon City being the end of the Oregon Trail."

"How about Sage's Tea Room," Verne said, a little less ill-humored than previously. Even his shoulders were less slumped. He shrugged. "It's your place. You should pick the name."

She looked at Charlie, but though he was grinning like a puppet master in full control, he didn't seem to have a suggestion for the name of this new adventure. "Why do you guys care so much about doing this?"

Charlie's grin slipped. "Because we're getting older." He glanced at the others before continuing. "We have more days behind us than we do ahead, and we don't want the time we have left to be squandered sitting in the old folk's home being bored to death while we play bingo and wait for the end to come. Your tea room is exactly what we need to add some spice to our lives."

All eyes settled on Sage. She got it. The book club needed her to be brave and take a risk. Not just for her mother's memory, but for the sake of all of their immediate futures, hers included.

"All right. I'll give it a try but don't get your hopes up. If by some miracle I get a grant, you all have to promise to pitch in and help make the tea room a reality."

Lily clapped her hands as she bounced up on her toes. Bette calmly lifted her chin as a smile spread across her classic features. Verne grunted his approval if a grunt could be called a sign of approval. Charlie straightened, the sudden shrewdness in his gaze momentarily giving Sage pause. What was her grandparent's best friend up to?

"This deserves a toast." Charlie went to the pantry and found Grams' stash of sparkling cider while Lily searched the cupboards until she found some flutes her grandmother had left behind.

Charlie filled the glasses. Sage lifted hers. "To Amelia's Cuppa Tea—after my mom—and a successful opening." She hoped.

"Excellent choice," Lily said, raising her glass.

"Here here." The kitchen erupted in cheers.

Sage took a deep breath. This was the biggest, scariest thing she ever attempted. Maybe she *should* get some advice from Luke. What did she have to lose? If she was turned down for a grant, then that was that. They'd all be disappointed, but they could go back to their normal lives knowing she'd given her mom's tea room her best shot. And, if she had to, she could still sell the house and return to her interrupted life on the Emerald Star.

Charlie's cell rang. He fished it out of his pocket. "It's Luke. I'll be right back. I'm sure he'll have some great recommendations for how to get Amelia's Cuppa Tea off the ground."

Sage should have mentioned she'd run into his nephew earlier, but Charlie hadn't given her a chance. Watching the older man as he cast a quick look in her direction before leaving the kitchen, yup, he definitely had the look of a man who was getting up to a boatload of mischief.

It was a good thing she'd cleared the air with Luke earlier. He wasn't looking for a girlfriend. She wasn't looking for a repeat performance like the one she'd had with Gordan.

All she had to do now was convince Charlie they were perfectly happy living separate lives in towns that were far enough apart, a romantic partnership wasn't convenient for either of them.

Chapter Six

With his phone pressed to his ear, Luke tossed his room key-card on the bed and waited for his uncle to answer. So far, uncovering why Sage was okay with taking Charlie's money was a bust. Instead, all he'd come up with were arguable scenarios that pointed toward innocence rather than any guilt.

"Hey, Luke. So glad you called. That was quick. Have you started the process of getting the grant papers ready to mail?."

"There hasn't been enough time for Gabi to draw them up. I wanted to talk to you about it one more time before we proceed. I'm staying at The Oak Hotel."

"You're in Wally Creek?"

"Yes, and—"

Charlie didn't give Luke a chance to tell him he'd met Sage Dawson.

"There's nothing to talk about," his uncle said in a tone Luke recognized. He'd been right to think, in this instance, changing the old man's mind would take a miracle. "I need you to get the award letter in the mail as soon as possible. The grant money can come later, but I want Sage to know the money is coming."

Luke could hear voices in the background. "Where are you?"

"I'm at Sage's. She has a big house on River Road. Bette, Lily, Verne and I are staying here for a while."

Very little surprised Luke, but this wasn't his uncle's normal behavior. The old man liked his space. "Your friends from the book club? Why?"

"It's a long story." Charlie paused, then, "The short version is we can't all fit into my place. And we're helping Sage open Amelia's."

Luke walked to the window and stared in the direction of his uncle's cottage. A plan was cooking in his brain. "What's Amelia's?"

"A tea room." Charlie's voice faded for a second before he came back with a gruff, "Don't make any waves, young man."

Charlie rarely scolded Luke, but he hadn't spent all those summers with his uncle not to have learned a thing or two about how big his heart was and how far out of his way he'd go to help someone he thought was deserving.

Luke had also learned not to give up so easily. "Do you mind if I stay at your place for a day to two?"

He smiled at the sigh that sounded more like irritation. "The spare key is inside the rock in the flower pot. Come for brunch tomorrow, but I don't want you to mention the grant to Sage, or the others, either. I want it to be anonymous. Oh, be surprised about Amelia's. You didn't hear that from me."

Charlie wasn't making any sense. What in the heck was going on? "Uncle Charlie—"

"I'm serious, my boy," his uncle interrupted quietly, which was way worse than if he'd raised his voice. "If you won't do this for me, I'll find someone who will."

And the old man would too. The situation was more serious than he'd thought.

"I'll have Gabi start on the letter first thing in the morning." He'd do that much, but he wasn't ready to raise the white flag quite yet. "Can you at least tell me why keeping the origins of the grant secret is important?"

"Sage won't take the money if she knows it's from me."

That, at least, was one point in the lady's favor. But from where Luke stood, that was a very good reason to tell Sage she had an angel investor and who that investor was. Only in her case, Charlie didn't appear to be asking for equity in the new business, which wasn't in his uncle's best financial interests. Nothing good could come of keeping his name out of the deal.

"She needs Amelia's more than I need the money," Charlie said seriously.

"I see." He didn't, but it would take Gabi a couple of days to take care of the legal details. Days that Luke intended to put to good use.

"I'll need Sage's address. What time do you want me to come tomorrow?"

Charlie gave him the information. "You'll like her, Luke. She's a very sweet girl."

Like her? Charlie hung up before Luke could say he'd already met Sage. Unfortunately, against his better judgment, he *did* like the woman, but no matter what his uncle said, that didn't mean she was entirely innocent in this dodgy scheme to get the old man's money.

Pretty sure he couldn't keep his uncle's connection with the grant quiet for very long, Luke hoped Charlie didn't disown his favorite nephew when the information came out. Secrets were hard things to keep for long.

He pictured Sage sitting across from him at the hotel. The way her dark hair framed her face. How her stunning eyes had snapped at him at first, then turned sad when she talked about her parents. How she'd abruptly left him sitting there when he'd pushed too far.

Playing secret detective didn't make him feel that great, but it wasn't about him. This was for Charlie, the bighearted guy. The least he could do was spend a few extra days in Wally Creek and get to know Sage better. Then maybe he'd feel better about complying with Charlie's wishes.

He hit the speed dial number for Gabi. It took a few rings for her to pick up. "Hey, listen, I'm staying a few extra days in Wally Creek." He explained the situation with Charlie and what his uncle was requesting. "If you'll put together the grant approval letter and email it to me when you're finished, I'll approve it before you send it out."

"Are you sure there's nothing shady going on?"

Luke could picture Gabi's frown. He knew she wouldn't like this situation anymore than he did. "That's why I want you to legally cover our bases. And drag your feet as much as possible. So far I haven't been able to change Charlie's mind. At least with a few extra days here, I can snoop around some more." He pushed his hair off his forehead, running his hand over the top of his head. "Any updates on the Portman project?"

After she gave him an update, which wasn't much, he pocketed his phone, put his things back in his bag, and went downstairs to check out. He didn't run into Emerson, which was unfortunate. He'd hoped to casually pry some information about her friend out of the hotel owner. She probably wouldn't tell him much, but it would have been worth the try.

After Allie completed the paperwork for his short stay, Luke drove to his uncle's place, found the key right where Charlie had said it would be, and let himself in. It didn't take long to get settled into the spare bedroom. Opening the curtains to let in the waning sunlight, he took a moment to look out into the backyard.

The small patch of grass was shaded by towering trees. He could see why Charlie liked the little cottage and why he'd decided to buy the compact house. It was like living in the woods. And Wally Creek was a charming town. But all that didn't explain why his uncle was currently staying at Sage's house. Especially since he had this sweet little sanctuary.

Luke's business back in Seattle with Portman couldn't wait forever, probably not even another week or two, which meant he had to finish up this business with Sage fast. How to do that was the question. If she could convince him she wasn't out to take Charlie to the cleaners, then he'd get out of their way. In fact, maybe even give her some advice on opening this tea room Charlie had mentioned.

Luke shoved his hands in his pockets. A tea room, fancy or not, in a small town on a long road into the mountains didn't seem like a profitable idea. The problem was the woman who he still had to be convinced wasn't taking advantage of his uncle. He liked her. She was pretty, of course, but more than that, interesting. She made him feel like they could talk forever about nothing at all, and she'd still be listening. She definitely ran his motor hot.

Put the breaks on, buddy.

He had no intention of cheating on his business. Not now. Not anytime in the near future. Not if he really intended to take MR Investments to the next level.

Unfortunately, his promise to not reveal Charlie's secret tied his hands. Still, if the older man was right and Sage wouldn't take the grant if she knew her benefactor was his uncle, Luke needed a better plan than confronting the lady head on. That kind of clash wouldn't get either of them anywhere. There had to be a workaround. There always was.

He went to the kitchen to see if he needed to make a grocery run. As usual Charlie was stocked up, which left Luke free to plan for a nice, calm conversation tomorrow, where he didn't accuse Sage Dawson of being an unscrupulous woman. If she had the right answers, maybe he could save his uncle's retirement fund by becoming her benefactor in Charlie's place.

Gabi was always looking for a charity to support. It wouldn't be hard to change the important elements of the grant letter, maybe add a couple of enticing carrots. And, if the numbers looked good on paper, the seed money for the tea room could be their next charity. Not just a grant for Sage, but maybe an annual grant for new start ups. The more Luke thought about it, the more he liked the idea.

There was just one snag with the whole thing. If she wouldn't want Charlie to be behind the grant—Luke still wasn't sure he believed that, but he'd try to keep an open mind—it wasn't likely she'd want to be his company's charity either. Even if they chose her over the two other competitors he was certain he could round up.

Leaning against the island, he stared at the bottle of pop on the counter he'd pulled from the fridge. It probably wasn't smart on his part to keep more secrets than he already was.

He wasn't good at it, anyway.

How in the heck did he resolve this dilemma without crossing the line and going against Charlie's resolve? No matter how fast his pulse raced every time he saw Sage—either in frustration or surprising attraction, he wasn't sure which—his relationship with his uncle was too important to put it in jeopardy over a pretty stranger who could quite possibly be the best con artist he'd ever run across.

~ * ~

What with swearing off men, her grandparents' move south so soon after her ex had dumped her, acquiring their house, the Sunnybrook book club relocating upstairs, helping them get settled in, and now all the talk about reviving her mother's dream of opening a tea room, and on top of all that, literally falling into the arms of a guy who was more handsome than Gordan any day of the week, Sage was pretty sure her life had taken a hard turn toward complicated beyond normal expectations.

If she looked beneath Luke's all-business-all-the-time facade, he was much more charming than she'd thought at first glance. He was more . . . everything. Their clumsy introduction was all her, not Cupid doing his thing.

She was wrong about Gordan. With her luck, the man across the table, apparently enjoying Verne's excellent scrambled eggs and French toast while he talked to her housemates like they were his best friends, wasn't a better choice. Not that she was looking for a new guy. She didn't know what kind of package her forever guy came in anymore, she just knew that man wasn't Luke Marshell.

Super good looks and an uncanny ability to prompt a girl into blathering on about something as personal as being orphaned at a young age, and on the first day they'd met no less, did not show his dreamy attributes. Or hers, for that matter. She scooped up another bite of French toast dripping with strawberry syrup. It made her more than a little uncomfortable.

Thanks to Gordan, it appeared she had no self-preservation left.

That's right, she said to the girl in her head on the other side of her inner debate. *Luke Marshell should make you suspicious. He's too well put together and asks too many questions to be, you know, The One.*

No way would she play the fool again. Not so soon after Gordan had shown his true colors. Jack was right. Her brother didn't let anything interfere with his search and rescue business. Even when he was a senior in high school, he was on a straight-line course to the military. She'd thought there was something between him and Em that might change his mind, but neither confided in her. When Jack joined the Marines as soon as he graduated, Em stayed behind in Wally Creek. There had been one girl in Jack's life since then. Briefly. So brief, in fact, Sage couldn't remember the lady's name.

Her brother never claimed to be looking for happy-ever-after, and if she didn't want to get hurt again, she should be clear on that point herself.

Laughing at something Lily said, Luke glanced in her direction. She saw the questions swirling in blue eyes that seemed to miss nothing.

She shot him a silent, No more questions, buddy.

Shifting her glance away from him, she swallowed a gulp of cooled tea to wash down the last of her breakfast . . . lunch . . . whatever, and glanced around the table. Her new housemates were counting on her to make Amelia's a reality. If she could get a grant like Bette suggested, she'd do her best not to let them down, but what if she didn't get the grant? Well then, no problem. She'd move on. Her new friends would also move on to other diversions. Maybe Charlie would even move to Seattle to be closer to Luke.

In the meantime, she had questions to ask of the gentleman. "Now, what exactly do you do, Luke?"

"I own an investment company."

Charlie had hinted that Luke could give her some pointers on opening a small business. It was time to find out if big city businessman was on the same page. She could always ask Em if he wasn't. Her best friend in high school had started The Oak Hotel from scratch five years back. She was more likely to know the potholes of opening a beverage and food business in Wally Creek than a big investment broker from Seattle.

"What does that mean?"

"I evaluate investment opportunities and inherent risks for clients." He glanced at his uncle. "Then I make recommenda-tions."

Charlie's sudden frown at Luke wasn't reassuring. But then the line between his bushy brows was quickly replaced by a crooked grin the old codger sent in Sage's direction. "Luke's very good at his job. He's helped a lot of businesses with their financial options. I'm sure he could draft up a road map for Amelia's."

Sage didn't think so. From the speed at which his lips thinned into a firm line, Luke was *not* on board, which was odd, considering Charlie's assertion that his nephew's company supported new businesses. Not that it mattered to Sage. She had plenty of support right here in Wally Creek.

The conversation at the table turned to the Seattle art scene. Sinking back in her chair, she guessed by the disgruntled look he sent his uncle's way, Luke didn't think opening a tea room in Wally Creek was a good idea. And if she asked him why, with the tension building between him and Charlie, she wasn't sure he'd give her a straight answer.

Her cell rang with The Turtles ringtone *Imagine you and me* that signaled Grams was calling. It had been her and Grandpa's song for as long as Sage could remember.

"Grams." She jumped up. The weight of Luke's gaze followed her up the stairs. "I'm so glad you called. Did you find a place to stay?"

"We did. An adorable mid-century house in Sedona. And there's plenty of room for you and Jack to come visit." The soft sigh of a cushioned chair as Grams sat down made Sage wish she was having this conversation in person instead of across too many miles to count. "Now tell me everything that's happened since we left. Charlie said the book club is staying with you?"

Sage flopped back on her bed and laughed. "Do not ask me how that happened."

"Don't have to. I know Charlie. He usually gets what he wants." Grams chuckled. "So have you decided to keep the house?"

Taking a deep breath, she admitted, "Maybe— Remember when we used to talk about opening a tea room? I'm looking into putting Amelia's Cuppa Tea on the first floor. Well, we're checking the possibility out, anyway. Charlie, Verne, Bette, and Lily all want to help."

She might not be so good at the happy-ever-after thing, but she could do her best to make her mother's dream come alive, so she told Grams everything.

"Sage, that's wonderful. Your parents would be so proud."

"I hope so, but don't get too excited. I have to apply for a grant to pay for it. And if I don't get it, I'll probably have to sell the house." She crossed her fingers that it wouldn't come to that, because more and more, she didn't want to sell the house that her grandparents had made into a home when they first moved to Wally Creek.

"Grandpa and I can help financially."

"Thanks for the offer, Grams, but I'll figure it out."

"Okay. Just remember we're here for you." Her grandmother went silent, then said softly, "You can do this."

"Thank you, Grams. I hope so." Sage wiped away the lone tear slowly making a track down her cheek. She cleared her throat. "I'd better get back downstairs. We have a dinner guest."

"Oh, who?"

Sage hesitated, then shook her head. Grams probably already knew. If she didn't, she would more than likely find out soon enough anyway. "Luke's in town visiting Charlie."

"Really . . . " An ultimate romantic, Grams' voice hummed with speculation and the history of a happy fifty-six-year marriage.

"Put your matchmaking wand away, Grams. Luke is— I don't know what, but I'm sure he's not looking for a long-term commitment. And neither am I," she hastened to point out.

"If you both weren't so focused on your jobs—"

Before the idea of her and Luke dating got out of the starting gate, Sage made sure her grandmother knew the score. "Luke lives in Seattle. Wally Creek isn't his idea of the perfect port of call. And he doesn't strike me as a small-town kind of guy."

Right? Right!

"You could be wrong about that. He certainly comes often enough to see Charlie." Grams chuckled softly in Sage's ear. "Besides, you can't blame a grandmother for hoping. It would be so nice to have great-grandchildren."

Those great-grandchildren were not in the cards. Unless Jack gave them to Grams sometime in the future. "I love you, Grams."

"I love you too, sweetheart."

"Hug Grandpa for me."

"I will. Say hi to Luke for us," Grams chuckled, then hung up.

Sage shook her head. Downstairs, she walked right into the middle of a conversation that had nothing to do with possible plans for Amelia's or the Dan Brown novel the book club had selected to read next.

"I think that since Luke is in town for only a few days, we should have the birthday party Friday night," Bette argued, clearing the table.

Lily nodded. "Me too."

Sage wrapped her hands around the cup of hot tea Charlie sat in front of her on the breakfast bar. "Who's birthday is it?"

"Verne's and Uncle Charlie's," Luke said. "The ladies are lobbying for an over-the-hill party."

"That sounds like a fun idea." She took a swig of her tea while she swung between appreciating how Lily and Bette were happy to tease the older gentlemen, and wondering what was so important a smiling Luke would leave his office to head south and visit his uncle in the middle of the week, even if he was the boss and could make his own hours.

Luke took Charlie's place at the sink, quite sexy with his sleeves rolled up to his elbows. Water dripped from his hands as he prepped the dishes to go into the dishwasher.

"It's a milestone," Bette went on. "It's not every day that a person turns—"

There wasn't a single woman in all of Wally Creek who wouldn't be attracted to Luke's confidence, uber-success, and seeing the handsome man tackle a domestic chore with the same calm attention he would probably give to the woman he chose to share his life with.

Except her. Despite the tug of attraction that was more an irritation than a life-changing event, Sage had no plan to move off the sideline.

"Don't say it," Verne warned in his most grumpy tone.

"—seventy," Bette and Lily said together.

"Or seventy-five," Bette finished as she glanced at Charlie, a little sparkle in her smile.

Charlie snorted. Verne tossed the towel he'd been using to wipe down the counters on the bar and stomped out of the kitchen. Heavy steps on the stairs punctuated his discontent.

Lily poured hot water from the kettle whistling on the stove into a cup, dunked in a tea bag, and came to stand next to Sage. Her pale blue eyes teased. "He's a little sensitive about his age."

"Is that why he's been grouchy?"

Lily shrugged, humor lifting the corners of her mouth as she sipped her tea.

"I'll go talk to him." Sage wasn't sure what she'd say, but—"I've had lots of experience talking people out of their funks."

Lily handed Sage her steaming cup. "That's okay. I'll talk to him." And off the older lady went.

"Speaking of experience. I wonder if you'd do me a favor?"

Charlie said, studying her with a calculating look.

Sage raised her brows. Here they went again. Charlie liked to talk her into things she didn't want to do. Of course, she had to ask. It was either that or hide out in her bedroom, like Verne. She teased, "You have another favor to ask? I'm shocked."

"If you don't mind," Charlie said with a jolly wink. "Will you plan the party for us? Nothing fancy. Just something where Verne doesn't have to cook. I can give you a list of a few people to invite."

"I'll help Charlie with the guest list. And I can host." Bette said as she nudged Luke aside, then put her teacup and saucer in the dishwasher. "It'll be good practice for when Amelia's opens. I want to be the hostess."

Sage glanced at Luke. He was drying his hands on the towel Verne had tossed down. His back was straight and he looked almost as unhappy as Verne before he'd marched upstairs.

So, when was the city slicker going to tell her he thought Amelia's was not a great idea? It didn't take a mind reader to figure out the man wasn't impressed with the idea. Sage wasn't a psychologist or mind reader, but she'd worked with enough passengers to be able to read body language pretty well. And right now, as he turned to stare at her, Luke Marshell was not giving Amelia's high marks for success.

Chapter Seven

Charlie clapped Luke on the shoulder. "Luke will give you a hand with the party planning. Two heads are better than one, I always say."

"Um sure." What else could Sage say?

If reluctance was a suit a guy might wear to a cruise-line dinner party at the Captain's table, Luke's would be a top-of-the-line tuxedo. Clearly he had as much trouble saying no to his uncle as she did.

"One day isn't much time to plan and execute a party." She hoped Luke picked up on her effort to get them out of partnering up for Charlie's newest attempt to throw them together. If he would back her up, that might get the message across to his uncle.

No such luck. When he sent her a speculative look that was so like Charlie when the older man was in the middle of a scheme to get her on board with whatever he had in mind, it was scary. Fortunately, it was all she could do not to roll her eyes.

"I actually had in mind that we might go fishing tomorrow, Uncle Charlie," Luke said.

Maybe he had gotten her subliminal message. That earned him a point or two.

"We'll go fishing after the party. I promise. Sage has lots of experience planning events, but she's going to need your help to get the thing organized on such short notice."

Charlie didn't play fair and did not act the part of an innocent bystander all that well, either.

Well, fine then. Sage gave up. Seventy-five was such a big milestone, she could let Charlie have his way. This time, anyway.

"Is there a special theme you want for this over-the-hill party?" She teased, "Have you lived long enough to be crowned king of the mountain?"

Charlie didn't even blink. "It's just another day around the sun, young lady." Then, not so easily outmaneuvered, he patted Luke's shoulder. "I appreciate you giving Sage a hand, son."

"It's no problem." Luke glanced her way. His thoughts weren't easy to read. More importantly, why in the world did she want to know what he was thinking in the first place?

"Glad to hear it." With a satisfied smile and a quick wave, Charlie made for the stairs. "I have to prepare for a town council meeting that's coming up. See you kids later."

With a look at each other that said they knew what Charlie was up to, Bette, Lily, and Verne followed him upstairs.

Sage sighed. From the way his brows knitted together, Luke liked being manipulated about as much as she did. She needed to have a talk with Charlie about his efforts at making something happen between them. And she would, but not until after the birthday party.

Luke, on the other hand, needed to be set straight right now. "Are you going to let your uncle get away with that?"

"Are you?" Watching her closely, he shrugged. "Have you ever tried to change Charlie's mind once he's decided to make a thing happen?"

"No and no," she said with a chuckle. In the meantime, until she could corner the shrewd old dude. "Cross my heart, I can handle a birthday party. You honestly don't have to help." She made the motion to prove her point. It would be better if Luke did his own thing, whatever that was, while she put her well-earned skills to work. "Charlie is just being Charlie. I've managed a lot of events. A party for two seventy-somethings will be a walk in the park."

She figured Luke would be grateful to be let off the hook, but the frown forming between his brows said otherwise.

His frown dissipating like an evaporating, he broke the silence and went to the refrigerator to pull out a tub of ice cream. "I brought dessert. How do you feel about a bowl of ice cream drowned in loads of chocolate syrup?"

Just the two of them?

"You should relax. Take a day off. You honestly don't have to spend tomorrow planning a party," she told him.

"Look who's talking." He raised the tub and the can of syrup he scavenged from the pantry and wiggled both.

Peppermint. Oh, for heaven's sake. She was in so much trouble. Instead of fighting it, she got bowls down, then hunted for spoons. "Okay, but just one scoop."

"A whole scoop." A smile slipped through Luke's normal reserve. "Sage Dawson, you definitely know how to live dangerously."

Before she could warn herself to be careful, the sudden sparkle in summer blue eyes tempted her to have two scoops just so she could linger longer in his company. Maybe even ask him a question or two about her new enterprise.

But really, it wouldn't be smart to get too cozy with the man his uncle was doing his best to pair her with. *Broken heart, remember?*

Sticking to her guns, she gave him one more chance to change his mind. "Listen, you don't have to go shopping with me tomorrow."

"I want to," he said with a brief look in her direction as he pried off the top of the tub. "When I was a kid, I spent my summers with Uncle Charlie. Every year, he threw me a birthday party. I haven't had many chances to return the favor. He's a good guy. And Verne is too." He scooped ice cream into the bowls. "It'll be fun."

Luke loved his uncle. How could she fight that? Even with Charlie's very obvious matchmaking, who wouldn't love the older man? Like her grandpa, he operated completely from the heart.

The polite distance Luke had kept between them narrowed, at least on Sage's side. Memories lingered in his smile drawing her across the line of *don't go there, girl. Don't repeat a bad mistake.*

Catching herself just in time, she pulled her cruise director's composure close. "When's your birthday?"

"In August." He handed her a bowl, one scoop slathered in more chocolate syrup than she would have added. Did she turn it down? No. The man knew his way around a girl's favorite foods.

Taking her bowl to the living room, she settled into the

chair closest to the fireplace. It was too warm to start a fire, but sitting close to the cozy whitewashed brick brought back memories.

Scooping a spoonful of ice cream into her mouth, she closed her eyes, savoring the taste of peppermint mixed with the sweet heaven of chocolate. If only she could find a man who had the same combination of sweetness and layers of unforgettable, mouth-watering, lingering sincerity.

"Do you like planning events?" Luke asked, interrupting her stolen moment with the best dessert ever.

It took Sage a moment to come back to reality, but finally, she shook herself free from her ridiculous fascination—with the sound of Luke's voice, not the ice cream. "I do. Except for making friends with the passengers, it's the best part of the job. Event planning is a challenge and different every day. The only downside is the long cruises kept me away from my grandparents too long." She took a deep breath and took a chance. She was probably revealing more than the man plying her with sugar and chocolate wanted to hear. "Now that they've moved to Arizona, in hindsight, I wish I'd taken more time to come home and see them."

"My work can get in the way of seeing Uncle Charlie too."

She didn't know how often he came to see his uncle—two or three times a year? As she'd found out, that wasn't enough. "You should see Charlie as much as you can."

His expression turned briefly thoughtful before morphing into something less sympathetic. He nodded, then said, "Uncle Charlie mentioned he and his friends are renting rooms from you. Is that going to be a problem? Aren't you anxious to get back to your job?"

She'd hoped Charlie wouldn't mention their rental agreement, not that she had anything to hide since her new roommates had insisted on paying rent and she'd agreed to a low monthly rate. Besides, they could move back to their previous accommodations anytime they wanted.

"Maybe. I'm not sure," she answered the second part of his question honestly. And why not? He was just a guy making conversation over dessert. "But Charlie, Verne, Bette, and Lily staying with me isn't a problem. It's fun. Why do you ask?"

"Because I love my job. I can't imagine leaving it to do something less exciting. May I?" His ice cream was all gone. When she held out her bowl to him, he reached over and scooped up a spoonful. "So it sounds like they won't interfere with any plans to return to your job."

She raised her brows at the dessert thief. He'd heard the talk about the possibility of opening a tea room. What would he think if she told him she'd almost decided not to return to the Emerald Queen?

It did feel odd after all this time to be thinking about leaving the cruise line. But the more she thought about it, the more she wanted to make her mom's dream come true. Setting aside her melting ice cream, she leaned forward in her chair. "What if, like you, I *want* to own my own business?"

His eyes turned an intense blue. He leaned toward her, copying Sage's posture. "Not as much adventure. No more seeing exotic ports of call. Or making friends with people who come from all over the globe."

"Maybe, but I could build something special, make my home here rather than on a cruise ship. That could be exciting. And with the right advertisement, tourists passing through Wally Creek would be enticed to come back over and over again."

Of course, that wasn't a sure thing, but with a lot of work, it could be.

His dark brows came together. The lips she tried hard not to think about kissing—if he wanted to; he didn't look like it—twisted with skepticism.

It was clear he didn't think she could pull off Amelia's. Well, he was wrong.

She straightened her back. Amelia's was her mother's dream, but the tea room was becoming her dream too. Wally Creek would be the perfect place to settle down. She could be a successful business owner in the cute little town. The idea was growing on Sage. And with the book club's help, she could have a life surrounded by family, even if they were adopted, regular customers who'd love Amelia's as much as she did. And that little hint of loneliness that occasionally showed its face could go away.

She eased back in the chair. Was she actually entertaining the idea of not going back to the Emerald Star? Luke watched her closely.

Collecting her bowl, she held out a hand for his empty dish. He'd practically licked it clean. "It's getting late. Tomorrow will be busy."

"Of course." He gave her the bowl. On the way out, he stopped with the front door half open. "What time do you want to meet?"

For now, her thoughts and dreams were her own. He didn't need to know how close she was to making a change.

She pasted a smile on her face. "I'll text you."

"All right. See you tomorrow." He hesitated as if wanting to say more, but then left, the door closing softly behind him.

Luke Marshell was nothing like the sweet, nice man she'd always thought she'd end up marrying. How could he be? He was suspicious. Too analytical. And not all that flexible. How could she spend more than a minute thinking—what? That someday in the distant future, he would suddenly check off at least three or four of the boxes on her perfect guy list?

Despite what Charlie and her grandparents thought, that was very unlikely.

It didn't matter. There was no reason to get her panties all tied in a knot. Luke would be heading back to Seattle as soon as he took care of whatever business had brought him to Wally Creek in the first place. And if that business was his Uncle Charlie, that at least was another point in his favor.

Taking their dishes to the kitchen, she rinsed them out and put them in the dishwasher. The whole time her thoughts wouldn't stop swirling around Luke and his apparent opposition to Amelia's.

Grams had said, when one door closes, a window opens. Even though she was so sure Sage would like him, she couldn't have meant Luke. When he was deep in conversation with Charlie and the others, his barriers came down and his not-so-ready smile added handsome wrinkles to the edges of his eyes. She *did* like him then.

It was only when he was talking with her, and asking all his questions, that his guard snapped back in place. Whether he'd intended to or not, he'd implied— She wasn't sure what, but he sure seemed in a hurry for her to get back to the Emerald Queen.

Mentally running through the events that had led to the septuagenarians moving in, she pressed her lips together. She hadn't done anything wrong. Maybe Luke hadn't meant what she thought he meant—that everyone would be better off if she gave up Amelia's and returned to her job. Except she had a feeling he did.

That was too bad. All four of her housemates deserved to live in a place that made them happy. If that was her home, then who was she to say it wasn't so? In the meantime, she'd give Charlie and Verne a birthday party they would never forget. She'd prove to Luke his suspicions were so off the mark.

Turning off the lights as she went, she made her way up to her room, put on her pajamas, and got comfortable at her computer. Scooting the statue of Tonatiah back from the monitor, a reminder of how much she enjoyed exploring the different ports where the Emerald Star docked, she resumed her search. Applying for a few more grants couldn't hurt and would only increase the odds of someone offering the money she needed.

Grams was right. A window had opened. Who would have guessed that someday—sooner rather than later—she'd be considering leaving the Emerald Star?

Spending the last few days in Wally Creek, seeing her grandparents—even if their visit was brief, then welcoming Charlie and the others into her home, all that had opened her eyes to what she'd been missing. It explained why the last few months she hadn't been happy on the Emerald Star. And why, secretly, she'd pushed Gordan, hoping he would want as much as she did to settle down and make a home with her somewhere on the mainland. And why she always saw that home in Wally Creek.

What surprised her most was that she hadn't figured it out earlier.

The good news was, Luke would return to his life in Seattle. If he was out of sight, he'd be out of her mind too, making it easier to concentrate on the new adventure ahead of her.

With an exciting future to explore—a future that included Charlie and the gang, and Amelia's Cuppa Tea—Sage tucked Luke and his disturbing insinuations out of her mind and filled out another application.

~ * ~

The next morning, Luke glanced at Charlie's kitchen clock and decided he still had a little spare time before he met up with the woman who was fast becoming a thorn in his side. Pulling his phone out of his pocket, he dialed Charlie, who picked up on the first ring. "Hey, Uncle."

"Hey, yourself." Luke could hear a lively conversation going on in the background. His uncle asked, "How's our little project going?"

"Is Sage there with you?"

"Uh-huh. We just finished up breakfast and our first planning session for Amelia's."

The tea room again.

"Are you sure she doesn't know you're giving her the grant? I could be her benefactor instead—"

"No." Charlie's tone took on that firm edge. "I promised her grandfather I'd look out for her. I want to do this. "

Pressing his lips into a straight line, Luke raised one brow. "Are you sure?"

"Positive." Charlie's voice dropped to a whisper as the background conversation faded. "She doesn't have a clue, and you agreed to keep it that way."

"I did."

"She's a sweet girl."

"She seems nice," Luke said reluctantly. He could understand why Charlie might have an elderly crush on Sage.

112

That wasn't true. Charlie was smarter than that. Besides, he hadn't had a romantic interest since the woman he was about to marry broke off their wedding the week before. At least, not that Luke knew of. He'd been about to go off to college that summer and had his own breakup to get over. They'd been two brokenhearted bachelors together, but they'd survived.

Sighing, he gave in. "Can I take you out to dinner tonight? Someplace nice and quiet?" And where he could find out what the heck was really behind his uncle's unusual behavior.

"Cliff House has great food."

"Pick you up about six?"

Charlie must have wandered back to the others. He could hear Sage clearly as if he was standing right beside her. "I have to get going. I'll see you all later."

"Six will be fine. I have to meet with several town council members today about the Summer Celebration and will need a break," Charlie said after he said goodbye to Sage.

His uncle was heavily involved with the town council. Had been since he retired to Wally Creek. Just because he was retired, that didn't mean the old man was sitting on a porch swing letting the years pass him by. Luke admired that about the older man.

"Okay. See you then."

He thought about calling Gabi and asking her to slow-walk selling the stocks he'd decided would do the least amount of damage to his uncle's portfolio but decided to wait until after their dinner conversation. If he objected too much, it would just get Charlie's backup. How would he protect his uncle financially if he did as he threatened and took his account elsewhere? A more subtle approach was definitely in order.

Luke opened his laptop and went to his favorite business site to do a quick exploration of tea rooms and new startups. His instincts had been correct. The cursory glance didn't make him feel any better. Who got to be the lucky one to tell Sage that new businesses like Amelia's didn't have a huge profit margin and that most failed in the first year? Probably not Charlie.

So, he was right. A tea room wasn't the best idea. Especially when it was Charlie's retirement that was bankrolling the thing. He glanced at the time on his phone. More thorough research would have to wait.

Wally Creek was small enough and had enough charm that exploring the little town by walking to where he wanted to go was too tempting to pass up. He liked that about the area where he lived on Mercer Island too.

With his hands in his pants pockets and with a slight breeze keeping him company, he let his thoughts roam free, a little more excited about meeting up with his party planning cohort than he should be. Sage was a smart woman. She would figure out he was batting for his uncle's team soon enough. And when she did, he'd be in plenty of hot water instead of making it onto her we-should-be-friends list.

The sidewalk took him past a cemetery with well-tended, weathered headstones shaded by strong, old maples. Butter-flies fluttered from sunlight to shade. Small brown birds he didn't know the name of hopped on the ground, digging for their breakfast.

Too bad he wouldn't be in town long enough to find out which variety of the bird family they belonged to. He'd always been fascinated, especially as a kid, by the chirpy little creatures. They lived their entire lives making homes in trees, searching for food, and taking care of their young.

Sage was like that. Making a home that now included his uncle and friends. Looking to open a business where she could take care of her customers. The more he was around her, the more he thought about having a home big enough for his own future family. More and more he wanted to be her friend instead of facing off on opposite sides of the fence.

Could he turn their give and take into a friendly undertaking that accomplished both their goals instead of competing for Charlie's bank account like it was a prized bread box? That was a question he didn't have an answer to.

His mind refusing to get off the merry-go-round, he passed by a high school on his right and a middle school with a large auditorium on the opposite corner. As he got closer to the market, many of the residential houses had been repurposed into quaint businesses. A woman waved at him from the front of a flower shop.

Stopping at the corner of a road that intersected Birch Street at the top of a small hill overlooking most of downtown, Luke took a deep breath. He could see almost the whole of the main thoroughfare as it gradually angled up from the Wally River bordering the west side of town.

Flower baskets hung from old-fashioned street lamps next to planters filled with bushy, flowering plants at every corner. Parking slots angled into colorful, brick-laid sidewalks. Luke started down the hill as a truck leisurely passed him going up. At the bottom across from the grocery was his destination, Wally Creek Pharmacy. And there, parked in the postage-sized parking lot, was Sage's Sunbeam.

Annabelle. Would a scheming woman give a classic car a name that brought to mind summer parties, bar-b-ques, and thick slices of juicy watermelon? That said something good about her, didn't it?

He ducked into the small garden area fenced off in front of the pharmacy. He wasn't usually so indecisive about people or his next step, but keeping a personal distance from Sage Dawson was a challenge. Luke had enough experience to know who he was dealing with. He just wished naming a Sunbeam, Annabelle, wasn't so . . . so charming. He didn't like feeling that his objectivity was slipping.

Walking slowly among the potted plants, not really seeing them, his misgivings give way to something else. For a lot of years, he'd set aside his private life in favor of focusing on business. Where would he be now if he'd gotten married to Hannah Berk right out of college as planned and had to divide his attention between MR Investments and a growing family? Probably not about to take MR international.

Hannah had taught him a valuable lesson. Some women were only interested in a man's assets, not in forging a relationship that would last a lifetime. If he ever took the plunge, he wanted it to be with someone who wanted the whole package, not just that he could give her a cushy life with prestige, which, interesting enough, Sage didn't seem to have much interest in.

Give it a rest, dude.

Impatient with the revolving door in his mind, he tracked the lady in question down in the back of the store, in what could barely be described as the party section. Sage was eyeing the various balloons while she tapped her finger on a small notebook opened to a page that appeared to contain a list.

Sage made lists. Wasn't that sexy? "Find anything that will work for the party?"

Spinning around, the concentration that pulled her brows together disappeared. "I'm not sure."

"Is there something I can help you with?" asked a sales clerk who came from the pharmacy area.

Sage turned to smile at Karen—according to the clerk's name tag. A spontaneous, happy smile. Not the careful, not-sure-if-I-trust-you, twist of lips she normally graced him with.

Sage was right not to trust him. And he shouldn't trust her. He just wasn't having much luck holding out against her sweet wiles—the way she smiled at everyone but him and how she blurted out what was on her mind, apparently without thinking the words through—

I'm not looking for a boyfriend, no matter what Charlie told you.

You should see Charlie as much as you can.

Despite how they'd started out, more enemies than mere acquaintances, he appreciated her honesty, at least on those two occasions.

"I'm—" She glanced at him before turning back to the salesgirl. "—*We're* planning a birthday party for two guys in their seventies. We need something fun and playful."

Karen went behind the counter and pulled a package of balloons from the shelf. "We have this pack of metallic balloons. It comes with this strip to attach the balloons to. With it, you can shape them into anything."

"That might work." Her reserve evaporating, Sage moved aside so he could see the packages better, and asked him, "Don't you think?"

He hesitated. He didn't want to ruin an opportunity to be her partner in crime, but— "That's a lot of balloons to blow up."

"We have an air pump that will make that a lot easier," Karen said with a smile that included them both.

"We'll take it," he said, hoping Sage wouldn't notice that Karen thought they were a couple. He added quickly, "How about that banner that says 'Happy over the hill party'? And that 'Happy 70+ years' streamer?"

"I like them." The beginning of a smile hovered at the corners of her lips.

He had a hard time looking away, but it was progress, anyway. As if he planned birthday parties all the time and was certain about what he was doing, Luke asked the salesgirl, "Do you have twinkle lights?"

He wasn't trying to impress Sage. At least he didn't think he cared about that. Suddenly, torn between telling Sage right out what he was doing in Wally Creek versus incurring Charlie's anger, well it wasn't a comfortable place to be. A very serious conversation would happen that night during dinner at the Cliff House.

Karen shook her head. "Not this time of year."

"We can check the attic at the house. Grams always keeps odd things like that there." Sage pulled a bank card from her wallet.

At the same time, Luke pulled his phone out of his pocket. "Let me pay."

"That's okay. I've got it."

"How about we go fifty-fifty?" Sage planning the party had been Charlie's idea, after all.

She stared at him for a long, full moment before she said, "You don't have to."

That was becoming a refrain used too often.

"I know. Besides, we're planning this party together, right?"

He widened his smile, hoping to bring back the easy woman he'd spent the last hour with.

"Okay," she finally conceded.

While they paid, he asked, "What's next?"

"Birthday presents, of course."

"Of course." He liked to do his shopping online. But after following Sage around the store, he had to admit, looking for birthday presents in person was more fun than he'd had outside of work in a long time.

She was cute. She touched everything. Asked his opinion. And when he didn't have one, had one of her own she was more than happy to share. He couldn't remember the last time he'd spent such an entertaining day with a woman who wasn't Gabi, Dara, or Fran.

After a lot of looking, they finally chose a funny superhero apron for Verne, with the words *a cape is just an apron put on backward* sprawled across the front, and a book on the history of Wally Creek for Charlie.

Luke couldn't believe how inexplicably he was drawn to the woman who'd landed on his chest the day they'd met. There was so much more to Sage Dawson than a pretty face or a lady who had a clumsy gene, or one who might be taking advantage of an older man.

"All that's left to do is stop by Luna's Books, and then get the cake ingredients and ice cream."

At Luna's, they went their separate ways. Luke was glad to have a minute to himself to catch his breath. While he was at it, he found the perfect gift for Charlie—a leather-bound journal. His uncle had kept a journal for as long as he could remember.

After paying for the book, he found a deep cushioned chair

where he could watch Sage. She was such a contradiction. She ran her fingers down the spines of the books in the cookbook section, occasionally pulling one out to flip through the pages.

There was something about her that wouldn't let him go. He just couldn't put his finger on what it was. If the situation weren't so dire, he'd give in to the attraction, just for the heck of it, to see where it took them. He would like to explore the feelings giving him a hard time. Despite his suspicions, he liked her, which made him the one who wasn't so smart, didn't it?

Maybe Charlie was right. Maybe he was on a wild goose chase. Charlie, who'd never misled him, was certain Sage didn't know where the grant was coming from. Why didn't he believe his uncle?

She finally selected a book. Luke joined her at the cash register. "Which book did you decide to get?"

She showed him the title before handing the cookbook over to the young man behind the register. *Summer Recipes*. It suited Verne.

By mid-afternoon, they'd finished shopping.

"I guess that's it," she said as he put the grocery bags in the backseat of her car. "So, I'll see you tomorrow. We'll start the party about one."

"I thought I'd come with you now and lend a hand with the decorating." That's what potential friends did, right? Help each other out?

Luke almost convinced himself that was why he wanted to hang out with the intriguing lady. Becoming friends seemed reasonable. He gave her his best, *I'm available* look—not in *that* way—but to convince her he was serious about getting to know her better.

Pausing with the driver's side door half open, she hesitated, brown eyes turning darker, making Luke all the more determined to go with her to the house. He still had questions and the only way he would get answers was if he convinced Sage he wasn't the enemy. Which was rich, because, from a certain point of view, he was. He just no longer wanted to be.

She slid behind the wheel. "No worries. I can handle it."

Chapter Eight

L uke leaned on the car door before Sage could close it in his face.

"I insist. I have a few hours before Uncle Charlie and I go to dinner at the Cliff House, so I have time to do some heavy lifting for you," he said, smiling in an effort to get Sage to let him come over and play—to use the vernacular of children. From the look she gave him, it was a long shot, but he wasn't a quitter and wasn't about to give up now.

"Okay, but there won't be much heavy lifting going on."

When she didn't immediately start the engine, he took that as an invitation. Moving quickly around the front of the Sunbeam, he got in on the passenger side and buckled his seat belt.

As she backed up, she gave him a sideways look. "You love your uncle, don't you?"

"He's the best." Luke shifted sideways so he could see her better. "Did you think I didn't like him?"

She'd pulled out of the parking lot and stopped at the only light in town. One shoulder moved gracefully up and down. "I don't know. It just seemed like you weren't happy with Charlie the first time you came to see him."

"I had a lot of . . . work on my mind." That part at least was true.

Now would be a good time to tell her why he'd made the trip down from Seattle in the first place, but all he could hear in his head was Charlie's warning not to say a thing about what he was up to. "Did Uncle Charlie tell you that when I was a kid I spent my summers with him?"

"No, but that must have been fun. He's a great guy." The light turned green. She drove smoothly across the intersection and turned onto River Road.

Luke unbuckled his seat belt as she parked. "We got to be pretty tight. I would never let anything bad happen to him."

It wasn't a warning exactly, but well— Yes, it was.

She turned off the engine and reached behind the console to grab her small backpack. "I feel the same way about my grandparents."

So, they had that in common. It could be that she didn't want anything to happen to her cash cow, though he was seriously starting to question his conclusion on that point. No longer as certain as he'd been when he first drove like a madman to get to Wally Creek, he was having a hard time believing Sage was a woman who had no moral compass.

That complicated things, didn't it? He didn't want to ruin the good time he was having with Sage, planning a birthday party for two old dudes and picking out Charlie and Verne's presents. Grabbing the packages on his side of the Sunbeam, Luke followed her into the dining room.

If he could get Sage to trust him, maybe he could avoid his uncle's order not to reveal the origin of the grant, and still get the information he needed. Aside from that, he didn't want to be 'the enemy' any longer.

"How long are you planning to stay in Wally Creek?" She glanced his way, her expression more curious than suspicious. Suddenly, feeling so much lighter, Luke almost hugged her. He could live with them doing more talking than playing tug-of-war over Charlie.

"A few days." He unloaded his arms on the table and put aside the journal to be wrapped when he got back to Charlie's place. If he was lucky, he wouldn't need much more than that to finish sorting out the mystery that was Sage Dawson. "So you think your grandmother might have twinkle lights in the attic? Should we look?"

She quickly put away the cake ingredients and ice cream. "Yes."

Grabbing the bags containing the presents, she went upstairs, then left them in a bedroom he presumed was hers while he waited by the stairs that continued up to the attic. Curious, but deciding it wasn't appropriate to invade her privacy, he studied the framed photographs hanging on the hall wall.

Each one told their own story. They were markets and iconic places, several of which he recognized. Pike Place Fish Market in Seattle. He'd been there many times. He could have stepped into the photo and been right in the middle of the market. In another, San Francisco's Golden Gate bridge played peekaboo through morning fog. He'd hiked across the bridge during one of his visits and could still feel the breeze pulling at his jacket.

"These are stunning."

"Thank you."

He turned to her as she came to stand next to him, close enough he could smell a subtle note of vanilla. "You took these?"

"Don't look so surprised." She laughed.

The happy sound washed over him, a pleasant surprise he wasn't expecting.

What would he have done if, when he was first starting out, someone had told him he couldn't make a go of MR Investments? Of course he wouldn't have listened. Nothing that he'd discovered about Sage Dawson since meeting her made him think she was any less driven than that young man who'd just graduated from college.

He stuffed his hands in his pockets. "I didn't mean—"

"Of course not. No worries," she said, giving him a light punch on the arm. "I've been taking pictures since I was a kid. I love it."

"Well, you're super-talented." He edged toward the stairs leading to the attic. "You could take pictures professionally."

Stepping around him to lead the way, she said, "My brother, Jack, is more serious about it than I am. I just take pictures for fun."

"Then I say, that's the rest of the world's loss." Luke meant that sincerely. Her smile said she might believe him.

The roomy attic was lit by two windows at the gable ends, one on each side. An industrial style light hung from the rafters in the middle. It didn't take them long to locate the twinkle lights.

A jaunty jingle from Luke's phone announced an incoming text. "I'm running about fifteen minutes late. Meet you at the Cliff House."

He sent Charlie a grinning emoji before saying to Sage, "I'll help you get these downstairs, then I have to take off."

"That was Charlie?"

Luke nodded. "He has a habit of showing up late. At least he doesn't mind admitting that time gets away from him."

"There are worse faults to have." For the first time she wasn't looking at him with wary fences braced up. "I had fun today. Thanks for the help."

Clearing his throat, he stacked the boxes she pointed to and carried them down the stairs. "I'll come back tomorrow morning and help with the decorating."

"You don't—"

"—have to," he finished for her and said over his shoulder, "I know. Watch your step here. That last one's a little creaky."

In the dining room, they put the boxes in a corner. He didn't linger. Grabbing the journal, he waved as he left. His last glimpse of Sage was the lady shaking her head at him before turning to go to the kitchen where he could hear Verne and Lily's voices.

Back at the bungalow, he went over the long conversation he intended to have with Charlie. He had to have a plan or his uncle would not take his concerns seriously. What still really bothered Luke was that if Charlie went through with the grant, the old man wasn't the only one who could be hurt. What was the point of giving Sage the money if, before a year's end, she'd have to close up shop because the tea room hadn't made a successful start?

After the twenty minute drive to the Cliff House and waiting at a table overlooking the Wally River below, Luke still didn't have a good argument that would convince his uncle to rethink this grant thing, maybe even get more creative about where the money would come from.

Helping Sage with the birthday party had been an eye opener. If she were a puppy, she'd be a GoldenDoodle—bouncy, loving, everyone's friend. He'd never been especially good at making friends, like she was. What he was good at was doing business, which was all he'd needed to make MR stand out on the financial map. Besides, the three ladies in his life, Gabi, Dara, and Fran kept him busy enough in the female friends department.

And speaking of his business partner— *Yes, Gabi, I had fun today.*

But that wasn't the most important part. Somehow, he had to convince Charlie to let MR fund the grant. If he couldn't, he would just have to be the one to tell Sage how rare it was for small businesses to succeed. His conscience demanded he at least be that truthful, since she wasn't about to hear it from his uncle.

Just as he decided he would keep talking until Charlie heard what he had to say, his uncle came into the restaurant. He wasn't alone. He'd brought Bette along.

Luke liked Bette—she was sweet—but tonight wasn't the best time for a social visit. He should have told Charlie he wanted to talk business.

Too late now. His chance to change Charlie's mind about the grant would have to wait until tomorrow morning when he went to help Sage with the setup. He could corner the old man then.

Hiding a heavy sigh, Luke stood and pulled out a chair for Bette.

~ * ~

The party was in full swing when Sage stopped circulating

and found herself standing near the window facing the front yard, right next to Luke, in an empty corner of the living room. It turned out Bette's guest list wasn't that short. Charlie and Verne knew a lot of people in town.

"Nice party, Ms. Dawson." As promised, Luke had shown up early that morning to help with the decorating.

"Your help was invaluable, Mr. Marshell," she responded in kind.

She smiled inside but couldn't look in his direction or she'd laugh out loud. He was funny. In a poker-face way. The aloofness that sometimes made him seem so unapproachable currently mingled with a flash of humor he was pretty good at hiding. Did he come by that reserve naturally or was that something he'd picked up along the way? The cruise director still lurking inside wanted to know.

Broken heart, remember?

Sage stepped away from curiosity insisting on finding answers. There was no time to fall for this charming man just because she had a nagging feeling that Luke Marshell was worth a second look.

Looking for a distraction, she moved to the dining room and the wall she'd turned into a gallery display. Luke followed.

It was pure inspiration if she did say so herself. "I appreciate your help with the pictures."

The photographs were of Charlie, Verne, Bette, and Lily. Smiles seeped into their eyes as they played Scrabble in front of the fireplace. They laughed in the kitchen while they cleaned up from dinner. The other three peered over Lily's shoulders as she finished her painting of the back garden.

It'd been fun, sneaking around to capture the precious moments. So had been clearing a spot in the attic for her printers.

This morning, after the decorating was done, Luke had given her a hand cleaning up the frames she'd found buried in one of the attic's far corners. She was impressed. He knew his way around wood restoration and tools.

"Gordan would have just gone out and bought new," she said under her breath.

"Gordan?"

She hadn't meant for him to hear that. "My ex."

He nodded but, thank goodness, didn't pursue her slip of the tongue. Her breakup with Gordan wasn't something she wanted to talk about with her party-planning partner. All shiny in dress trousers and a nice buttoned-down shirt that matched his eyes, he'd cleaned up nicely. When he pushed his hands in his pockets, lips curling up slightly, his gaze following Charlie as the older man mingled among his guests, she needed a quick reminder this was Verne and Charlie's day, not crush on Luke Marshell day.

With Amelia's hanging in the balance— Yup, she still hadn't heard back from any of the grant queries she'd made. It was too soon. And she was just too anxious to hear if the financing was going to come through or not.

Anyhow, now was not the time to get diverted by a guy who, like her brother, Jack, was not necessarily user-friendly. Though he did a good job of helping her with the party.

Last night, when she couldn't get to sleep, and just so she'd stop thinking about Luke, she'd imagined what Amelia's would look like. She'd even sat in the dark with only the light from her desk lamp, making sketches. In the light's glow, the tea room came alive as clear as day. Tongue-and-groove boards painted a heather green and run vertically on the walls on both sides of the wide open space. Round wood tables scattered across the main seating area, covered in lace-trimmed cotton linens. Nothing too fancy, but comfortable, with teapots filled with fresh flowers as centerpieces. Cushioned, ladder-back chairs, each one a little different from the others, surrounding the tables.

Somewhere she wanted to fit in bookshelves lined with the book club's current reading selection and journals and old-fashioned writing materials. For customers who wanted to enjoy a moment of quiet musing, colorful overstuffed chairs to anchor the bookshelves would fit perfectly against the walls. She wasn't exactly sure where she would fit it all in, or if she could save the fireplace, but the more she drew, the more the pages had stacked up.

"They're about to open their presents," Luke said at her shoulder.

By the time the party began to thin out, she was ready for some quiet time of her own. Standing by the door, she said goodbye to departing guests.

"What a lovely party," Maggie Tupper said with a smile. Maggie was the Mayor of Wally Creek. She also took charge at the town council meetings, with Charlie as her backup. She was in her fifties. Widowed. And the driving force behind the Summer Celebration. "You did a wonderful job of organizing this party."

"Thank you. I had help." At the last minute, Sage had roped Luke into helping her set up a board game station on the coffee table by the fireplace. It didn't take guests long to start a puzzle or a rousing game of Scrabble.

"Smart girl. I heard your helper was that nice young man from Seattle, Charlie's once-removed nephew."

Nice? She was still debating on that one, but she guessed she would concede the point.

"Charlie tells me you have lots of experience in the event planning department. I'll keep that in mind, just in case something comes up that needs your special skills." The Mayor's eyes twinkled. "Our annual Summer Celebration is in a few weeks. Everything is running smoothly so far, but you never know how things will go."

Sage felt obligated to tell the Mayor, "I'm not sure how long I'll be in Wally Creek."

"Not to worry. Circumstances can change on a dime." Maggie gave Sage's arm a gentle pat. "I know Charlie is hoping you'll stay in town."

And with that, off the mayor went.

Watching Maggie get into her Prius, Sage wondered if she was being realistic. She wasn't that worried. Not much anyway. But looking down the road wasn't really one of her best skill sets. She was more of a dreamer, a big-picture girl, and a hope-for-the-best kind of gal. What if opening Amelia's *was* too risky? Should she stick with what she knew best? Planning a birthday party or an excursion for tourists was a whole different thing than opening up her own business and then being responsible for its success, not to mention, her friends.

Luke had made his business work. Why couldn't she do the same?

The good news was she didn't have to make a decision until she got the grant. Which meant she had time to think about whether she was truly ready to settle permanently in Wally Creek.

The house emptied out fairly quickly after the Mayor left.

Luke helped Bette and Lily clean up the dining room and kitchen.

Verne found her putting away the games. Turning off the soft sounds of the Andrew Sisters (after much discussion, Lily had been the one elected to come up with the evening's playlist), he sat down across from Sage, muttering in his gruff way. "Thanks for the shindig."

"Did you have fun?" It was easy to figure out what Charlie liked. He was like her. Happy to be surrounded by folks who enjoyed good conversation. Verne, on the other hand, was more of a mystery.

One shoulder shifted up and down. "Sure, but I kept wishing you'd let me cook. Sub sandwiches would have been a good addition."

"The whole point was to give you a day off from your kitchen duties." Sage laughed. "But I'll keep that in mind for your next birthday party."

Verne nodded, bent over to retrieve a runaway letter, then closed the lid on the Scrabble game. "So, you're planning to be here for the next one?"

"I'd like to be." Sage let her shoulders slump. "We'll see."

The longer she stayed, the more she loved Wally Creek and sharing the house with her elderly roommates.

"You need the grant."

"Yeah." She put the last of the puzzle pieces in the box.

Verne gathered the games and stood. "Don't give up. Something will come along. I'm sure of it."

"You sound just like Grams and Grandpa." Despite his gruffness, underneath it all, Verne was a sweet guy.

A rare grin broke across his face. "Lucky me." He winked and carried the games away.

Getting the grant would definitely make her decision easier. Carrying dirty glasses into the kitchen, she spotted Luke and Charlie having a very serious discussion in a corner by the stairs. Neither man looked happy.

Glancing her way, Luke said something that didn't seem to go over well with his uncle. Whatever was going on, she told herself it wasn't any of her business.

A frown pulled at the corners of Luke's mouth as he caught up with her. "Can we talk? Privately?"

That didn't sound good. "Will the back garden work?"

He nodded. She straightened a pillow while he delivered the remaining dishes to the kitchen, then made her way out to the back.

At the end of the garden, with the scent and riot of color from blooming roses surrounding her, Sage paced back and forth in front of the garden bench made of iron and wood. The backyard lights had come on as night closed in.

What could Luke possibly want that required a private conversation? Fortunately, her wary curiosity didn't have long to wait.

"What's up? Did I overcook the cake or burn the cookies?"

Jack was good at cornering her too. The idea that she'd somehow done something wrong, but couldn't figure out what that might be, had started when they'd lost their parents. Jack had pulled away, leaving her even more confused and alone. She understood now—mostly—that was the way her brother grieved, but she'd never gotten over the feeling that there was something she could have done to keep him close.

"What? No! The food was all delicious."

"That's good news." What would he do if she batted her eyelashes at him and maybe flirted a little? The last time she'd put any effort into flirting was with her ex.

"You did a great job." He straightened his shoulders and shoved his hands in his pockets. This *was* serious.

"*We* did a great job," she reminded him, wondering how to encourage Luke to get to the point. Though he was kind of cute with his brows all scrunched together the way they were, she sincerely doubted he'd asked her into the garden to talk about her party food choices.

"I was talking to Uncle Charlie about this tea room idea you have, and I think it's important for you to know some things."

"It's not a sure thing yet." But he had her undivided attention. "I'm waiting to hear about some grants I've applied for."

He studied her face unnecessarily long. "And if you don't get a grant?"

"I'm not sure." She shrugged.

The more she could see Amelia's as a real thing, the less she wanted to go back to the Emerald Star. Unfortunately, she might not have a choice.

His gaze reached for hers. "I like you." And with her pulse suddenly taking off like a rocket with misfiring boosters, when she opened her mouth to say something, anything coherent, the words stuck in her throat.

She wanted to say she liked him too. How crazy was that?

If she got the grant, of course she'd stay in Wally Creek. Luke would go home to Seattle, probably sooner rather than later. And that would be that. The worst thing that could happen would be that she didn't get the grant. And at the same time, she developed feelings for the businessman that weren't returned in the same measure.

Been there, done that with Gordan. She didn't need more heartbreak because she'd misread a man's idea of friendship a second time.

Sage blinked. Realized it would suck if she had to go back to the Emerald Star. Any secret thought she had about finding a grand passion, even if her grand passion only turned out to be Amelia's, would be over.

"I feel obligated to tell you that tea rooms, even those in prime locations like Portland and Seattle, don't have huge profit margins. Most fail within the first year."

Suddenly getting the drift of where he was going with his little 'talk', she crossed her arms over her chest. "I see."

"I don't think you do." He reduced the space between them, reaching out as if taking her hand would show his sincerity. "I have a degree in finance. I know what I'm talking about."

"And because I don't have a degree, you don't think I know what I'm doing?" Sage managed to stay calm as she took a step back out of reach.

Was this the argument he'd been having with Charlie?

Charlie and the book club wanted her to keep the house and open Amelia's Cuppa Tea because it would give them all purpose. The biggest surprise of all was that it hadn't taken much for them to get her on board.

She curled her fingers into her palms. "I'm not planning to fail. How can you even say that? You barely know me. You don't know how hard I work. And even if I did fail, that's my business, not yours."

Luke's gaze shifted over her shoulder to the house. She glanced back to see what had caught his attention. Charlie was watching them from the kitchen window.

Plunking fists on her hips, she turned back to Luke. "Does Charlie have a problem with the idea of opening Amelia's?"

She hadn't thought so, but a person could change their mind.

Especially if their nephew was against the idea.

Luke hesitated, but finally said, "No. He and Verne, and Bette and Lily, they all think it's a great idea."

"So what's your problem, then?"

His expression went blank. "I just think it's too risky."

Luke was only echoing her own round-robin of arguments. But if she didn't take the risk, would she look back, regret not taking the leap, and by being so timid, miss out on something really good, like keeping her mother's dream alive? "What if I don't mind taking risks?"

She held her breath, not understanding why she cared what Luke Marshell thought.

His gaze narrowed. "I would say this particular risk is too big. It won't be just you who loses out if your venture fails."

"What do you mean?" She waited for his explanation. None came. Instead, he pressed his lips together.

Exasperated, she demanded lowly, "Don't you ever loosen up?"

He put more space between them. "I apologize if I over-stepped."

Not believing him, Sage spun on her heel. She threw over her shoulder as she walked off, "You're not the only one in town who knows how to run a business, Luke Marshell."

Charlie and the book club were depending on her to make Amelia's a success. *She* was depending on her skills and determination. It'd never really mattered to her, but just this once she wanted to prove to Jack and Gordan, and now Luke that she had what it took to make a long-term commitment.

She wasn't a butterfly flitting from one pretty bloom to another. She was a lady hawk building a nest and protecting the new family she was making. Charlie and the others weren't the family she'd been anticipating when she made plans to visit her grandparents, but they were the family she'd found.

Em would tell her straight out if she was barking up the wrong tree.

She spun around to tell Luke just that, but he had his back to her and his phone to his ear.

Fine. If he didn't get it, then too bad for him. Before poking his nose into other people's business, he needed to take a deep breath and chill. And she would make sure he got that message. As soon as she talked to Em.

Chapter Nine

The next morning, Sage sank back in her chair after telling Em about her plans and the confrontation with Luke. She blew out a breath and closed her eyes. "He said that?"

"Yes! But is he right? Will Amelia's fail in the first year?"

The waiter brought their food. They'd ended up at the Hargrove for brunch, named after one of the original settlers in Wally Creek. The restaurant was the oldest building in town. Perched above the Wally River, it had originally been built to accommodate the hordes of miners who came looking for gold and silver. On one end was the restaurant. On the other, a bar that still harbored the faint smell of tobacco, even though the whole place had undergone a full restoration a few years ago and inside smoking wasn't allowed.

Sage would bet Roy Hargrove—who, as the story went, wasn't an astute businessman but a miner who'd put all his mining gains into his namesake—hadn't worried about his restaurant failing in the first year.

"Just tell me the truth. I can handle it."

Sage reeled under the startling realization that she really *wanted* to open Amelia's and *didn't want* the tea room to fail at all, much less before it hardly got started. Em just had to tell her Luke Marshell was dead wrong. Opening her eyes, she unwrapped the silverware and placed the linen napkin on her lap while she waited for her friend's verdict.

Em took a sip of her wine, then proceeded to cut up her tofu meatloaf. She'd been a vegetarian for as long as Sage could remember and always, always, was careful about the advice she gave. "I've read the statistics, and Luke isn't exactly wrong."

Of course, he wasn't. Her shoulders slumped. At least he was honest about what he thought. Reluctantly, she admitted it couldn't have been easy to tell her the things he had. Sage had to at least respect that.

"However, from my personal experience, I don't think the studies take into account the motivation of the business owners." Em popped a bite into her mouth. "Mmm. They make the best tofu loaf here."

Sage's favorite was regular old meatloaf, a recipe that went back to the early days of the Hargrove. It was one of her favorite meals in town. When Em's words sank in, she perked up. "The Oak made it past the first year."

"Yeah. I was very motivated to make sure it did." Em took another sip of her wine. "My dream was a boutique hotel. When The Oak went up for sale, I had to go for it. My advice to you is, if you want to open a tea room, go into it with your eyes wide open, and don't let the naysayers make you question *your* dream."

She wanted Amelia's. Period. To honor her mother's memory and dream. There was no longer any question about it in her mind.

So she couldn't be accused of not thinking through all the angles—that would be Jack's voice in her ear—Sage gave it a shot and attempted to look at Amelia's from Luke's point of view. "A tea room probably doesn't have the same draw as a hotel."

Em snorted. "Says who? We'll bill it as . . . Amelia's, along with The Oak, the best places to get away from a noisy life in Portland and Wally Creek. We'll help each other target the right audience and market our places together."

Worry lifted from Sage's shoulders. "You are the best, Em."

"Yes, I am," her friend laughed. "Now tell me all about this stupid man who dumped you."

Sage winced. "Ouch."

"You know what I mean. And then, tell me all about the gorgeous places you've been to since we last talked. I can't believe you're giving up world travel to settle in Wally Creek, but I'm glad you are."

Sage couldn't believe it, either, except the timing just seemed right. Glossing over her breakup with Gordan, she took the rest of their meal and most of their glass of wine after to cover her travels.

Em leaned back as the waiter cleared their dessert dishes. "Will you miss it? Stopping in a new place every few days?"

Honestly? "I don't know. But I think it's time to do something different."

"And an old-fashioned tea room in Wally Creek is definitely different." Em laughed.

They were walking out of the restaurant when Sage suddenly stopped. "So, Amelia's. Good idea? Or a bad idea?" She really wanted to prove Luke wrong.

Em dragged her into a tight hug, saying with conviction. "Your mother's dream is a great idea."

"Not too risky?" Sage whispered.

"Everything in life is a risk. I say go for it." Em linked arms and predicted, "It'll be alright. We'll make sure you run into as little problems as possible."

Sage grinned, lifting her hand for a high five. "Here's to a new adventure."

They walked back to The Oak where she'd left Annabelle. She didn't need Em to tell her which fork in the road to take. Deep down she'd already known what she wanted to do. She'd just needed reassurance that it didn't matter whether Luke was right or not, and Em's opinion that Amelia's was worth taking a chance on.

Amelia's *would* be risky, but what was life worth if a person didn't take a risk or two along the way?

At The Oak, she unlocked the Sunbeam. "Thanks for letting me bend your ear."

"That's what besties are for." Em went to go inside, then spun back. "Hey, listen. The town council is having a meeting Monday night to talk about the Summer Celebration. The public is invited. You should come. You'll want to know what the town leaders are doing for Wally Creek."

"What time?" Until she was awarded a grant, Sage's evenings were wide open.

"Seven."

"I can meet you here at a quarter till."

"Six-thirty would be better," Em negotiated with a wink. "That way we don't have to be in a hurry."

Somehow she'd pay her friend back. Sage drove the short distance to the house. Em never did anything halfway, thank goodness.

Luke, on the other hand, by playing devil's advocate—whether it was his intention or not—had helped her decide which direction she wanted to go. And because of his analytical way of looking at things, he'd kind of become a friend who'd made sure her eyes were wide open. She hadn't expected that.

Pulling into the drive, she turned off the car and stayed there, staring at the house. She could envision outdoor seating on the generous porch, Amelia's Cuppa Tea elegantly scripted on the double front door that was mostly glass and original to the house. She could add more pots of blooming plants to enhance a cozy welcome. A new awning over the living room triple window would give the building that old-time feel.

Grabbing her bag, she slipped into the house. It was mid-afternoon and quiet. She found Charlie and Bette playing a quiet game of Scrabble. They were so absorbed in sorting through their tiles, they didn't see her pause on the way to her room. Deciding not to disturb them, she was at the bottom of the stairs when she heard a soft trill of laughter from Bette.

"Woman, you are a pain in my backside." Charlie's tone was laced with humor.

"I can't help it if you leave a triple score open. I have to take advantage."

A chair scooted back. "Do you want another cup of tea?"

"Yes, thank you." Bette sounded pleased with herself.

Changing her mind about going upstairs, Sage went into the kitchen to rustle up her own cup of tea. "Hi, Charlie. It sounds like Bette's winning."

"Hi, yourself. She always does." He poured hot water into a cup from the kettle on the stove. "She's nearly invincible when it comes to Scrabble. Did you have a nice brunch with Emerson?"

She'd let her roommates know she wouldn't be there for breakfast or lunch.

"It was fun. She invited me to the town council meeting Monday night."

"Are you going?" He plunked a tea bag into the cup until it was saturated with water.

"Yup." To check if Charlie was still on board—you never know; clearly, she had a lot of opposition from Luke—Sage added, "She thinks Amelia's is a great idea."

"It *is* a great idea." He grinned, adding honey to Bette's cup of tea.

Sage fixed her tea without honey. "Luke doesn't think so."

"Don't you worry about that boy. He'll come around." Charlie patted her on the shoulder, and taking Bette's tea with him, headed back to his game. "We're going fishing tomorrow. That will put my nephew in a better frame of mind."

"I haven't heard from any of the grants I applied for," Sage blurted before Charlie had taken more than a couple steps. He sounded so confident about Luke. "It's too soon, of course, but I'm a little worried that I won't qualify. I don't want you to get too invested in Amelia's and then be disappointed if it doesn't work out."

She couldn't read Charlie's expression, which was a little concerning. Usually, the older man's face was an open book.

"I'm not worried, Sage. I'm sure you'll hear from one of them soon."

With that softly spoken prediction, he disappeared into the

living room, teasing Bette when he got there. "I hope you didn't look at my tiles while I was getting your tea."

"Of course, I didn't, you old geezer," Bette said with a laugh.

Taking her cue from the two of them, upstairs Sage sank into the bedside chair and mulled over the clue Charlie had revealed. Luke liked to fish. In his off time? He liked rivers then. And maybe rafting. Like Gordan.

Dismissing her ex's invasion into something he had nothing to do with, she sat at her desk to do some exploration of her own. The best river in the county for recreation was right across the street, on the other side of a walking path. The Wally River and Wally Creek were named after the first prospector to strike it rich in the Willamette Valley region. The prospector moved on during the California gold rush, but his name stuck on the river and town where he'd worked his original claim.

The Wally River was mostly calm and peaceful. Perfect for a meandering rafting trip designed for relaxation and slowly catching fish. When she was a kid, Sage had gone fishing with her grandpa more times than she could count. Perhaps it was time to go again. Not with her grandpa, of course. And not tomorrow with Charlie and Luke. She didn't want to intrude into Charlie's day with his nephew. But if Luke was still in town next weekend—

It wasn't a bad idea. The picture of his back to her, phone plastered to his ear, nagged at her mind. Before he died of an early heart attack, the man really should learn to slow down a bit, and have more in his life than constant, unfinished work. She was sure Charlie would love to see Luke make time for his family and friends.

Unexpectedly, she would love to see that too. Not with her,

of course. He hadn't given any hint that his thoughts ran in that direction.

Sage straightened in the chair. Dang it! She liked him. Under different circumstances, they would probably be friends. They could be friends right now if he wasn't so sure he was right about Amelia's. According to Grams, life was a lot like traveling to the next destination. Either you stood by the rail and watched it all go by, or you got off and explored every stop.

Luke didn't strike her as a get-off-and-explore kind of guy. But maybe he should be. And as his friend, she could do him a favor, like loosen him up so he wasn't so intense about both of their businesses.

How many times had she brought out the inner explorer in her passengers? If she wanted to put in the effort—she was tempted—that's what she could do for Luke. Invite him to get off the boat. No point in freaking the man out, but just so he could experience a stop or two. That was all it would take to broaden his outlook and give him something more than his work to look forward to.

On top of opening Amelia's and making a home for the local Sunnybrook Book Club members, pulling Luke out of his bubble was probably more than she should voluntarily take on. On the other hand, why not?

~ * ~

Luke cast his line as far from the bank as he could and watched it plunk into the slowly moving river. "I'm not good company today, Uncle Charlie."

"Don't worry about it. Everyone needs a quiet day to sort out their thoughts once in a while."

His uncle knew how to take advantage of the relaxing

moments that came along. Luke wasn't that skillful at it. But he could be home and back to work first thing in the morning. "I'm heading back to Seattle tonight."

"I'm sorry to hear that. I've enjoyed having you around, son." Charlie glanced his way. "It reminds me of when you used to visit when you were a kid. I was hoping you'd hang around for a few more days."

Guilt pinched at Luke's gut. Seattle wasn't that far away from Wally Creek. Sage was right. He should make more of an effort to spend time with his uncle. But this time, staying longer wouldn't solve anything.

When he'd warned her about the percentages of new businesses that failed, he'd seen the disappointment in her dark eyes. Because of his background and experience, he'd hoped to get her to believe him. Maybe she had, but she hadn't backed down. The way her chin had angled up was something he found quite charmingly attractive actually. He'd almost gotten on train Sage Dawson right then and there.

It wouldn't do them any good. And there was no way that she would consider taking a job at MR as their company event planner. No matter how much he paid her. She was determined to chase her dream. Could he blame her? He'd seen Dara do the same thing, with the same drive. And he'd done it himself.

"It's been a nice break." A surprise given the reason he'd come to Wally Creek in the first place. Just as surprising as Sage.

"Are you sure you have to leave?" Charlie adjusted his pole, then cast out his line.

He *could* stay. He was the boss after all, but— "It's time to get back to the real world."

Charlie's brows shot up. A sly look replaced his usual go-with-the-flow manner. It was not a good sign. "Come for dinner. I'll have Verne cook up the fish we catch. I have a town council meeting after. You should come along and see a small town 'real world' at work."

Clearly, he'd chosen the wrong words.

"I didn't mean that how it sounded, Uncle Charlie." When he managed to insult his favorite relative, it *was* time to get back to his own routine. "I have a lot to do in Seattle."

"I know. I'm just busting your chops." Charlie winked. "If you change your mind, we'll be going over the last-minute changes to the Summer Celebration. It would be nice to have another set of ears, in case there's something we've missed."

That wasn't likely. Charlie had been involved in the Summer Celebration practically from the day he'd moved to Wally Creek. First as a volunteer. Later as a member of the town council. It had always been his passion. Over the years Luke had received more than one invitation to come for the party.

He cast out his line again, regretting he hadn't taken Charlie up on any of the invitations. "I'll stay for dinner. You'll have to let me know how the meeting turns out."

At least if he went to dinner, he could find out if Sage had gotten her award letter. After their disastrous conversation, he'd called Gabi and instructed her to overnight the letter she had ready to go. It should have arrived today.

Except for being a little nomadic, Sage didn't seem to be the grasping woman he'd first thought he would encounter. Look how she'd taken in his uncle and the older man's friends in their hour of need. "Does Sage have a site picked out for her tea room?"

"Amelia's? She's remodeling the first floor of the house."

Charlie reeled in a fish that nibbled his line and added it to the others they'd caught. The older man cast him a sideways look. "I'll let her tell you about her plans."

They packed up their gear and their catch. Back at Sage's house, Verne took charge of dinner, as usual, including the tartar sauce ingredients they'd picked up at the grocery on the way back. Charlie disappeared upstairs.

Sage sat at the dining room table with Bette and Lily. Her hands pushed back her hair from her face as she leaned on her elbows and stared at a letter on the table.

From where he stood, Luke recognized the letterhead.

"I can't believe I got a grant. I mean, I hoped I would, of course, but I was skeptical too, you know? To be honest, I didn't think I would hear this soon."

Lily picked up the letter. "No one deserves it more than you do, dear."

Sage scrubbed her face, then took the letter from Lily. "The letter says it's an anonymous grant. Is that a real thing?"

"Must be," Lily said, equally confused.

Sage dropped the letter and looked up to see him standing there.

"Congratulations." Though he still thought the tea room was not the best idea, at the same time, Luke was relieved the grant was on the way. A small part of him hoped, against all odds, Sage would prove him wrong.

All three ladies studied him—Bette and Lily curious, Sage wary after her excitement.

Lily was the first to move. Cheeky mischievousness lifted the corners of her mouth when she smiled at Sage. "I think I'll give Verne a hand with dinner."

Scooting her chair back, she disappeared into the kitchen.

Bette hugged Sage. "I believe I'll go upstairs and see what Charlie's up to."

He was alone with Sage and the well-deserved suspicion she directed at him.

"I'm happy for you." He sat next to her, resisting the urge to fold her hand between both of his.

And he was. His uncle believed in Sage. Why couldn't he? It was time to give Charlie credit where credit was due and trust the old man's instincts. In any case, Sage had enough optimism about the success of Amelia's for all of them.

"Even though you think Amelia's will fail in the first year?" She dropped her hands in her lap and leaned back in her chair, daring him to revise his original opinion.

Luke didn't like having to apologize, but in this instance, he had to, especially since he wanted to keep the relationship with Charlie they'd built over all the years his uncle had given him a soft place to land while his parents traipsed around the world.

"I'm sorry. Of course, not every new business fails. I was too blunt, I know. I—" He couldn't tell Sage why he'd been so determined to stop her project from moving forward. Not until Charlie released him from his gag order or *he* concluded that she was sweet, out of this world caring, and not the vile person he originally thought she was. "Gabi keeps telling me it's one of my least endearing qualities. I get too focused on whatever I'm working on and neglect to be user-friendly in polite company."

Sage's assessing gaze didn't waver. "Are you working on something as important to you as Amelia's is to me?"

MR Investments and this thing for Charlie.

"I am, yes." And just like that Luke realized he had a lot of rethinking to do.

"I think I like Gabi." She smiled slowly as she leaned on her elbows, fingers splayed across the table for support. "Is she your girlfriend?"

That's when he knew. Sage was a woman—if he let her—who could take hold of his heart and steer him completely off course.

Chapter Ten

L uke had no intention of going off course where his company was concerned or forgetting why he was in Wally Creek. Maybe Sage *was* who she appeared to be, but he had to be absolutely sure.

"Gabi is my partner at MR Investments. She's married to the most talented glass artist in Seattle. Dara wouldn't take it kindly if I made a move on her wife."

He covered her hand with his, the touch instantly sending a hot charge up his arm. Everything went still, except the voices laughing in the kitchen and the creaking sounds of the house as evening came on. Luke wanted Sage to believe his apology about coming on too strongly.

Their gazes collided, hers seeing more than he wanted her to, he was afraid. Sage turned an intriguing shade of pink. "Good to know."

"She's my best friend." She searched his face. Fierce. Adorable. More tempting than he was prepared for. In his head, Gabi said, *I told you so.* "Thanks for letting me help with the birthday party. It was fun."

It said a lot about her that Sage hadn't been put off by Charlie's insistence on his nephew lending a hand with the party. The person he was looking for when he first came to Wally Creek wouldn't have been so accommodating.

With a half-smile, she shrugged her shoulders. "No problem. An extra pair of hands is always welcome."

His defenses sagged. There was no doubt she liked making people happy. The woman was impressive. And appealing, dang it. Stunned at the feelings making his pulse uneven, he let go when she tugged on her hand and eased back in his chair.

Don't be an idiot, Marshell.

Before he could stop himself, he blurted, "We should be friends."

His mind—the mind that could untangle any business problem—went blank. What was he doing?

Her brows shot up, causing the cutest furrows on her forehead. She choked on a laugh that sounded a little strangled, then cleared her throat. "Aren't we already friends?"

"Maybe." It made Luke feel better that she seemed to be as off-balance as he was. Since he'd opened Pandora's box, he had no other choice but to follow through. "What do you think? Should we shake on it?"

He held out his hand when what he wanted to do was kiss the surprising woman. A friendly kiss on the cheek. It would be a first for him. Usually, a handshake was all that was needed to cement any agreement he made.

"Maybe," she echoed him. "As friends, would we be able to tell each other the truth? Like you did by telling me that

Amelia's could fail in the first year?"

"Exactly. Yes. That is what friends do." He was pretty sure it was.

She took the hand he offered. "So I could tell you—and you wouldn't get mad—that I think you don't have enough fun? And, that it's something you should work on?"

Had he created a monster?

"Yes, and as your friend, I would take your counsel under serious advisement. Just like I know you're keeping in mind my advice about Amelia's." He pumped their clenched hands up and down once, barely missing banging the table.

A grin spread across her face as she let go. "I think we'll have a deal."

"Me too," he said softly and hoped he wasn't throwing a kink into his efforts to untangle Charlie's thing. But who couldn't use another friend? And was it legit to ask, "What does your brother think about you opening Amelia's?"

She shrugged, her smile staying in place. "I haven't told Jack yet. His work keeps him on the move, and makes it hard to stay in touch."

So the brother wasn't involved. Amelia's was all Sage's idea, with a little assistance from her new renters, from what he could tell. "When did you and my uncle meet?"

Her bows shot up. "Are you asking as a curious friend or for another reason? Because it feels like we might be back to square one."

"Both?"

"And you don't want to tell me the other reason?"

He had to be honest. "Not yet."

Her smile dimmed slightly, but she didn't retreat. Instead, she leaned toward him on the table. "Okay, friend. I met

Charlie when he moved to town a few years after we did. He and Grandpa hit it off right away. They started the Sunnybrook Book Club together, and they've been tight ever since. Is there anything else you'd like to know?"

Luke ignored the snark that tempted him to kiss Sage. "And now your grandparents have moved to Arizona," he confirmed, determined to look into every corner of her life while he had the chance.

"They've been wanting to go on an adventure for a while. And as you know, I'm away on the Emerald Star for long stretches at a time. They probably thought, if not now, when?"

It would appear that when it came to family, they had a lot in common. They both cared about their elder family members. And currently, they both had Charlie influencing their decisions.

She leaned closer, meeting his gaze straight on. "You must not have many friends, if you put everyone you meet through this kind of interrogation."

"I'm out of line." But he was beginning to like this game they were playing. He offered a smile in apology. "I can be intense, I know."

"Since we're friends now, I won't hold that against you. You can make up for the thousand-question inquisition by telling me, what's your favorite activity?"

She was so cheeky, he decided to play along. His favorite activity was a no-brainer. He started to tell her when she interrupted him. "And your answer can't have anything to do with work."

Which was exactly what he was about to tell her. MR was his life and the funnest thing he'd been doing for a long time.

He held up a hand to hold her objection off. "I love my work.

But okay, I like to go to Dara's art shows too."

"You like to go fishing," Sage offered, with a smile in her dark eyes that drew him out.

"I do." He had to think for a minute, but— "Oh, and I like to throw birthday parties."

"There you go. Life outside of work." Her laugh invited him to join in the fun. She asked more seriously, "When do you have to go back to Seattle?"

It looked like 'his friend' Sage had won this round. As much as he'd like to hang around to see how things worked out with Amelia's, he still had MR to run and a meeting to take with Portman. If he didn't get back soon, he ran the risk of losing his opportunity with Portman Technologies. Portman's international arm wouldn't come on board without a little persuasion.

"After the town council meeting tonight."

"You'll be there?"

"Uncle Charlie asked me to go," he explained.

"Em asked me to go."

He leaned forward in his chair. Something was going on, but he couldn't believe Sage's friend and his uncle were in cahoots behind their backs. Charlie might do something like that but Emerson didn't strike him as the type to get up to shenanigans over her best friend's romantic life.

While he kind of appreciated the effort, his luck with the fairer sex wasn't that great. And besides, country girl versus city boy. Not a great equation.

Before he got farther involved, it was time to put Wally Creek and the more-intriguing-by-the-minute Sage Dawson in his rearview mirror. The sooner, the better.

Lily came back carrying a large bowl of salad. "Hey, you

two. Will you set the table?"

"Sure." Sage immediately headed for the kitchen.

Luke followed more slowly. He wouldn't mind staying another day or two—just to see what would happen next in this house of unlikely roommates.

Verne passed him plates stacked with napkins and silverware. Sage had already grabbed the tray of glasses sitting on the breakfast bar. Together they headed back to the table.

As the dinner conversation swirled around him, Luke watched Sage talk to everyone at the table, including him. She had a way of tilting her head when she laughed that made him want to be funny, which wasn't one of those things that came easy. Pure joy sparkled in her brown eyes as she quickly popped into the kitchen for another forgotten item.

She'd finished her meal—the fish he and Charlie had caught and tater tots—and was telling stories about her passengers, the families she'd encountered, funny onboard entertainment, dress-up affairs, dress-down excursions. Even Luke had to lean back and enjoy the ride. She definitely had the gift of entertainment.

She spared him a sweet look and smiled. "You're friend's grandmother, Fran, was my favorite passenger. She's so cute. A little reserved at first, but we made sure she participated in every event. It didn't take her long to get accustomed to cruise life. Her favorite was game night."

Okay, that was enough. Sage was way too charming.

He turned to his uncle. "You know, Uncle Charlie, I think I'll skip the meeting. I have a lot to do at the office."

Not waiting to see Charlie's reaction to his abrupt change of plans, he picked up his plate and carried it to the kitchen. He'd put it in the dishwasher when another plate was plunked down on the counter by his elbow.

A too-familiar voice hissed, "What are you doing?

"What do you mean?" he asked Sage calmly. Not an easy feat, given that it'd been a long time since a woman had tempted him to leave behind everything he'd worked so hard to build.

Not since his college sweetheart, Hannah Berk, had he thought he could have it all. A family and a thriving business. He couldn't. He knew that about himself. And it was the reason why it was time to go back to the life that he was familiar with.

Luke hadn't felt this unsettled since that first summer when his parents left him with Charlie, while they went off to explore the opal mines in Australia. The heat of the desert and the mines were too dangerous for a kid, they'd said as they waved goodbye. That was the beginning of his summer holidays with his uncle. Every year his parents would go to Coober Pedy. He went to Charlie's.

But he made his own decisions now. And he decided that it was time to be on his way before he made the mistake of thinking the woman frowning at him, fists perched on her hips, was more than a friend. Just because Seattle seemed unexciting in comparison, that didn't mean he should hang around until his life got all tied up in knots he couldn't unravel.

"Charlie was looking forward to you going to the meeting with him." Her tone was frustrated. *Well, join the club, lady.* "You can spare a few hours before you have to leave. What made you change your mind, anyhow?"

He couldn't tell her, *you*, could he? Or that the reason he was so selective about who he let into his life was that he didn't want to be on the receiving end of disappointment when he was proven wrong about a potential friend's, or girlfriend's, likely longevity. He'd had enough of that already, starting with his parents, and then Hannah.

He was good at business. Never disappointed. He would stick with that.

"I have a lot to do." *Portman.* "I've already been away too long."

A look of sudden understanding replaced her frustration. Luke's heartbeat kicked up a notch.

"As your friend, I'm telling you, Charlie wants to show you off to his friends on the town council. He misses you." Slender fingers tugged slightly on his forearm. "You'll regret not spending the time with him. You can always leave after the meeting like you originally planned."

Friend. And regret. "Like you regret losing your parents," he said softly.

She nodded, still clinging to his arm. "And not spending time with my grandparents when I had the chance. You don't want that."

"I have an important deal on the table. Charlie understands how important MR Investments is and that it's not wise for me to delay getting back any longer."

"Are you sure he understands?" She persisted, not giving in an inch. "Don't you ever take a vacation?"

"I don't need a vacation. I love my work," he said stubbornly but then saw the twinkle in her eyes and the grin she barely stopped from spreading across her face.

Sage knew what buttons to push and was so cute standing there, taking him to task while trying to look very serious. Really, what she said had merit. A couple more hours in his 'friend's' company wouldn't do damage to his deal with Portman. But the thing was, what he wanted and where he was going wasn't here in Wally Creek.

"I'd better go say my goodbyes."

"I was hoping you'd change your mind." She shook her head. "You're smarter than that."

"Guess not." So, this is what it felt like when he was championing his own agenda, but no one was listening.

He went to find Charlie. The old man wasn't a happy camper.

Pulled into a bear hug, the slap on Luke's back and Charlie's next words were the same ones he always said when they'd said goodbye at the end of their summers together. The words were saturated with the same unhappy emotions. "Travel safe, son."

"I'll text when I get home," He promised.

Before closing the front door behind him, Luke chanced a glance over his shoulder to see if he could get a glimpse of Sage. All he saw was her back, shoulders slouched as she climbed the stairs.

At Charlie's, he told himself he was doing the right thing, it didn't take long to pack. The business he'd worked so hard to get off the ground didn't need him to be distracted. He'd locked up, replaced the key in Charlie's hiding place in the flower pot, tossed his bag into the back of his Camaro, and was about to turn over the engine when his cell rang.

Gabi. Before she could speak, he asked, "What's up? I'm about to head home so I can be in the office tomorrow."

"No need to rush."

Rushing was exactly what he was doing. "I have to finish the prep work for the Portman project—"

"No, you don't. I just got a call from Edward. He had a business emergency and had to cancel the meeting. He said he'd have his assistant call and reschedule as soon as he takes care of things."

Luke balled his fingers into a fist on the steering wheel. "We worked hard to get that meeting."

"Yeah, not the best news," Gabi grumbled before her tone brightened. "But it does mean you can spend a few more days with your uncle. There's nothing to do here at the moment. It's quiet enough, I'm taking a day or two off with Dara. She wants to go to the San Juan Islands for some inspiration."

Luke frowned. "I think I'll come home anyway. I have some things I can work on at the office."

"For heaven's sake, Luke. Take some time off. You deserve it." There was the Gabi he was used to. Bossy. Always pushing him to slow down. "Before you hang up on me," she laughed. "How did Sage Dawson react to her award letter?"

Picturing Sage at the table with Lily as she read the letter, something hard inside his chest loosened. "She was excited."

"So not the grasping woman you were expecting?"

"Um, no." If Gabi laughed at his mistaken judgment—

He could hear Dara in the background. "Does he like her?"

"If I want to make it to Seattle before midnight, I've got to go," he said and hung up.

Ignoring the stirred-up feelings in his chest at Dara's question, he tossed the phone on the passenger seat. Of course, he liked Sage. Everyone liked the woman.

Starting the engine, he backed out of the drive. He hadn't gone more than a block when he pulled over.

Who was he kidding? Images of her taking pictures of Charlie and Bette, hosting the party for her two roommates, they wouldn't let him go. She deserved a shot at her dream. And if he would get past his stubbornness and admit it, he was just the guy who could help. With the Portman deal on the back burner, he didn't have to go back to Seattle, at least right now, so he could do . . . what? Sit at his desk and drum his fingers?

He'd built MR Investments to withstand the rough spots that came along. He should listen to Gabi. She wouldn't steer him wrong. An extra day or two or three in Wally Creek wouldn't hurt him or the business. His baby could survive without him for a few more days.

He grabbed the phone, and before he changed his mind, texted Gabi. "Changed my mind. Going to hang out with Charlie for a couple of days."

That's right. Charlie. Not Sage.

He got a bouncing happy face in reply.

Next, he texted his uncle. "Where's this meeting?"

An address popped onto the screen. Luke checked the clock on his phone. He had just enough time to go back to Charlie's and unpack.

"Okay then." He pulled back into the bungalow's drive. "Let's do this."

He wasn't sure what *this* was, but a surge of unexpected excitement rushed Luke. Retrieving his travel bag, he plopped it on the bed in Charlie's spare room. As he unzipped the main compartment, he considered his options.

Sage hadn't responded well to his advice about the fragility of new businesses, even though she'd agreed they could be friends. If he held back his natural tendency to take hold of the reins, it was possible he could give her some valuable advice that wouldn't raise her hackles.

After all, how many times had he steered new clients in the right direction when they wanted to make new investments or start a business? He hadn't been so overbearing then. At least he didn't think so.

By the time he finished hatching a plan, he was walking into the brick and cedar building that was City Hall. A low buzz of multiple conversations filled the public meeting room. Five people sat at a long table at the head of the large room. His Uncle Charlie and Mayor Maggie Tupper, whom Luke had met at the birthday party—sharp lady—were in a heavy discussion. The others he didn't know.

He searched the small groups until he found Sage on the other side of the room with Bette. They both laughed at something Bette said. Suddenly, and quite surprisingly, he wanted to be part of that conversation.

Make a big impact or go home, he'd decided on the short drive to City Hall. It was time to put that plan in motion. He grinned at the unlikely motto that had motivated him all through college and made his way to Sage's side. "Hi."

As if she'd known he would show up—Charlie must have told her—Bette turned an irreverent grin on him. "Hi, yourself."

He could see why Charlie was attracted to Bette, not that his uncle had come right out and said anything. She definitely would keep his uncle on his toes. Luke was glad the old man had found someone he could be happy with.

A gavel pounded. Everyone who wasn't already seated moved toward the rows of chairs.

Luke leaned close to Sage. "I changed my mind. I'm going to hang around for a few more days."

When she flashed him a surprised look, he knew exactly what his next move would be. The trick was convincing the lady that he was serious about lending her his business expertise.

Chapter Eleven

L uke's shoulder brushed hers as he settled into the empty seat next to Sage. Startled, all she could think was, the man she found attractive in a careful-what-you-wish-for sort of way, was supposed to be on his way to Seattle.

She'd all but begged him to come to the council meeting, for Charlie's sake, of course, and still he'd brushed her off. She shouldn't have been so surprised. Being brushed off was becoming a regular happenstance in her life.

"Why are you here?" she hissed fiercely, trying the best she could to leave some space between their shoulders. Her brain scrambled for a good reason why Luke would change his mind. "I thought you had work to get back to."

"My meeting was canceled, so I decided to stay for a little longer." He leaned close, their shoulders bumping despite her best efforts. The warmth of his breath hijacked any rational thoughts she might have claimed as her own.

Just for a second—only one—she was attacked by a spark of excitement before she managed to get it under wraps. Exactly how long was Luke, who had not proven he could be her friend, much less a dream guy, going to stay in Wally Creek before he changed his mind? Again.

She shook her head. It was so maddening. She liked being a mellow, go-with-the-flow kind of girl. Luke Marshell was not that kind of guy. Because he had her questioning everything, he made it so difficult to look ahead and enjoy the journey.

What she wanted was for Luke to stop telling her Amelia's wouldn't be successful.

Her grandparents always told her to go after what she wanted and take a chance that her dreams could be everything she wanted them to be if she just tried. That was what she was doing. Taking a chance on Amelia's Cuppa Tea.

Luke didn't look at new opportunities that way. He went straight to the worst-case scenario.

She pulled her brows together and turned to glare at the man sitting next to her. He wasn't looking. His gaze was locked on Charlie sitting at the table on the stage at the front of the room.

What the guy needed was a good push in the direction of looking on the bright side. Sage took a deep breath and smiled. Since he was here, she would quite enjoy giving him that push.

"I'm sure Charlie will like that very much." She twisted so their shoulders weren't touching. She refused to go down the rabbit hole with the man sitting beside her in a tee shirt emblazoned with a well-known British Ferris wheel. "So you like the London Eye? Have you ever taken a ride?"

As she leaned in her direction, his breath brushed across her ear once more, distracting Sage. The attack on the normal function of her brain was worse than before. She knew better than to play with fire.

"About a year ago. I was in London scouting out locations for the office we're planning to open there."

See? Exactly what she was expecting. He wanted to move to London. The United Kingdom wasn't someplace she could get to by taking a two to three-hour drive. Which was a good thing, in case she was on the brink of changing *her* mind about the possibility of engaging in a long-distance relationship.

Well, whatever the reason for his change of heart about coming tonight, she was certain Luke wouldn't be in Wally Creek longer than he had to be. And she was sure it wouldn't be long before he told her exactly what he thought about her ongoing efforts to open her tea room.

So while she waited for him to come up with more reasons why Amelia's wouldn't pan out—because he had the hardest time not butting into her business—she glanced around the room to see who else was attending the council meeting.

Em was in the second row. Betty was farther down the row. Sage gave Em a quick wave, then tried to focus on the Mayor who was about to open the meeting.

Mayor Maggie stood at the podium and banged the gavel. "Thanks for coming, everyone. Let's get down to business. Nina Oakley, who has been organizing this year's Summer Celebration parade, was urgently called away on a family emergency."

Sage's thoughts drifted. Opening Amelia's would be the adventure of a lifetime. The grant. A new project she could sink her teeth into and that, with a lot of hard work, could turn into a comfortable income.

Luke pushed on her arm.

She looked at him sharply but kept her voice down. "What?"

With a quizzical look on his handsome face, he nodded toward the front of the room. All five council members were staring at her.

Her cheeks warmed. "I'm sorry. I must have missed what you were saying."

Maggie leaned forward on her elbows and smiled. "You did such a great job on the event for Charles and Mr. Winsten, and with Nina going back east to take care of her mom—" Maggie spread her hands wide. "I know organizing a parade is more complicated than putting together a birthday party, but since everything is nearly done, and the Summer Celebration is barely two weeks away, we're hoping you'll be willing to take over for Nina."

Sage stood. "I, um, I'd love to help, but I'm not sure I can. I have a lot on my plate at the moment."

"We've heard about your plans to open a tea room. Don't worry. The town council will be happy to help you navigate through permitting and the paperwork to get started. Frankly, we're desperate." An excited murmur spread through the room. The mayor was calm and steady. "In addition to the committee, we'll get volunteers to help so all you have to do is keep everything running smoothly and give the team their marching orders, so to speak."

More than one head turned in Sage's direction. Even with the promise of extra help, it was a lot to take on at the last minute, even if she was just overseeing the final results. She was about to decline the mayor's request when Luke raised his hand. "I volunteer to help Sage with the parade."

Ahead of her, Bette stood. "Me too."

A grin spread across Charlie's face, but he wasn't looking at

Sage. He only had eyes for Bette. "Me three," he said.

"Excellent. That settles it then." The mayor clapped her hands together. "Glad to have you on board, Sage. Now, let's move on to the next agenda item—ideas for new plants for the planters on Birch Street."

"But—"

Luke tugged her back into her seat. "It'll be okay, Sage."

She spun to face him. "You don't know that." He'd said he would help, but most likely he'd be gone before the Summer Celebration even got started. "How do you know this will be okay? You probably won't even be here."

"I've been in your shoes," he said with a quiet assurance that was so different from the way he'd informed her he didn't think a tea room would make it past the first year. "One way or the other, I'll be here. I promise. Besides, weren't you the one who said, if you want something bad enough, you can make it happen?"

"No, but I do believe that." She squinted at him. "What have you done with the Luke Marshell who believes my new business doesn't have a chance?"

He burst out in a deep, hushed laugh that finished shattering Sage's composure. The room went suddenly quiet. He waved a hand at the council and squelched his laughter, choking out, "Sorry."

Surprised by the rich timber of his laughter, the prickle of her skin reminded Sage of rides at the county fair, deep-fried cookies, and turkey legs.

She turned back to the meeting. Fortunately, it ended not much later.

Maggie caught her at the door just as Sage was about to escape before she did something stupid like fall under the spell of Luke's laughter. "I have a meeting tomorrow morning, but why don't you come to my office in the afternoon, and we'll go over the details for the parade? About three?"

Clearly, there was no fighting the inevitable. "That would be great. Thank you, Mayor."

"Heavens, please call me Maggie."

Sage nodded. "I'll see you tomorrow."

"We can talk about the steps you'll need to take to get started on your tea room too." Charlie waved to catch Maggie's attention. Before going back to the other council members, she turned a last smile on Sage. "Oh, your committee members are Emerson Finn and Rickie Harrison. I believe you already know Emerson?"

"Since high school," she acknowledged. It took a huge load off her shoulders to have a friendly face on the committee. She scanned the room but Em had already left. "I appreciate you making time to walk me through the small business process."

"We're all glad to help." They shook hands. "You're doing the town a huge favor. It's the least I can do. What I don't know, my assistant will."

Relief took a huge burden off Sage's shoulders. Opening Amelia's was going to work out.

"Do you want to stop in at the Hargrove for pie and ice cream?"

Sage tilted her head and studied the man she was sure could have any girl he wanted. Blue eyes calmly studied her face. His brown hair curled on the ends, snuggling low on his neck was an enticement that was hard to ignore. Her fingers itched to reach out and see how soft the curly ends were.

She shoved her hands in her dress pockets.

Like a soccer player—her favorite sport—who made every

goal he attempted, Luke carried himself with complete confidence. If he ever decided to bottle that certainty and put it up for sale, she wouldn't be able to stop herself. She'd be the first one in line and she'd buy a dozen bottles.

He waited patiently. Surely he wasn't suggesting a date. Just that two people, who were kind of friendly, could go out at the same time for her favorite dessert.

She should stick with her new no-dating rule until after Amelia's was open and providing a steady income. There was only one problem. She *wanted* to have dessert with Luke. How ridiculous was that?

And she wanted to ask his advice. She barely stopped herself from rolling her eyes. He would love that, wouldn't he? And he'd tell her the same thing he'd already told her. That Amelia's wasn't worth the effort she would have to put into the project.

Well, he was wrong.

Reluctantly, she shook her head. "Can I get a reign check? It's late and tomorrow's looking to be a pretty full day."

"Of course." He held the door open.

Immediately, she regretted turning down his invitation. Now who was the one who was all work and no play? But what else could she do? If Amelia's was going to get off the ground, she couldn't waste time flirting, over ice cream or otherwise, with any guy, which now that she'd set up that boundary, flirting was exactly what she wanted to do. With Luke.

"We could have ice cream and pie at the house? If you want. Verne makes a mean apple pie."

"What time?"

They left City Hall together. Luke walked her to her car.

Acutely aware that he was waiting, his keys in hand. "Maybe

after I meet with the mayor tomorrow? I'll text you."

Luke Marshell was definitely too much of . . . everything.

Sage quickly climbed in the Sunbeam, started the engine, waved, and forced herself to drive sedately home.

Verne had iced tea waiting when she got there. He and Lily were making cookies. The sweet smell of warm chocolate chips filled the kitchen. Oatmeal Chocolate chip cookies weren't the same as apple pie and ice cream, but they would satisfy the sweet tooth Luke had woken up with his unexpected invitation.

"Hi, guys," she said to the bakers.

Lily was dusted in flour. One of Verne's aprons nearly wrapped around her twice. Mixing a batch of cookies with a wooden spoon while Verne scooped spoonfuls of dough from his bowl onto a cookie sheet, Lily glanced at Sage. Her eyes twinkled. "How was the council meeting? Charlie said he'd talked you into going."

"It was interesting. I have a meeting with the mayor tomorrow afternoon to talk about what I need to do to get started on Amelia's."

Lily gave her mixture one more push around the bowl. "Are you excited?"

"And nervous too." She didn't want to bring the man who was taking up too much room in her mind into the conversation. Verne and Lily would just have questions. Questions she didn't have answers to, since she was getting too comfortable having Luke around. It didn't matter what she wanted because the words tumbled out anyway. "Luke was there. I was volunteered to take over the Summer Celebration parade."

Lily's brows shot up. She wiped her hands on the towel

slung over her shoulder. "Luke volunteered you?"

"No, the mayor did. But Luke said he would help. Bette and Charlie said they'd help too." Sage bit off the rest of her ramble.

She didn't know why she was so rattled. She could handle the unexpected load. How many times on the Emerald Star had she juggled multiple balls at a time? Managing a parade along with making room in her home for the book club besties and planning a new business was no different.

Maybe it was Luke asking her to go with him for pie and ice cream. That was no biggie, right?

Amelia's and the parade were important to more people than just herself. Charlie, Bette, Verne, Lily, the mayor, and the town. They all needed her to get these things right.

"We'll all help," Verne said in his grumbling way as he put his loaded cookie sheet in the oven.

Dismayed that it sounded like she was asking for their help, Sage paused in the act of stealing several cookies that had been cooling on racks on the breakfast bar. "I didn't mean . . . you don't have to—"

"But we will." Lily patted Sage's hand. "We're family now. And families help each other. Isn't that right, Verne?"

"Yup." Vern had another cookie sheet almost ready to go in the oven.

The warm, sugary smell of baking cookies reminded Sage of when she used to help her mom bake. Cookies were definitely on Amelia's menu.

"That's very sweet of you." Surrendering to their generosity and Verne's undeniable baking skills, she hugged them both, though she was surprised Verne let her wrap her arms, even loosely around his middle. About to leave the kitchen with her stolen goodies in hand, she turned back. "Luke is coming for pie and ice cream tomorrow night. I told him you make the best apple pie, Verne."

The corner of his eyes crinkled. Lily winked at her. "He makes the best apple pie in the county."

Sage grinned back, then headed for the staircase.

Stopping for a moment, foot on the lowest stair, her free hand hanging onto the baluster, she edged back a foot or two until she got a good view of the front room. It wasn't going to be easy to turn this part of the house into a tea room. There was probably enough space, but where to put everything might be problematic.

She hadn't really believed it. Sage had seen the vision, but not completely believed she would get to this point of planning out the actual space. And to be honest, she had to admit, her *family*, as Lily put it, had always believed. It was time to be all in with them.

How bad could it be to accept the help that was offered? Suddenly, she was wondering how horrible it would be to include Luke. As long as he was in Wally Creek, of course. Maybe he would have some good ideas about how to make the first floor functional for good customer flow. The only way to find out was to take advantage of his business insight when he came for pie and ice cream.

In her room, she settled at her computer and continued researching the steps for opening a cafe or coffee shop, the closest things she could find to opening a tea room. They were close cousins, she hoped. Armed with a list, her meetings the next day would go a lot better if she had an understanding or overview of what to expect.

The next morning, Sage didn't waste any time texting Em.

"I guess we're partners on the parade committee. Can we meet to discuss the details this morning?"

Em's response was immediate. "Eight-thirty at the Gold Cafe?"

That was Grams' and Grandpa's cafe. After school and during summer breaks, they'd spent a lot of their teenage years waiting tables at the retro eating house. Since she'd returned to Wally Creek and found out her grandparents had sold the business, Sage hadn't had the heart to stop by and check out what the new owner had done with the place. It wouldn't be the same without her grandparents behind the counter, waiting on tables, and visiting with longtime customers.

She texted back, "I'll be there."

Meeting Em for breakfast meant she would miss eating with her housemates. Her gang. *Family.* The idea that she'd acquired a new family was funny and not funny at the same time. And confusing. She had Grams and Grandpa and Jack, but now that Lily had her thinking about the book club renting her rooms on a more permanent basis, it put a whole new spin on her relationship with the elder folks. She'd always considered the passengers on board the Emerald Star her family too. Just not in a familial sense. And since Luke was Charlie's great-nephew, did that make him part of her family too?

"Of course, it doesn't," she muttered under her breath.

Glancing at the time on her phone, she grabbed her bag and keys, then headed downstairs, following the voices coming from the kitchen. She just missed running into Charlie, who was carrying a plate of stacked French toast to the dining room. Bette followed with a platter of bacon.

"Smells wonderful." Almost good enough to miss her

breakfast meeting with Em.

"Grab a seat, girl," Verne said.

She stole a piece of bacon. "Can't. I have a breakfast date with Em at the Gold Cafe."

Taking the piece of bacon with her, Sage waved on the way out. The morning was somewhat cool for early June, but the sky was cloudless and blue, and before the day was out, it would be hot as the dickens.

Getting sucked into Wally Creek's easy rhythm wasn't the adventure she thought she'd be on when she waited for Gordan to pop that special question. But it turned out the window opening Grams had promised had turned out to be much better than the door that closed. Even the uncertainty of Amelia's success was better than hanging out, hoping Gordan had the same future in mind for them that she did.

Maybe the problem wasn't Gordan or that he'd broken it off between them. Maybe she had it all wrong. Maybe what she'd been looking for was to recapture her passion, her zest for life that seemed to have gone missing. Instead of realizing that, she'd pinned her hopes and dreams on Gordan, the jerk, being her grand passion. Not the best move she'd ever made.

Wishing she'd had this much clarity when she was pining to be Gordan's wife, Sage parked in front of the cafe and just sat there for a minute.

Not much had changed. The new owner had given the building a paint job, a soft white instead of the red brick Sage had grown up with. *Gold Cafe* was still painted in large, gold, scrolling script on the front window. Through the glass, she could see Em was already there. Standing next to her, pouring coffee, was a woman about her and Em's age. Her long mahogany-colored hair was pulled into a ponytail that hung over one shoulder.

Grabbing her bag, Sage went into the cafe.

"I hope you haven't been waiting long." She dropped into the closest of the two empty chairs at Em's table. The waitress had already moved on.

"Only long enough to get coffee and order our favorite breakfast." Em poured a long stream of cream into her coffee. They both said at the same time, "Eggs Benedict." And laughed.

Boy, it was good to be back.

"How many times, when we were teenagers, did we sneak in early on a Saturday morning to have Grams' Eggs Benedict before we started work?"

"Too many times to count." Eyes sparkling, Em leaned back in her chair. "Did I ever tell you, a few years ago, I convinced Vanessa to give me the recipe?"

"Grams never could say no to you when you raved about her food."

"Yeah, she's sweet that way, and I'll be the first to admit when I took over The Oak and added the dining room, I shamelessly lobbied her kind heart."

Grinning at her friend, Sage leaned on her elbows. "She knew what you were doing."

"I know." Em smiled too. Their food arrived. The waitress put a third plate loaded with one egg and several pieces of bacon, in front of the empty chair before sitting.

"This is Rickie Jamison, Sage. She bought the cafe and is the third member of our parade committee."

"Nice to meet you." Rickie held out her hand. "Your grandparents saved my life."

"That sounds like them." Sage was starting to believe they'd also saved *her* life, figuratively speaking anyway, by giving her the house. She shook Rickie's hand. "How long have you been in town?"

Sage glanced around. Other than the whitewashed brick on the exterior of the building, the inside was just as she remembered except for the addition of colorful, quilted placemats.

Rickie shrugged, her smile turning down around the edges. Her gaze dropped to her plate, but she didn't touch the food. "About four months, I guess. John and Vanessa hired me the day after I came to town. When they decided to sell, they insisted I buy the cafe, so I made an offer."

Sage was confused. "They told me they'd sold, of course, but they shouldn't have pushed you into buying."

Green eyes flecked with gold snapped up. "They didn't push, but in the interest of full disclosure, I should tell you I know your brother, Jack. They were aware of that. He's best friends, or was best friends with my husband."

Before Sage could make sense of the sadness beneath the words, a little blonde-haired boy rushed through the door. He was closely followed by a woman who looked like a younger version of Rickie.

"Eli, slow down," the woman chasing him said.

"But I want to show Mom my new book," the little guy said. Nonetheless, he slowed down to a fast walk until he reached Rickie. "Mom. Look."

The sadness instantly retreated. Rickie took the book her son held out. When she flipped open the cover, Sage's heartbeat bounced. *The Bears' Picnic.* Her dad, and later, grandparents had read that book to her and Jack until the pages were frayed around the edges.

Pushing her untouched plate back, she leaned toward Rickie

and her little boy. "My dad used to read that book to me. It's my favorite."

Eli was adorable as he shifted from foot to foot in excitement. Someday she would love to have a son or daughter just as cute as this little guy. Though getting a husband first was probably a good idea.

Luke's face popped into her mind.

Eli turned trusting blue eyes on Sage. "My daddy can't read to me anymore." Her heart sank as he straightened and drew his little shoulders back. "My daddy died."

Impulsively, she reached out and took the boy's hand. "I'm so sorry to hear that, Eli. My dad died when I was little too."

"You don't have a dad?" He moved closer and leaned against Sage's arm.

Her breath caught on the sudden grief lodged in her throat. She glanced at Rickie, whose mouth wobbled a little at the corners. Even after all this time, the loss of her parents still caught Sage by surprise. She wrapped Eli in a hug. "My mom and dad are in heaven with your dad."

Animated, Eli scooted back. "My mom can be your mom too if you want. She'll read to you." He twisted to look at Rickie. "Won't you, Mom?"

Rickie's eyes misted up with pride and love. Pulling her son close, she looked at Sage and said as seriously as her son. "I'd be happy to read to you."

"Thank you. I'd like that," Sage said, playing along. Every once in a while, it would be nice to sit down and listen to someone read her a story that would take her away for a bit.

Em leaned over the table to get closer to the little boy who was wringing all their hearts. The woman who'd come in with him placed her hand on his shoulder. In the quiet that followed, Sage was certain this was it. Without a doubt, this is what she wanted. She was home. It was time to give Human Resources at the cruise line her notice.

"Eli, why don't you and Aunt Kendra go to the kitchen and get a scoop of ice cream," Rickie said, gently shooing the two on their way.

When they disappeared into the kitchen, Luke stepped up to the table. Startled, Sage looked up. His eyes were shiny with sympathy. He'd witnessed the whole thing with Eli. "Uncle Charlie sent me to pick up a lemon meringue pie. "I'll put the order in at the counter."

When he was done, Luke returned, bringing a chair with him. "Mind if I join you, ladies?"

He might be talking to the table at large, but his gaze rested on Sage, compassion softening the lines fanning out from the corners of his eyes. The man saw too much.

For the first time, Sage wasn't embarrassed by the emotions she wore on her sleeve where anyone could see. She was who she was, and she was done playing any other role but Sage Dawson.

"Please do." She turned to Em and Rickie. "Luke is Charlie's nephew. He volunteered to help with the parade."

He was smart, had organizational skills, and was willing. At the moment, that's all she needed to know about the man.

Welcome to the village, Luke.

Picking up her knife and fork, she pulled her neglected breakfast toward her and, why the heck not, asked Luke. "Want half?"

"I probably shouldn't since I've already had breakfast, but the food smells delicious." He reached across the space to the nearest table and grabbed a set of silverware wrapped in a napkin and a clean plate.

Sage pointed with her fork. "Luke . . . Rickie. Rickie . . . Luke."

After splitting her Eggs Benedict and hash browns, she convened their impromptu meeting. "Ladies, tell us everything we need to know about the parade."

Chapter Twelve

A fter following the excited boy, and the woman trying to corral the little guy, into the Gold Cafe, Luke shouldn't have been surprised to find Sage huddling around a table with her girlfriends. That was just how his luck was running since he'd come to Wally Creek. And how his Uncle Charlie rolled.

He should have guessed being sent for a lemon meringue pie was just a ruse. If he'd been at the top of his game, he would have remembered Verne made the pies in Sage's house and wouldn't appreciate desserts from anywhere else being brought in.

Charlie was up to his usual shenanigans. He'd mentioned more than once over the last year that he was ready for great-great-nephews and nieces, and the old man wasn't shy about playing matchmaker.

If Luke had the time, he'd turn the tables on Charlie. He'd seen how it was between his uncle and Bette, but it didn't seem they were ready to admit to anything serious. *He* wasn't ready to admit to having serious feelings for Sage, either. While two could play the matchmaking game, the problem was that he was starting to believe in the cause too.

He dug into the food Sage had shared and let the conversation swirl around him. It felt good to just sit there without any specific agenda and be part of her team. It had been a long time since he'd felt this relaxed with a woman, comfortable just sitting without a plan to get much done during the rest of the day.

He gave himself a mental pat on the back. Gabi would be proud, maybe even buy *him* a new book to read.

When the ladies had closed ranks around Eli, a stab of envy had almost taken Luke out before he reminded himself he had a tribe who had his back no matter what.

Immediately, he'd wanted to join the ladies and make sure the kid knew he was loved like Charlie had for him when he was a boy and left for the summer by his parents, a pattern that had continued until he'd left to go to college.

Eli seemed to take it all in stride, a testament to his mother's love and guidance. Luke guessed that was the part he envied.

Luke let out a deep breath. The kid was holding his own. He'd stated his case, and all three ladies' hearts had melted. His had too. For Eli. And Sage. He didn't have the best relationship with his parents, but at least they were still alive. And they were happy to see him when he occasionally made time to take the long trip to Australia.

Despite being on opposite sides of their argument, he liked Sage. Maybe he even more than liked her. Which complicated things. He didn't want to see her hurt.

When she talked about opening Amelia's, her gorgeous eyes

lit up and dragged him into her dream. He found himself wanting to help. He could guide her through the process and even wanted to have her take advantage of his experience, but his life was in Seattle.

Hers was here. The three-and-a-half-hour driving distance didn't sound like a lot, but once he went international with MR, every minute would be taken up with expanding his business. He wouldn't have time to answer any remaining questions she might have, even by way of connecting online.

Except for the look on her face when Eli had said his dad couldn't read him stories anymore, the hint of loneliness that was familiar from Luke's own childhood and that still plagued him on occasion necessitating a call to his parents, made him want to get off the sidelines and make sure she knew she wasn't alone. The parade was a good place to start.

To get his bearings, he listened with Sage to Emerson and Rickie as they laid out the scope of the parade that included the local fire department, the high school band and cheerleading squad, the Wally Creek Chamber of Commerce, the bicycle club, rodeo barrel racers, clowns, local businesses, and more. Enough more that Luke was convinced this wasn't a chintzy country parade. This was the real thing.

He leaned on his forearms. "Who's the grand marshal?"

"The Mayor," Emerson pushed her empty plate to the center of the table. "What we don't have is a theme and a car for Maggie to ride in."

"Do we have time to incorporate a theme?" Sage asked, putting her napkin on the table.

"I think so. The Summer Celebration starts in nine days." Rickie said as she got up to clear the table. "Nina took care of all the advertising for the parade, but it's mixed in with the promotion for the Summer Celebration. If we want the parade to stand out, a theme would help. What I don't know is if that's enough time to get the word out."

Luke gathered up the dishes she couldn't carry in one trip. Kendra and Eli had found a window seat that looked out on a sunny side street. Their ice cream cones were almost gone.

Luke smiled at the kid and was rewarded with a grin in return. He'd always thought that someday he'd have children, but MR had kept him too busy to make having a family a priority. Eli had him questioning that decision.

Back at the table, he took his seat. "The car is no trouble. We can use my Camaro." Which meant he'd have to stay in town longer or come back.

Sage grabbed his arm. "Are you sure?"

Her voice was rough with more than one question. Surely she was referring to his offer to use his car and not the sudden flare of something very male-female between them.

Luke weighed his options. Go or stay. Staying a little longer in Wally Creek won. "I'm sure."

"That's wonderful. Thank you." Realizing she was still hanging on to him, she quickly tucked her hand in her lap.

She's the one.

She can't be the one, he silently fired back.

"Okay then." Sage cleared her throat as she eased back in her seat. "To even out the numbers, we'll find three or four other classic cars to line up behind you."

He had his own ideas about evening out the numbers. Just because he'd volunteered, didn't mean he wanted to be in the parade all by his lonesome. "You ladies could follow me in the Sunbeam."

"Annabelle?" Her lips twitched at the corners. "Perhaps, but someone has to have shoes on the ground to make sure the parade goes off without a hitch."

If he doubted it before, he didn't now. Sage knew how to take charge of her own undertakings. He could use that take-charge attitude at MR, and probably not solely as the company's event planner. Outreach coordinator was a thing, right? Edward Portman would love her decisiveness.

"So, all we need now is the theme?" He didn't know enough about the town's history, except unexpectedly he was half in love with its future small business owner. "Is there something special Wally Creek is known for that we can play off of?"

The way Sage's brows came together was so cute. "Well, when Wally Creek was first incorporated, it was a gold mining and tourist town. The gold mines slowly went bust, but the tourist trade survived for a long time. Every weekend, especially in the summer months, sightseers would come out on the train that ran along the Wally River from Portland. They'd come for walks on the waterfront, bicycle rides, and canoeing. Tourism is still the main attraction, but the primary industry in this area is Christmas trees. Did you know, in Oregon, Christmas trees bring in over one hundred million dollars a year?"

For someone who spent most of her time on a cruise ship, Sage sure knew her Wally Creek history. Luke loved how she had to bite her lip to come down from her soapbox.

"It's not the right season for a Christmas theme." Emerson eyed them both. "How about something relating to the gold mines?"

"Wally Creek, a history of gold mines?" Rickie suggested, then shook her head. "Not catchy enough."

"I've got it." Sage straightened. "Wally Creek is a gold mine."

She looked around the table, her excited gaze landing and staying on his face.

His pulse jumped. Luke could no longer fight back a smile at her enthusiasm. "I like it. It's catchy. And has the benefit of being true."

"I like it too," Rickie laughed. Not a full laugh, but a soft sound that made him think she didn't laugh often. Eli came to lean against his mom.

"Perfect." Emerson stood. "I have the list of parade participants on my laptop. I'll email it to you all tonight. Right now, I have a staff meeting I have to attend."

The bell over the door chimed softly as she left. Rickie abandoned her seat too. "Looks like the lunch rush is about to start. When it's over, I'll set up a group email and send an invitation." She turned to her son. "Eli, go with Aunt Kendra. She's going to take you to the park."

He took his aunt's hand but didn't look excited at all. "But Mom. I want to be here with you."

Luke didn't blame the little guy. He remembered being sent away when all he wanted was to hang out with his parents.

"Next time, my love." She leaned down and kissed Eli's forehead. "How about when I'm done here, I read your new book to you?"

"Okay." He ducked his chin but must have quickly decided that it was a good bargain. "Can we have macaroni and cheese for dinner?"

Rickie smiled at her son. "That's a great suggestion."

"And I can help cook?"

She nodded.

A happy grin lit Eli's cherub face. "Come on Aunt Kendra. I want to play on the slide."

Luke watched the boy and his aunt go out into the sunshine. The kid literally bounced in his excitement.

Turning to Rickie, Luke said, "You have a great family."

Her relationship with her son and sister was exactly what Luke wanted. A wife. His Uncle Charlie living close by. A little boy or girl who had the striking smile of a sweet angel. Silently he swore he would be a good dad and husband to his future family. Not once would he leave his son behind while he went on adventures. *His* family would adventure together.

Instantly, he frowned. That would also mean he had to make changes in how much time he spent at work. Something to think about.

"Thank you. I think so." Rickie grabbed a cleaning towel from behind the counter and started wiping down their table. "Eli can be a handful, but I love him to pieces."

And wished her husband was still with them. Luke could read it on her face even as she buried the emotion and turned to the customers who were lining up to be seated. If it wasn't inappropriate, he would have pulled the still-grieving widow into a comforting hug.

Outside, he stopped Sage before she got in her car. "Would you like company when you go see the mayor?" He raised his hands. "I won't say a word, I swear. I'll just be there for moral support only."

Her gaze pinned on his face, Sage didn't answer right away. She was thinking so hard, he could almost hear the words. *Trust him? Don't trust him? Trust him? Don't trust him?*

"I take good notes," he coaxed her. "And my startup experience could come in handy."

She surprised him by agreeing without argument, "That would be useful. You'll think of questions I won't know to ask.

My appointment is at three."

"I'll meet you there." Holding open her car door as she got buckled in, Luke congratulated himself. If he got her to trust him—

He was only doing what any friend would do, right? She smiled and waved, then backed out of the parking slot.

This was ridiculous. He absolutely could not fall for Sage Dawson, just because she had guts and was brave enough to try something she'd never done before, and had lots of spunk, things he admired in a woman. She drew him to her like a—

He didn't know what. But he felt like he'd just hit a home run out of the park.

She was nothing like the girl he'd almost married or the woman he'd thought she would be before he came to Wally Creek to check her out. Thank goodness. But just being friends? Surely that was enough.

He drove back to Charlie's. Standing in front of the sliders, looking out at the patch of grass and wooded backyard. Sunlight dappled the greenery. He dialed Gabi.

Her phone was never far from her elbow. She picked up right away. "Hey. How's the time off going?"

"Fine." His heart bounced. That had everything to do with Sage. He rolled his eyes. "Has a meeting with Portman been scheduled yet?"

"No. He had to go back to London. We'll set up something when he gets back."

Luke rubbed his temple. If Portman didn't return to Seattle soon, that would mean a trip to England. For now though—"Do we have anything important going on in the next two weeks?"

"Nothing urgent."

Leaning his forehead against the glass, he gave in to the reason for his call. "Promise you won't laugh."

"You know I can't keep that promise." Laughter bubbled up in his ear. "I can't help it. You're a funny guy."

Gabi was the only one who thought that.

"Great. Just what I always want to hear." His plan was to convince Sage he wasn't all business. If he could. "I need you to clear my schedule for the next two weeks."

"Why?"

In for a penny, in for a pound. "I volunteered to drive Wally Creek's mayor in the Summer Celebration parade."

"How did that happen?" Yup, she laughed. He didn't blame her. This wasn't something he usually did during his rare times off. As everyone in his world knew, he wasn't good at walking away from his desk.

He took a soda out of the fridge. What the heck? He may as well spill all his beans. "Until then, I'm working on the Wally Creek parade committee with Sage."

"I see." Luke was pretty sure she didn't, but did it matter? "I'll have the intern clear your schedule."

"You don't have to sound so happy about it," he grumbled, feeling like a teenager whose mom insisted he get off his electronics and go hang out with his buddies.

"I am happy," Gabi said suddenly, very serious. "I've been worried about you."

"What do you mean?" Opening the slider, he sat in a deck chair. Sunlight danced through the small maple trees snuggled close to the pines. A soft breeze cooled the hot temperature. He took a long draw on his pop.

"Well—don't tell me it's none of my business—but it seems to me, you observe life. You don't participate. It's nice to see you involved."

Luke let the pop bottle settle in his lap. What was she talking about? Of course, he participated. All the time.

"Luke? Are you still there?"

"I went to Dara's show with you," he said quietly.

Firmly, but just as quiet, she came back with, "Yeah, you did. But that was work-related and had nothing to do with doing something for yourself."

His business was what he did for himself.

In the background, he heard, "Is that Luke?" *Dara.* "I want to talk to him."

Gabi must have handed over the phone because the next second Dara, unrestrained, was in his ear. "How's your uncle? And Wally Creek? Are you having fun?"

"I am." Amazingly enough, that was true.

"When are you coming home?" Her current sculpture must be going well. She had that satisfied purr in her voice.

"I was just telling Gabi—about two weeks."

"Wow!" Wow indeed. Luke shook his head as Dara rushed on but a little bit more subdued. "Promise me you'll do something wild and crazy."

He laughed. Wasn't being in a parade crazy enough?

How could he resist the two most important women in his life? They knew how to live big, for sure. "We'll see. I'm hanging up now."

Luke clutched his drink and let the laughter drain away. A tiny bird, wings beating a mile a minute, zipped by in front of him. It landed on a tree branch close enough he could see the green sheen across its back. The hummingbird tilted its head to the side.

Feeling the necessity to dispute Gabi's claim, he mumbled,

"I don't just observe life. I live it too."

Wild and Crazy. Talking to a wild creature. That had to fall into the category of crazy, didn't it? The bird cocked its head to the other side as though he had an opinion on the matter.

When *was* the last time he'd had unplanned fun?

Luke polished off his drink and put the bottle on the small cafe table beside him. Flying to see his parents once a year probably didn't count. He wouldn't call seeing his parents fun exactly, though most of the time he didn't hold their lack of parenting interest against them, either. And he did find them more user-friendly now that they'd retired. One thing he knew without a doubt was that he'd be a better parent than they'd been, if and when he had kids of his own. He'd make sure of it.

So, what could he do for fun? "Watching Sage throw jewelry over the side of the Emerald Star and seeing the shocked look on the guy's face. Now that was fun," he said to the little bird.

At the time he hadn't thought it in terms of what was fun, but looking back and knowing what he knew about Sage, how independent and spontaneous she could be, and how crazy the guy had to be to let her go? Luke chuckled.

Not having anything to add to the conversation, the hummingbird flew off, wings beating in the dry air with a soft whirl. Taking the empty soda bottle to the kitchen, he left it on the counter by the sink until he could figure out what his uncle did with his recyclables.

That was enough wild and crazy for one day. Eli had the right idea. A new novel to read was just what he needed to pass the time until he met up with Sage at City Hall. Visiting the local bookstore to pick out the perfect summer read—one that wasn't work-related—would definitely fall under Dara's definition of fun.

Five minutes later, he parked in front of Luna's Books prepared to spend the next few hours searching for the perfect book. Anything about dragons or ancient Greece set in a dystopian future would be perfect, except all that wrapped into one story or a series was a rare find. Eventually, he settled for an Anne McCaffery he'd read as a teenager but had no problem reading again.

He'd paid for the book and settled in a comfortable, over-stuffed chair bathed in sunlight from the front windows. He had a perfect view of the sidewalk and a lavishly blooming planter. As he opened the book a familiar silhouette caught his eye. Tucking his purchase under his arm, he left the store, pausing briefly to look right and left. Camera hanging from a strap around her neck, Sage had stopped in the shade on the next block over. She stared at her phone but didn't look happy.

"Hi there."

She spun around and sighed heavily. "Oh, it's you."

That didn't sound as welcoming as he would have liked.

"Were you expecting someone else?" he teased, hoping she would tell him what had caused the furrow between her brows.

Instead, she gave him an odd look, then glanced once more at her phone before sliding it into the pocket of her dress. Her frown disappeared at the same time. "Nothing important.

She walked backward until he got close enough that they could walk side by side. The floral dress—wow—with its big white flowers on a rust-colored background, hung from two thin straps. The flowing garment hinted at what he already knew was a trim figure. The dress hung to her knees. Sturdy bronze sandals matched the bracelets on her arm.

Taking her hand, Luke threaded her fingers through the crook of his arm as they walked down the sidewalk. She didn't object, which was a good sign. He would have liked to pull her whole arm through his, but he wasn't sure, from the wary smile in her eyes, if she'd welcome the fuller contact or not. Scaring her away wasn't his intention anymore. When she reached for her camera, it was too late to go for the risky move, anyway.

She pointed the camera down Birch Street, clicked, and then showed him the picture on the view screen. She'd caught the essence of the main street through downtown Wally Creek. It was picturesque, one of those pictures you'd find in a glossy magazine that make you want to visit on your next vacation.

He didn't normally take time to absorb his surroundings, but watching Sage as she took pictures of every detail opened a window into a very different perspective.

"You love it here, don't you." Not a question, just an observation. He obviously needed to have more in his life than a fourteen-hour workday.

"Wally Creek?" Taking her hand back, she turned and took several shots of the streets behind them before lowering her camera. The smile that had captured him from the first time he'd found it aimed in his direction, hovered at the corners of her mouth. "I guess I do. I didn't realize how much until I came home this time."

Her phone alerted her to a message with a brief bar of music. She ignored it.

"Do you need to get that?"

"No." She turned the camera on him and snapped a picture. "How about you? I think Charlie told me you live on Mercer Island. Do you like living there?"

Before this trip to see Charlie, he used to. "I like it a lot. It's a little like Wally Creek. Easy to walk. Small community. Cute place with lots of cafes and shopping."

"Does everyone know your business?" She took another picture of him.

"I think you've got enough pictures of me. I may break your camera," he half-joked. "My work keeps me pretty busy, but I have a favorite coffeehouse if that counts. I don't have much time to mix with my neighbors."

Luke winced. Even to his own ears, he sounded like a hermit. No wonder Gabi and Dara were on his case about finding time for something other than his job.

"I know just the fix for being too busy to get to know your neighbors," Sage said, a spark of mischief turning her dark eyes a molten brown. "I won't let you say no."

Gabi and Dori were right. Participating was a lot more fun than standing back and watching. "What do you have in mind?"

"Follow me." They walked a few blocks to Cedar Street. Sage threw open her arms. "Ta-da."

She'd taken him to a bicycle rental place. The sign over the door had Ben's Bike Repair and Rental in black letters on a bright yellow background.

"Ben has three-wheeled bicycles we can rent to explore all of Wally Creek. Are you game?"

"It's been a while since I've ridden a bicycle," he laughed. If only his partner could see him now. "Of course, I'm game."

For the next few hours, they explored every block of the town and its neighborhoods. They stopped for lunch at a food truck serving Mexican food, which they ate at a nearby park. Leaving the bikes in a bike rack, they walked through the water garden at the library. Sage snapped picture after picture.

With summer in high bloom, Luke couldn't help but fall in love. And not only with Wally Creek.

Three o'clock came too quickly. After returning the bikes, they made it to City Hall just in time to meet with the mayor. Luke kept his promise. He was there for moral support and nothing else. He did take notes under Sage's watchful eye.

She didn't need much from him. Pulling a list of questions out of her bag, she had everything covered. The mayor was informative. Sage asked all the right questions. She made it easy for him to follow what she was thinking for Amelia's.

How could he not fall completely under this clever lady's spell? She was everything he could want in a companion. A lifetime companion.

"You were brilliant in there," he told her on the way out.

Her cheeks turned a light shade of pink. "You think so?"

"Absolutely." Taking both of her hands, he pulled her to a stop outside City Hall. "You covered all your bases. You were clear and concise." He drew her a little closer and said, his voice a little rough as he spoke. "I could kiss you right now."

Her eyes went wide, the brown color melting.

A throat cleared nearby. "Sage?"

She broke away. Luke felt the loss deep inside where no one had touched him in a long time. Facing the dude who'd interrupted, though he'd only gotten a glimpse of the other man, Luke recognized him immediately. He was the guy from the Emerald Star.

A dainty necklace dangled from his fingers.

If he thought Sage would let him, Luke would tuck her close beneath his arm and rub his chin across her soft hair.

She notched her delicate chin and straightened to her full height. "What are you doing here, Gordan?"

The ex. Luke hoped that was freezing winter he heard in her voice.

"You didn't answer my texts." Gordan sent a hard look Luke's way.

Too bad, dude. You snooze, you lose.

"I was hoping we could talk," Gordan held out the necklace to Sage. "And I wanted to return this."

That Sage didn't immediately tell the guy to get lost spoke volumes. When she reached for the necklace, Luke could feel painful disappointment stabbing him in the chest.

Breath log-jamming in his throat, he turned to Sage. "I just remembered. I promised to meet up with Uncle Charlie and Verne for a poke game tonight." Which would be true as soon as he called them and invited them to Charlie's for chips and beer.

"Luke? Wait."

But he was out of there. No way was he going to make a fool of himself just because all of a sudden he wanted there to be more between him and Sage than there really was.

Chapter Thirteen

Confused, Sage watched Luke walk away. He wanted to kiss her?

"Sage?"

Gordan. Her ex's timing couldn't be worse. "What are you doing here?"

Before he answered, she realized she was holding the faerie necklace she'd thrown overboard. She thrust it back toward Gordan. "Where did you find this?"

Instead of taking the necklace, he pushed his hands into the pockets of his khaki pants. "I found it caught on the edge of the gangplank when I was leaving the ship."

Funny. She could have sworn it went into the water.

"So why did you come?" she demanded, making a fist around the necklace that had once been a symbol of her forever dreams.

A smile played around his mouth. "You invited me, remember?"

"And if I recall correctly, you decided to go whitewater rafting with your buddies instead." Suddenly chilled, she crossed her bare arms across her chest.

Smile disappearing, Gordan reached for her. She took a step back.

"Come on, Sage. I admit I made a mistake. I shouldn't have canceled on you at the last minute like that."

She took a calming breath and wiped the grimace from her face. What was done was done. She asked quietly, "Why did you?"

He took her in from head to toe. There was a time when she would have been thrilled at the close appraisal. Not so much this time.

"I got scared, I guess. I knew you wanted something more permanent than dating, but I wasn't ready."

"But you couldn't talk to me about it. And you're ready now?"

He threw up his hands, a very un-Gordan-like gesture. "For Pete's sake, Sage. You wanted to introduce me to your grandparents. That was big." He searched her face. "Wasn't it?"

If she'd learned anything from their breakup, it was that it was best to be open and honest. "It was. We dated for nine months, Gordan. I thought you were as committed as I was to you, that we had a long future ahead of us."

"I was a fool." Reaching across the space that separated them, he gingerly took her hand, gently uncrossing her arms. "I shouldn't have let you walk away."

Running as fast as she could was more like it.

Unfurling her fingers, he retrieved the necklace and fastened it around her neck.

His breezy cologne took her back to their life on the Emerald Star. The sunny days. The job they both loved. Entertaining all the passengers. They'd done everything together. Eventually, even spending their vacations as a couple. They were the perfect fit. And by that fateful day, she'd known exactly what she wanted. At least she'd thought so.

It seemed so long ago now, her dream of having the man she could completely love and who would love her just as much back. She'd wanted the house, the family, a future that included children and the two of them growing old together.

Well, it turned out, she had a family if she counted Charlie, Bette, Verne, and Lily, which she did. She had the house. She had a future here in Wally Creek, with Amelia's Cuppa Tea on the horizon. She could even happily grow old here. She had it all. Without Gordan. And she was okay—in the best possible way—with all of it.

There was also that kiss Luke had half-promised. Okay, he hadn't actually promised, but he had said he wanted—

Gordan's hands came to rest on her shoulders. "Give me, give us a second chance. Please?"

Be present. Sage didn't know where she'd heard that sage advice, but at the moment, it seemed spot on.

"I'm not that girl anymore, Gordan." She backed up until his hands dropped.

"Of course, you're that girl," he insisted. "It's barely been two weeks. The girl I knew couldn't have changed so much in such a short time."

"She did." Which only proved how well he didn't know her. He might be hoping that showing up like he had changed how things were left between them, but Sage couldn't forget. "I don't think—"

"Listen, before you turn me down flat," He put his fingers across her mouth. "I saw a restaurant when I was texting you. How about we have dinner, and you let me talk you into forgiving my stupidity."

She removed his hand. "Are you talking about the Hargrove?"

"Yes, that's it. Come on, Sage. Give me a chance to make amends."

It wasn't a good idea, but because of the years they'd been together, she owed him the chance to explain himself. Didn't she?

"All right," she relented, against her better judgment. "I need to make a call first."

Walking several feet away, she dialed Luke's number. It went straight to voicemail. "Hi. It's me. I'm sorry Gordan showed up when he did. I'm sorry he showed up at all. Can we talk later?"

Frowning, she hung up and called Verne. When he picked up, she raised her chin. What in the world was she doing? Gordan had already proven he wasn't the sticking kind. "Hi, Verne."

"Hey, girl." His gruff tone reminded her why she'd made up her mind to stay in Wally Creek.

"I just wanted to let you know, I won't be home for dinner."

"Got a hot date with our boy?"

Luke? The idea of going on a date with Luke was way more exciting than having to sit through a meal listening to Gordan making excuses.

"Um, no." Kicking a tuft of grass growing along the sidewalk, she glanced at Gordan. "A friend from the Emerald Star is in town. He wants to catch up, so we're going to dinner."

"Is it that chump who broke your heart?"

Grams must have filled them all in. Sage wanted to hug the older man. She could easily imagine the growl in Verne's voice blooming on the rugged landscape of his face.

"My heart's not broken, Verne." Which, surprisingly, was true. That keen sense of belonging she used to feel with Gordan just wasn't there any longer.

She rubbed the faerie between her thumb and finger. Some couples got a second chance. She wasn't sure she wanted to be one of them. Could Gordan get on board with her plans for Amelia's? Would he leave the Emerald Star for Wally Creek? Most likely not. But then, she didn't see Luke leaving Seattle, either.

"Where are you going?" It warmed her up that Verne cared enough to be concerned. Certainly, her grandparents would have been.

Gordan watched her, his brows merging. Turning away from his scrutiny, she walked further away. "The Hargrove."

"At least they have decent food," Verne harrumphed.

She smiled. She would take him as a substitute grandfather any day. "I'll see you guys later."

"You should bring your friend by to meet everyone."

And from the tone of his voice, throw Gordan into the lion's den? She might agree but— "Not tonight."

She poked the disconnect button, pocketed her phone, and walked back to Gordan. As he had before they'd broken up, he took her hand and laced their fingers together. "All set?"

A silver Camaro zipped by. Luke stared straight ahead without looking in her direction.

She pulled her hand free. It was too confusing. Here she was with Mr. Adventure, her former heartthrob. Was she seriously wishing she had a chance with Mr. Died-in-the-wool, I'm-all-about-Business? Just because he wanted to kiss her?

"I'll get my car and—" she said, unsettled by the comparison of the two men.

"We can take my car. I'm parked right over there." His usual rental, a new red Mustang was just up the block. She used to think that was so charming.

"That's okay, I'll meet you there." She headed for her to the car before he could stop her.

What had happened to giving him a chance? Sage shrugged. By the time she parked Annabelle, he was waiting outside the Hargrove, hands in his back pockets as he stared off across the river.

When he saw her, he dredged up a lopsided grin, the one he used to get his way—how had she just realized that—and sauntered over to open her car door as if they still met every day to share a meal. "I thought for a moment you changed your mind"

"I would never do that to you," she said without thinking. He winced. Sage wrapped her hand around his arm. "I'm sorry. I didn't mean for that to sound so judgmental."

"I get it, Sage. I know it's not going to be easy to earn back your trust."

What could she say to that? She couldn't deny how she felt.

They were seated at a window table overlooking a patio with scattered outdoor dining and had ordered their food before she responded.

The sun dropped below the horizon.

"Except for a very few people—" He used to be one of them. "—I don't trust easily, Gordan."

He reached across the table, his fingers resting against hers. "Let's talk about your grandparents instead. Will I get to meet them this trip?"

"They moved to Arizona the day after I got here." Missing them, she stared at their touching fingers. She should feel a spark, shouldn't she? They used to have sparks when they touched.

"They didn't tell you before you got here?" He sounded genuinely surprised.

Had she been too hasty on the Emerald Star? Let her dreams get ahead of reality?

Placing her napkin, and her hands in her lap, she eased back. "They wanted to, but the Emerald Star was out to sea for its longest cruise, and I wanted to surprise them, so I didn't let them know we . . . I was coming."

If there was a next time, she would know better than to assume her grandparents were hanging around just waiting for her to come home. She wouldn't be that self-absorbed again.

The waiter brought their food, salmon on a bed of rice for Gordan and a taco salad for Sage.

He dug into his meal. "Are you staying at a hotel, then? Maybe I can get a room at the same place."

"They gave me their house," she said quietly as she added guacamole and sour cream to her salad. Why was it so uncomfortable keeping a casual conversation going with the man she'd thought she would spend the rest of her life with?

"That's generous of them, but we have to be back on the Emerald Star in little over a week. Are you going to sell the house?" He gave her his best smile. This time she didn't have any trouble resisting. "Hey, I can stay with you until we leave—

"

She gave him a long look. Even if she was inclined to let him have one of the rooms for a few days, there was no room at the inn.

"Or not." Cluing into her silence, he laid down his fork.

"The Oak Hotel is the best place in town to stay. The owner is a good friend of mine. She might have a room available."

"Thanks for the suggestion." The shine faded from his smile as he retrieved his fork and went back to his salmon dinner. "So, what are you going to do with the house?"

As the summer days grew longer, Sage was happy to be in Wally Creek. The warmth of the season drew neighbors out into their yards to visit. Flowers bloomed in all the best places. Bees buzzed from bloom to bloom collecting nectar for their honey. Birds provided a happy, chirpy background. By the end of summer, Amelia's would be open. There was no place in the world she wanted to be for the foreseeable future.

"I'm going to open a tea room," she said to see what Gordan did with the information.

His fork landed on his plate, only this time with more clank. "A tea room? That's crazy. What about your job?"

There was no reason why she should defend her choices. Especially not to an ex-boyfriend who'd at the last minute gotten cold feet.

"I have some vacation time saved up." She angled her chin. Amelia's wasn't whitewater rafting, but it was still an adventure. Because he looked so confused, she answered his question. "I'm giving notice as soon as the financing comes through."

"You don't have to do this. Not because of my stupid timing." Gordan leaned forward. "You don't have any experience running your own business."

Sage shortened the distance between them. "That might be true, but I have plenty of experience helping customers have a great time."

"You're serious," he said, backing off.

"Very serious." She was past sugarcoating her dreams, especially her new ones, so that whoever her boyfriend was or wasn't would be happy for her and get on board with her plans.

It wasn't that she blamed Gordan for figuring out before she did that what she'd wanted all along was to settle down, have a family, and make a home. She'd been the last one to figure that out, thinking her dreams began and ended with being with a special guy. But now her dream had expanded into something bigger, she would wager her first day's earnings at Amelia's this new version wasn't what Gordan wanted any more than he truly wanted to be her grand passion.

They finished their meal with idle chatter. At her car, he took both her hands in his and kissed her knuckles. His gaze turned sad. "We're not going to work, are we?"

The Hargrove's lights softly illuminated the parking lot as stars began to twinkle in the night sky. Slowly, she shook her head. "No."

"I guess I won't be needing that room at The Oak tonight."

"Probably not." She smiled gently at him, grateful that all her uncertainty about her future had finally dissipated like a low-lying fog along an Oregon beach in the first rays of morning sunshine.

The smile she remembered came back in full force as he squeezed her hands. "Be happy, Sage."

Opening her car door, he waited until she buckled her seat

belt and started the engine before heading for the Mustang.

About to take the left that would lead to River Road and her house, she checked her rearview mirror. Gordan was pulling onto the highway going through the edge of town. Eventually, it would take him back to Seattle.

Was it bad that she felt relieved? She searched her feelings. Nope. It was okay. Gordan, the Emerald Star, that chapter of her life was finished.

When she walked into the house, all was peacefully quiet. Perfect for taking a moment to catch her breath. Not that she regretted the finality of her and Gordan's breakup, it was just that his visit made it very clear it was time to move forward, not hang on to the past.

Pouring a glass of red wine, she carried it out to the back porch where she found that Bette and Lily had the same idea. The porch light illuminated the nearby garden.

Lily sat on a stool in front of an easel, painting a nightscape, a bouquet of chrysanthemums, peonies, roses, and snapdragons in vibrant colors that filled the whole canvas edged in the darker color of dusk.

Bette was knitting a shawl with delicate pale fuchsia yarn. She looked up as Sage sank into one of the remaining chairs. "There you are. How was your visit with your friend?"

Sage let out a breath. "It was good." She smiled. It had turned out alright. "Gordan wanted to get back together, but— Anyway, he's on his way back to the Emerald Star."

"The man who broke your heart?" Bette raised perfectly arched brows.

Sage rolled her eyes. "But?"

Lily swung around, a paint-blotted wooden paint palette in one hand, brush in the other. A swatch of red was smeared across her chin. "He's not the right one for you."

Sage almost spit out the sip of wine she'd just taken. Coughing, she half-laughed. Lily could be very astute. "What makes you think that?"

"You were pretty sad the day we first met. We wanted to know why, so we called Vanessa." Of course. Lily put her painting tools aside. "If this man wanted to get back together, a 'no' over one dinner wouldn't have sent him on his way."

Two or three dates wouldn't have made any difference. She wasn't the same heartbroken girl who'd come to Wally Creek to see her grandparents and mend a broken heart.

Sighing happily, Sage closed her eyes and leaned back in the chair. It'd been a long time since she'd taken time to relax with girlfriends. "So, where are Verne and Charlie?"

"They're at Charlie's playing poker with Luke," Lily said. She joined Sage and Bette on the porch.

Ah, the poker game. She'd forgotten that's how Luke would be spending the evening. Her only excuse was she'd been busy sorting out her surprising lack of feelings for Gordan.

"Is poker a regular thing with the guys?" Sage breathed in the garden's floral concoction. The click of Bette's needles offered background music. "Who do you suppose will win?"

"Charlie. He's been playing since his university days." Bette's needles went quiet. "They wanted to get in a game before Luke left."

Wondering what kissing Luke would be like, Bette's words didn't sink in at first. Despite their precarious beginning, Sage couldn't help but think about where their friendship could go from here. The man's love affair with logic and facts, and his determination not to keep them to himself was growing on her.

Suddenly, she sat straight up. "Luke's leaving? When did he decide that?"

"This afternoon, I think" Bette's needles started back up.

Before or after Gordan showed up? "Did he say why?"

Lily looked as relaxed as a kitten napping in a warm patch of sunlight. Without opening her eyes she said, "No, only that he was leaving first thing in the morning."

"He can't leave." Sage jumped up and started pacing.

Rousing, Lily sat up, and using one foot, stopped her chair from rocking. "Well, he's a grown man. I guess he can leave if he wants."

She faced the ladies. They looked innocently confused by her reaction, but Sage wasn't fooled. They both had a keen sense of humor and a mischievous streak a mile wide. Both were on display at the moment, in the twinkle of the two pairs of eyes pinned on her face.

"He agreed to drive the mayor in the Summer Celebration parade." Sage popped her hands on her hips. "If I have to find another car and driver—"

"I believe he talked Charlie into doing driving duty." Bette glanced up coyly and kept knitting. "Is that what you heard too, Lily?"

As serious as the best apple pie winning the blue ribbon at a local fair, Lily chirped, "Yup. I believe I did."

Did he even intend to say goodbye before he left? That was a short trip, going from wanting to kiss to leaving town without so much as a wave before leaving Wally Creek in his dust.

Disappointed, Sage rubbed her arms. Walking to the edge of the grass, she stared unseeing at the backyard.

"Come sit down, dear." Lily patted the chair she'd jumped out of moments before. When Sage perched on the edge of the seat, she asked, "You like Luke, don't you? That's why you couldn't make up with Gordan."

Bette put her knitting aside and scooted her chair until the three of them were in a close circle. She patted Sage's knee in sympathy.

Be honest, Dawson. "Sure. I like him." Sage had a feeling she wasn't the only one in this confusing predicament. She put her hand on top of Bette's. "What about you? Do you like Charlie? It seems pretty obvious that something is going on between the two of you."

"I do." Bette's face twisted into an amused grimace. "But, I'm still deciding what to do about it."

Sage was the one doing the patting now. "Me, too."

"Well, you better do something pretty quick, young lady." Lily raised her wine glass between them. "That boy's gonna be gone in the morning."

Muttering, "Men can be so much trouble," Sage stood. She dragged her cell out of her pocket and started to call but suddenly stopped. "I don't have his number."

"I have it. Charlie gave it to me in case of an emergency." Bette disappeared into the house and came back with her phone. "Here you go."

After putting the number in her contact list, Sage dialed. The call went to voicemail. "Hi, Luke. It's Sage. I heard you're going back to Seattle tomorrow morning. I'm hoping we can talk before you leave?" She looked at Lily and Bette, arched her brows, then shrugged both shoulders. When the ladies shook their heads, offering no other advice, she finished with, "Okay. Well, call me as soon as you get this message."

Disturbed more than she should be, Sage put the phone away. "I'll keep trying, but if he's not answering his phone, I don't know what to do."

"Maybe he just needs a little incentive." Lily and Bette looked at each other. It was Lily who clarified what their silent communication meant. "A small push in the right direction, you know?"

"Maybe." Sage couldn't guess what kind of incentive that would take. Luke hadn't been the least bit bashful to tell her what he thought when he'd first come to Wally Creek. But now he was going silent?

Maybe he didn't want to kiss her anymore. She couldn't blame him. Gordan's arrival had been ill-timed. Rinsing her wine glass out and leaving it in the sink, she headed upstairs to her room. After changing into her pajamas she tried one more time to call Luke but again got voicemail. Leaving another message, she crawled into bed.

She turned on her side and vowed, no more hiding. If it wasn't Gordan and her life as a cruise director that got her all excited, what did? The answer came immediately.

More than anything, she wanted a new life in Wally Creek. It wasn't just the town that brought a smile to her face. Every day was an adventure. A ray of sunshine. She wanted Amelia's Cuppa Tea to be a gathering place for her customers. And she wanted a chance to see if there could be anything between her and Luke. Something more than the possibility of a kiss. She wanted one kiss to lead to another and then another. She wanted— Luke.

Willing the cell she'd left on the nightstand to ring, she tucked her pillow close under her head and closed her eyes. What she needed was an incentive, as Lily had suggested. A plan. And she had the perfect thing in mind. Logic, the best coffee and pastry in town. Good thing she was an early riser.

Hopefully, Luke wasn't.

Chapter Fourteen

The hour was late when Luke closed the door behind his uncle and Verne. The poker game had done little to eliminate the restlessness caused by Sage's ex showing up, but it had at least provided a momentary diversion. He glanced at the large Route US 66 clock on the wall. It was too late to return Sage's call. In any case, what would he say to her?

Putting away the cards, he cleared the table.

Fortunately, at dinner, Charlie had agreed to drive the mayor in the parade, so there was nothing else to keep him in town. Not the Summer Celebration, not the ladies working on the parade committee who he'd come to enjoy working with, and certainly not Sage Dawson. During the game, there had been no talk about lost opportunities or the one who'd gotten away. Luke figured he was okay with that.

Fortunately, he had a very full life in Seattle to take his mind off how much his heart hurt. In comparison, his breakup with

Hannah had been child's play.

It wasn't until the last hand when he'd been staring at two kings, two eights, and a five of diamonds for far too long, wondering which to throw away, that a different distraction popped into his head and refused to be dismissed.

Charlie had a cute place here.

His uncle won that hand with a full house, aces over queens. The Queen of Hearts, determination reflected in the set of her chin, had reminded him so much of Sage. But what did it matter? After he went back to Seattle, the only time he would run into her was when he occasionally made the trip back to Wally Creek to see Charlie. And if he was successful in bringing Portman Technologies on board which would result in expanding MR Investments to London, the times he returned to the mountain town would be even less.

Finished with the cleanup and not wanting to pack his bags just yet, Luke toured the two-bedroom, two-bath bungalow to see if his sudden idea held any water.

If Charlie planned to stay at Sage's with the rest of the book club, listing his cozy home on the vacation rental market could bring in enough money to replace the funds that were going into Sage's grant from his uncle's retirement account. It would be a win-win for both sides.

The house had outstanding curb appeal. Bedrooms and a bath were upstairs. The living area was on the first floor. It needed some updates, maybe a lick of paint here and there, and new appliances in the kitchen, but otherwise it was in good shape. They might even be able to talk Bette and Lily into managing bookings and housekeeping if the ladies weren't too busy with Sage's tea room. He wouldn't have to come back for business at all that way.

The best part of this plan was that Sage didn't have to find out where the money for her grant had come from. Especially since Charlie hadn't told her, and Luke was still under strict orders not to make any disclosures. Truth be told, he no longer wanted to reveal where her grant was coming from.

When he first came to Wally Creek, he had no idea he'd have to choose between his sense of right and wrong and the only family member he went out of his way to see. Avoiding the question of whether he'd made the right choice to leave in the morning, Luke returned to the living room with a pad and pencil to run the numbers, but his mind kept going back to Sage and the necklace she'd taken back from Gordan.

That had to mean something. He wanted her to be happy. Not just in her day job or the place where she lived, but in her heart too. If her ex was that guy, who was he to stand in their way?

It was a lousy conclusion to come to. Luke set aside his calculations and went to make coffee. It was clear Sage wanted Gordan. They were holding hands when he drove by.

"What are you saying?" he demanded of the empty kitchen as coffee dripped into his cup. "That you want to be the one promising her a future?" Of course, he did.

Wouldn't happen with Gordan hanging around. And anyway, Sage hadn't shown any signs that she liked him that way. Except, when he'd told her he wanted to kiss her. She'd leaned toward him, just a fraction, but enough that he was hoping she would welcome his kiss.

Gordan What's-his-name was not her guy. Look how he'd left her high and dry. At least that was the story he'd gotten at dinner. All he remembered was seeing the necklace sail over the railing of the ship. The man and woman watching, and by their body language, the man horrified, the lady really ticked off.

Sage deserved to be happy. Whether she was conscious of it or not, the pictures she took showed just how deep her hopes ran. He would wager all the money he had that she believed in Ron Weasley and Hermione Granger, Aladdin and Jasmine, and Queen Victoria and Prince Albert.

Falling in love was something he'd never enjoyed. Would she believe him if he told her before he left that her ex was not Weasley, Aladdin, or Albert?

Probably not. He hadn't exactly made a great impression when they first met, and he had no evidence against Gordan to prove his case.

The next morning Luke was up early and was still trying to work out how to convince Sage that Gordan was not the guy who could fulfill her wish list. Not that Luke knew what was on that list, he was just pretty sure she had one.

He still hadn't packed. Instead, he was typing up a proposal on his laptop to present to Charlie for turning the cozy bungalow into a vacation rental. In the back of his mind, he was also working on ways to let Sage know, before he went back to Seattle, why he wanted what was best for her.

She was smart. She had courage galore. And the lady cared so much about her friends and family. Look how she'd offered Verne, Bette, and Lily a place to stay after the fire at their senior home. She was going to be a hard woman to forget.

And, she had Gordan.

Ten minutes later, he was finished with the proposal. For the bungalow, not the list of why he would never forget Sage no matter how hard he tried. Maybe he should return her call after all. There had to be a way he could show her that she deserved better than a guy who didn't have the stamina to stay when things got complicated. But how?

The doorbell chimed. He went to answer the summons.

She'd be the first to tell him, what she did was none of his business. Still, he couldn't just stand by and watch her ex break her heart a second time. Before Sage, Luke would never have said he had any mojo when it came to making a romantic relationship work, but the situation with Sage was different. She was different.

The doorbell rang a second time as he opened the door.

"Um. Hi." Sage stood on the doorstep juggling two coffees and a bag sporting The Oak's logo that smelled suspiciously of gooey sugar. "You didn't return my call, so I brought treats."

She looked so pretty in the dark green jumpsuit that stopped just below her knees. The style was one of Dara's favorites though her color choice ran more to shades of lavender.

Sage's thick mahogany hair was pulled into a messy bun on the top of her head. He couldn't stop staring.

"Luke?"

"Of course, come in." Untangling his tongue, he managed to inform the woman scooting past him, "I was going to call—"

Her brows came together in that delightful way she had when she didn't quite believe him.

Handing him one of the coffees, she went to the kitchen. "Black, right?"

"Thanks. What's in the bag?" She'd noticed how he liked his coffee? Unexpectedly, his pulse settled. Closing the door, he followed her as far as the table where his laptop was still open. He quickly flipped it closed.

"Bear Claws. I wasn't sure what you'd like, so I got my favorite."

"They're my favorite too." As of this minute.

He grabbed plates and napkins and joined her at the table, where she'd taken a seat, and was waiting.

He wasn't the jealous type and didn't want to sound like he was, but if the lady wouldn't look after herself, someone had to. "Look, I know it's none of my business, and if I were you, I wouldn't be interested in my opinion, but I have to be honest. That Gordan guy, he's not good for you."

She bit off a bite of her bear claw. Covering her mouth, she finished chewing before swallowing. Her delicate brows raised. "Why?"

So, not as offended as he thought she would be. He was improving in his relaying-the-facts-without-putting-his-foot-in-his-mouth skills. "Well, first of all, he left you. Big mistake. If he cared about you, he wouldn't have walked away. He would have hung around and worked things out."

"Maybe I'm a real pain in the neck as a girlfriend." She leaned on her elbow and put her chin in her hand. "It could be he was right to dump me."

"Not hardly," Through rising hackles, he demanded, a soft growl sticking in his throat, "He said that to you?"

"No." She laughed. "I appreciate the vote of confidence, but you don't know me that well."

She was teasing. He let his frown fade into an internal smile. Leaving Sage right now wasn't going to convince her there were better guys out there than her ex. And that one of those guys was Luke Marshell. It was his turn to hang around and work things out. If she'd let him.

"I expected too much from Gordan, and for him, I was moving too fast. Some guys don't see themselves living in a house with a white picket fence, a minivan in the drive, and the father of two kids."

"Some guys see that as a trap." That had never been his plan, either. But with the right woman, Sage, for instance, it could happen someday. "Is that what you want?"

"I, maybe, I guess." She shook her head. "No one was more surprised than me. I thought I wanted to travel the world before I did all those things."

"Gordan wasn't interested?" If the other man hadn't turned Sage's dreams down, *he* wouldn't be sitting here talking to the most interesting and tempting woman he'd ever met.

She shrugged. "He was not."

"But he's here, so he must have changed his mind." Swallowing his disappointment, Luke leaned back in his chair. He was too late. The lady was taken.

Sage tucked a stray of hair behind her ear before settling her gaze on his face. "Gordan's not here. He's on his way back to the Emerald Star."

"No kidding?" He straightened and leaned on his forearms. He couldn't tell how she felt about this new development, but he wanted to jump up and down like a kid who'd just been promised his first prom date. "Whose idea was it for him to leave?"

"Mine." She gave him a quick smile, easing his worry that she was pining for the dumb guy. "We're not a good fit. Things have changed for me. I've changed."

Oh, man. Did he want to know this? "Amelia's?"

"That and Wally Creek. Charlie and the rest of the book club. A lot is going on here that I want to see through." The sincerity in her dark brown eyes captured Luke. She tilted her head to the side. "It's like you and Seattle. I'm home. While he was here, it was so clear that Wally Creek could never be

Gordan's home."

He and Seattle. Home. He might like her—a lot—but he had no plan to pick up his life and move to Wally Creek any more than Gordan was going to give up his shipboard lifestyle. In that way, he wasn't much different from her ex. Luke cringed at the comparison.

"Luke, you can't leave," Sage said on a firm note. "Not yet."

Surprised at her determination and curious about what reason she would give to keep him in Wally Creek, he cautiously asked, "Why not? Charlie's going to drive—"

"—Drive the mayor in the parade. I know. But that's not the point."

If he didn't already find her fascinating, this conversation would seal the deal. "It's not?"

"No. The point is you're already taking time away from work. What better way to spend that time than staying in Wally Creek to help with the parade? As you promised, I might add." She sipped her coffee and watched him over the rim. Eyes twinkling, she put the cup back on the table. "Have you ever been to a small-town parade?"

"Not that I can recall." The woman had an undeniably attractive verbal skill. A skill he couldn't resist. It was a good thing he hadn't packed his bags yet.

"See? Another good reason to stay," she said, a hopeful lilt in her tone that went a long way toward encouraging Luke to change his mind.

She'd had him at *'things have changed for me'*, but the lady didn't need to know that. "What other reasons?"

"There's Charlie, of course." Leaning on her elbows, she counted on her fingers. "And Verne. And Bette. And Lily. They all love you."

Love was a strong word, even when it was applied to the woman looking more and more determined to change his mind about staying. The coziness of Charlie's bungalow and the woman trying so hard to persuade him, suddenly made him wonder if he could downsize to Wally Creek.

Not if he still wanted to take MR international. Which he did. He hadn't changed his mind about that. So scratch Wally Creek off the table.

"And I, uh, thought that since you're this big shot business guy—" he almost missed the sparkle in her dark eyes. She was playing with him. If he was a younger, less experienced, man heading for his first crush, he'd be driving off the cliff right about then. "—I'd like to have an opportunity to get some advice about Amelia's. If you wouldn't mind."

A sparkle of his own started to blaze a path in his chest. "It will cost you."

When her teasing turned into a grin, breathing became difficult. "Name your price, Marshell."

Tilting the chair back, he crossed his arms over his chest. Gesturing toward her half-finished pastry, he said, as serious as a hundred-dollar bill, "You'll have to get me a few more of those bear claws. They're delicious."

"That's asking a lot, you know."

"I figured."

She tried to bury her laughter but wasn't successful. "So, you'll stay?"

Popping the last bite of his pastry into his mouth, he nodded.

"It's a deal then." She jumped up, taking the remnants from her impromptu bribe to the kitchen.

After wiping his hands on a napkin, Luke followed. "I've already taken time off, so I'm at your disposal."

She spun around to face him. "Now that was just plain ornery, making me work so hard to talk you into staying."

"I know." It took all the strength he had not to hug Sage when he saw that she wasn't really upset with his game. "I'll apologize, but I still want to get paid in Bear Claws."

She grinned. "You give me a headache, you know that?"

"So I've been told." By Gabi. More than once. "What's next on the agenda today?"

"I want to finish cleaning up the attic and see what it would take to turn the space into an office and photography room." She cast him an expectant look. "Wanna come?"

He couldn't help teasing the delightful woman. "So you can keep an eye on me and make sure I don't leave town?"

"Something like that." A wink turned into a satisfied smile.

He would like to believe she'd come over this morning, and bearing gifts too, because she was afraid he wasn't staying. The truth was, he was afraid he *would* stay for longer than it would take to help Sage with the parade. As a kid, he hadn't felt like he was part of the family. In his twenties, Hannah had only been interested in his assets, not him as a person struggling to put his heart out there. What if he still wasn't enough?

"Luke?" Sage waited, one hand gripping the open front door.

Outside the summer sunshine and the inviting scents of June warmed by the sun beckoned. Sage's wavering smile was the final straw. He grabbed his key and joined her, ushering her out of the house. "Did I ever tell you I worked my way through college as a carpenter?"

"No, you did not, but if this is an offer to lend me your skills, I'll take it." Preceding him down the front walk, she glanced over her shoulder at him and laughed. "Carpenter skills, Marshell? Perfect timing. Meet you at the house?"

The woman was killing him. In a good way. Luke nodded and headed for his Camaro.

After he parked behind Sage at her place, they went straight to the attic after making a brief stop in the kitchen for drinks. Charlie and Bette were putting the last of the breakfast dishes in the dishwasher.

"My favorite vacation is Hawaii." Bette flipped the tea towel she was using to dry pans over her shoulder.

"No place beats Durango, Colorado, my dear." his uncle countered back before turning to greet them. "Hi, kids. What are you up to today?"

His uncle had that look. He was plotting. Could it be he was finally going to tell Sage where her grant money had come from? That would take a load off of Luke's shoulders, but he was pretty sure that wasn't what was on Charlie's mind.

Sage didn't give his uncle a chance to confess. "We're going up to the attic to do some cleanup. We need an office for the business and I want to put my photography computer and equipment up there too."

Her enthusiasm was infectious. Except for Gabi and Dara, he'd never met a woman more focused on projects and who was as determined to step into her future as Sage was.

"When you get a chance, we should all sit down and discuss what you want Amelia's to look like inside and how you want the space to function," Charlie suggested. "Lily volunteered to do some drawings once she knows what you have in mind."

"That would be wonderful. I don't see any reason not to start planning. Even without the grant money. Will tomorrow work?"

"Yup." Charlie closed the dishwasher.

With a big grin, she left the kitchen and went upstairs. Luke followed Sage. He could feel Charlie's hard stare. His uncle wasn't a patient man when it came to moving forward once he'd made a decision. His patience was probably wearing thin, but there was nothing more Luke could do. It would take time to evaluate and liquidate the stocks from Charlie's portfolio that would do the least harm. Gabi was overseeing the process, but even she couldn't move things along any faster than they were going.

Up in the attic, he could see why the sprawling room appealed to Sage. He hadn't taken a close look at the space when he was up here last, but now that he had an idea of what she wanted, he could envision what the room would look like.

With a little insulation and sheetrock, the attic would be perfect for the space she wanted. Standing in the light from two good-sized windows in the gable ends, he couldn't believe he'd honestly thought Sage was after a cozy nest egg from Charlie.

It was finally clear he'd lost that argument with his uncle, and himself, shortly after he'd arrived in Wally Creek and just didn't know it. That was why he found himself between a rock and a hard spot; still stuck between keeping his word to his uncle and being honest with the woman who was coming to mean more to him than a casual acquaintance. Or Charlie's landlady and potential future employer, if he could believe that the roommates really were going to work at Amelia's once the tea room opened.

When he told Sage the truth, he was pretty sure it would not go well. Mentally crossing his fingers that everything would work out in the end, he pushed aside his misgivings and concentrated on the task at hand.

Stacks of boxes lined both sloping sides of the attic. Miscellaneous furniture was stacked neatly down the middle. Sunlit particles floated in the filtered light from the windows. The floor was unfinished with wide planks. For an attic, where most homeowners stashed their old memories, it wasn't badly organized.

"Where do you want to start?"

"Let's sort the boxes first." She headed for the stacks on the farthest end of the attic. "We can make a keep-it stack on one side of the room and a look-at-later stack on the other."

Luke asked when he couldn't guess which pile his box went into. Fortunately, they were marked, so it didn't take long to get through them all. When they finished with the last box, his partner in crime—he was starting to think of Sage that way—sat on a stool, wiping off a picture frame with a rag.

"What do you have there?" He looked over her shoulder at a photo of a younger Sage standing next to a young man with lighter hair and the same dark eyes.

"A picture of my brother, Jack, and me, just before I went off to college."

Her younger version looked like she was ready to take on the world. Luke didn't remember having that same excited energy when he'd gone off to university. It was a practical matter for him. He had to go to college to get where he wanted to be—owner of a successful business that would give him stability and a home of his choice wherever he finally landed. He'd picked the University of Washington in Seattle because the school reminded him a little bit of Oxford, and Seattle was a thriving city with an international airport.

"Are you and your brother close?"

"Mostly. He doesn't come home much." Frowning, she

shifted on the stool and laid the picture face down in her lap.

"Well, I'm jealous. Growing up, I always wanted a brother or sister."

She nodded. "That part was very cool. We were close back then. At least we were until he left home." She picked up the picture and took it to the window, standing it up on the sill before turning back to him. "So, how handy are you, Mr. Carpenter Man?"

One brow raised as humor replaced the serious moment. She missed her brother. It wasn't until he met Gabi that Luke stopped feeling like a lone stranger wherever he went. He still wasn't sure love was worth all the trouble, but Sage Dawson made him want to take the risk. What the heck? Why not give them a try?

"I'm handy enough to know you're going to need insulation, new electrical, lights, and lots of drywall to make this space usable. Which do you prefer, painted walls or tongue-and-groove?"

Chapter Fifteen

⚜

Generally, Sage saw no point in dragging her feet. Starting over in Wally Creek with Amelia's was no exception. And yes, she had a list. What self-respecting organized woman wouldn't? On that list was to make sure the details of the parade were in order, which they were taking care of. Finish the floor plan for Amelia's, also in the works. And determine if there was something special happening between her and Luke, though this last one wasn't written on the list. And with her recent failure in the romance department, she wasn't quite certain how to go about untangling that knot.

"What are you thinking so hard about?"

Startled, she glanced at Luke as he joined her. Along with Em, Rickie, and Eli, they were charting the parade route to make sure there wouldn't be any snags on parade day, only five days away. The route made a loop along the two main streets of town, starting on Birch Street and ending on Elm in front of the fire station.

"Nothing much."

"It can't be nothing. You're twisting your hair into a knot." He pointed at the loop of hair she'd wrapped around her fingers.

Unwinding the chunk, she attempted to relax, not an easy feat with Luke walking so close their arms almost brushed. She shrugged. "I'm thinking about the paintings Lily promised to show us tonight. I can't wait to see them."

Which was partly the truth.

Lily's sketches had taken Sage's breath away—not Luke's hand that had been flattened on her shoulder blade as they both looked at Amelia's Cuppa Tea come to life right before their eyes. After they'd all told Lily how much they'd loved her drawings, her resident artist promised to have several watercolors ready by dinner tonight.

"I can't wait to see them myself." He shoved his hands in his pockets, apparently not as discombobulated as she was while they walked side by side.

It'd been two days since he'd worked with her to sort through the boxes in the attic. He'd been a big help, and she was surprised at how easy it was to work with him on that simple project. Together they'd figured out exactly how she wanted the space to look and feel, with improved insulation covered by white beadboard on the ceiling, a painted checkerboard on whitewashed wood floors, and soft gray walls. All she needed to finish was the arrival of the supplies she'd ordered at Hardware Nuts and Bolts.

Then, yesterday, they'd all gotten together, including Luke, and walked the first floor of the house—living room, den, the kitchen with a walk-in pantry, and appropriate bathrooms.

Every angle was explored. The fireplace stayed on the must-have list. Sage couldn't bring herself to tear it down. It held too many memories she didn't want to forget.

Luke kept up every step of the way. She really could fall in love with the man. Not just your average everyday love, but if she wasn't careful, deep OMG, in L. O. V. E. without any hope of return of the same emotion on his part. She sighed heavily. Been there already.

He'd been so against Amelia's in the beginning. Wally Creek must have won him over just like it had her. More and more over the last few days, she could picture him, laptop in hand, sitting at one of her tables, eating a bear claw with his coffee.

Or better yet behind the counter taking orders and customer's payments. She knew she shouldn't indulge in the fantasy—this was her dream, not his—but it was getting harder and harder to separate him from her desire to someday have her own family in this lovely town.

Gordan had done her a huge favor by turning up in Wally Creek expecting everything between them to go back to the way they were. She hadn't been lying when she'd told him she'd changed and wasn't the same girl he knew anymore.

She'd completely fallen under Wally Creek's spell. Was inspired by the slower pace that was the lifeblood of the sleepy mountain town. Living in Wally Creek and becoming a business owner here, somehow had come to fit her like a beloved, comfortable glove. It hadn't been like that when she was a kid, and then a teenager, determined to spread her wings. She'd had enough of flying away.

"Are you coming to dinner?" she asked Luke, catching hold of Eli's shoulder before he could hopscotch off the curb and into the street.

Eli slid his free hand into Sage's. Luke grabbed the boy's other hand. "I wouldn't miss it."

The boy skipped between them with a six-year-old's energy Sage could only envy. He tugged on Luke's hand. "Is there going to be a fire truck in the parade?"

Luke glanced at her. Sage nodded.

"There sure is," he told the little guy.

Together they lifted Eli so that his hops were much higher and longer than his steps. "Can I ride on the fire truck?"

Luke was just as cute. Cut off guard, he again turned to her, dark brows lifted in question. She shook her head and mouthed, "I don't know."

"I'm not sure, buddy. You'll have to ask your mom." Helping Eli to hop even higher, Luke grinned at the boy.

Sage's heartbeat swelled. If she ever got that far, Luke was exactly the parenting partner she wanted—protective, caring, and kind. She wanted her family to do things together, like going to parades. And taking trips to the High Desert Museum in Central Oregon, where her parents had taken her and Jack when they were kids. And later when she and Jack moved in with Grams and Grandpa, exploring the rivers around Wally Creek.

Gordan would never be as patient with kids as Luke. His preferred audience was the party age group.

Luke caught her eye. "Everything's going to work out. The parade is going to be great."

Holy cow! Could he read her mind? With his sweet assurance, she was suddenly certain, everything *would* work out.

Sage couldn't help the new spring in her step. Every choice she'd made since leaving Wally Creek had brought her home.

Even her breakup with Gordan, surprising as that was. She was living in the best house, with four wonderful friends, who encouraged her every step of the way. She was about to embark on a great new adventure, even if it was a little scary. And then there was Luke. If her roommates could start a new chapter in their lives, then so could she.

Eli ran up to his mother. "Mom. Mom. Can I ride on the fire truck in the parade?"

"I don't know, honey." Rickie glanced back at them before kneeling in front of her son. "We'll have to ask the fire chief."

Eli jumped up and down. The boy had enough enthusiasm to power his own fire station. Sage hoped that someday she would have a boy as cute as Rickie's son. She glanced at Luke. He was watching Eli too, a smile curving his lips.

"Can we ask him right now?" Eli grabbed his mom's hand.

"Not right now, kiddo. We have a lot to do at the cafe." And when Eli's enthusiasm melted away, Rickie rubbed his head with her knuckles. "How about tomorrow?"

"Yes!" He pumped his little fist.

"Way to go kid," Luke whispered under his breath.

Laughter bubbled up in Sage's chest. Pushing away the crazy thought that she might not have to look any further for her dream man, she finished walking the parade route with the others. Everything looked good.

"I have to get back to the cafe." Rickie picked up Eli, who immediately wiggled to get down. She lowered him until his feet touched the ground, but hung on to his hand.

Sage knelt in front of the boy. "Can I get a hug?"

Little arms wrapped around her neck. She closed her eyes and held on. Luke would probably freak out if he knew he'd taken on the lead role in her growing family fantasy, but even without him, someday she would have one of these.

Her phone pinged. She let Eli go, waved to mom and son, then checked the incoming text. "The wood and drywall have been delivered to the house," she read out loud. "Charlie and Verne are taking it up to the attic."

"I'd better go help them." Luke took his car keys out of his pocket. "See you there?"

For someone who wasn't planning to hang around very long, the man was getting very cozy with her projects. Not that she was complaining. But what had happened to the cranky dude who'd come to Wally Creek and given her such a bad time about opening a potentially unsuccessful business?

She could honestly say she liked this version much better. "I'm going to stop at the hardware store first and pick out paint colors for the attic floor."

"I'll go with you." Em threaded her arm through Sage's. "I want to talk to you about something."

Sage watched Luke go to his car. Man, he was good-looking, mostly charming, and quite handy to have around. No wonder he was starting to grow on her.

Em pulled on her arm, and when they were out of hearing range, said, "Now, tell me what's going on between you and Luke."

She swiveled to look at her friend. "What—? No. Nothing is going on."

"That's not what it looks like to me," Em smirked, dragging Sage down Elm toward Hardware Nuts and Bolts.

"He's a nice guy, that's all," she finally conceded. "And he's being helpful."

"I can see that. Based on the look on your face the first time you followed him into The Oak, that was not what you were thinking then. I thought you were going to clock him like you did Ben Neville when we were in the tenth grade."

"Ben deserved it." Sage matched her steps to Em's. "He pinched my butte. I had a bruise for a week."

Em chuckled. "Boys. Did you know he married Anna Colter?"

"The one who was voted the nicest girl in our graduating class?"

"That's her. They got married right after college and live over on Tenth Street. They have three kids, two girls and a boy. He teaches math and metal shop at the middle school. The consensus is they are very happy."

"Wow." Even despicable Ben was able to find love.

"Wow is right." Em held open the door to the hardware store. "So, tell your BFF all about hunky Luke Marshell."

Distraction. That's what she needed, not another conversation about Luke, who had his own life far away to live. Sage went directly to the paint section. "What do you think about this color of blue, matched with rusty brown?"

Em took the color swatches and stared at them. "The blue is too in your face." She handed them back. "I'm not leaving until you tell me everything, starting with, when did you begin to like Luke?"

That's what she got for staying friends with Emerson Finn through thick and thin. Her friend knew everything about her. "Okay, yes, I like him."

"You like him a lot. I can tell," Em said, forming her hands into a heart over her chest.

Jeez. Sage gave her the look. The one they'd perfected over the years that said, *you're pushing it, my friend.* "It doesn't matter how much I like him. He's not staying. When the summer Celebration is over, he's going back to Seattle where his life and business are."

"I knew it!" It took a second for Em to catch up with the fact that Wally Creek wasn't Luke's final destination. "You can't talk him into staying?"

Sage shook her head. Did she want to? That was the real question her friend wasn't asking, thank goodness.

"This blue." Em handed over a swatch. "Long-distance romances can work, you know."

"I know. But tell me this— Could you have put any kind of effort into a new relationship when you were first opening The Oak?"

"You've got me there. I didn't have the time or energy to juggle a romance." Em grabbed brushes and a paint roller.

"And there you have it." She'd known what Em's answer would be, but it still made her feel deflated. If she was going to give romance another try, Luke wouldn't be as good a partner as he was working on her attic or on the parade.

"If I had the right guy, I might have given it a try."

Sage put Em's blue swatch against the rust-colored one. Her friend hadn't exactly said, *go for it. You* can *open a business and start a new relationship. Easy peasy.*

"These will go well together." Sage paid for the paint and supplies.

Em hugged her. Before taking off for The Oak, she whispered in Sage's ear. "Hang in there. It'll all work out."

"I'm sure you're right." She believed that too, didn't she?

She could make a long-distance relationship work if she wanted to. She just didn't know if Luke wanted the same thing. Not so easy peasy.

She hurried home. When Sage got to the house, all the

building supplies had been moved upstairs. She could hear the whirl of a drill overhead as she stepped into the entrance hall. Grabbing bottles of water from the fridge, she took them and her paint supplies upstairs to see if she could lend a hand. And thinking of Em's advice, while she was there, she'd gently quiz the Seattleite on how he felt about long-distance relationships. Especially the ones where the participants were separated by a mere two-hundred-ish miles.

Once he was back in Seattle, he would be as busy with his company as she would be with Amelia's. And wouldn't it be embarrassing if, when she broached the subject, he looked at her like he wasn't on the same page? Asking about his thoughts on the matter might not be such a good idea after all.

Lily's door was closed when she passed by on the way to the third floor. She must still be working on the promised paintings. Passing by without knocking to see if she could get a preview, Sage slipped into the attic before she realized Luke wasn't alone. One wall was already covered in drywall. The drill Charlie held in his hand was silent.

She'd interrupted their conversation. Both men looked in her direction. Luke's brows were pulled together, his expression closed off. Charlie didn't look any more approachable. If she was a girl who was naturally suspicious, which she was—

She lifted the bottles. "I brought water."

"Thanks." Luke recovered first and took the offering.

"I promised Bette I would take a look at her sewing machine." With a quick nod, Charlie put the drill on the floor by the window. "I'll see you kids later."

His footsteps echoed on the stairs.

"What's wrong?" she asked, then studied Luke closely. He did not have the appearance of a happy man. There went her conversation with him about how he felt about long-distance relationships.

"Nothing important." Uncapping the water bottle, his mouth, a very tempting mouth by the way, twisted into a crooked smile. He gestured at the partially finished wall. "What do you think?"

Twisting the top off the other water bottle with a little too much force, she sloshed some of the water onto the floor. "Is there anything I can do to help?"

"Have you ever put up drywall?"

Pretending he didn't understand her question only made Sage more curious. If that's how he wanted to play it, she would go along. She didn't have any experience building things—including a relationship that lasted longer than a minute—but surely she could learn.

"I was out of town the day Hardware Nuts and Bolts was giving a class," she said with a quick smile in his direction while she put the sack of painting supplies out of the way in the far corner.

He laughed, as she intended, and they spent the next few hours with Luke showing her how to introduce screws to drywall. They didn't talk about relationships, long-distance or otherwise, but by dinnertime, they had the walls done and closets framed for storage along one long wall.

Standing back, she admired their work. Who knew, along with her overdeveloped people skills, she also had building skills?

Not bad Dawson. "So, what do you think, teach?"

That got his attention, something she wasn't opposed to at the moment.

"You get an A+. Best student ever."

"I'll bet you say that to all your students," she said, having fun. She put the hammer she'd been using aside.

Verne called up the stairs, "Dinner's ready."

"I know it's hard to believe, but you're my first one," he teased back, then indicated she should precede him down the stairs.

"First student?" she tossed over her shoulder as she descended the stairs. "So hard to believe,"

Maybe that question about long-distance relationships could be broached at another time.

When they got to the dining room, Sage stopped, causing Luke to almost run into her. On easels against the far wall were Lily's paintings. In soft pastel watercolors, their combined dream had been brought to glorious, colorful life.

"Oh, my, gosh." Sage rested the palm of her hand against the base of her neck. Behind her, Luke gave a low whistle.

Lily came into the dining room carrying a bowl of salad. Bette followed with a large pan of enchiladas.

"Lily! Look what you did! These are magnificent."

Lily put the salad on the table, then wrapped her arms around Sage's shoulders. "They did turn out good, didn't they? Is this what you were envisioning?"

"Good? They're so much better than good. They're extraordinary!" Sage walked toward the paintings, reaching out to touch the closest one.

The fireplace was center stage in a large open room. Tables with white linens, tulip-shaped vases, and mismatched chairs filled the foreground. In the background, a counter, glass display case, and culinary delights stretched the length of the room. Behind that was a gray brick wall, interrupted by a simple door, presumably leading into the kitchen.

Sage lost her breath, and not just because the painting was stunning. Luke had stepped up behind her, one hand giving her shoulder a gentle squeeze. A shiver she hoped he didn't notice raced down her back.

His deep voice didn't help matters any. "You are one talented lady, Miss Lily."

"What do you think of the last one on the left?"

As her gaze landed on the painting, Sage had to laugh. It was all of them. Verne lounged in the doorway to the kitchen, an old-fashioned chef's hat perched on his head. Sage sat regally in the foreground at one of the tables, wearing an early 1900s dress. The red skirt with lace edging hung to mid-calf. Lace fluttered at her wrists. A quill draped over the hand that pressed parchment paper to the table.

Bette and Lily stood at flanking tables facing Sage. Lily wore an attractive purple, early century dress; Bette, forest green with matching gloves up to her elbows.

Even Luke was there, behind the counter, placing dollars in an ornate brass cash register. Round wire glasses sat on the bridge of his manly nose. His sleeves were rolled up to his elbows. She had to admit, he was very yummy in the painting, not that he wasn't super-yummy in real life.

"Oh, Lily." It was like stepping back in time and exactly what Sage wanted Amelia's to be. "This one of all of us is going on the fireplace mantel." She spun to face her housemates, her gaze touching each dear face, including Luke's, as she took the chance that he saw the same future in Lily's paintings as she did. "You guys, we can do this."

Everyone talked at once as they gathered close around the extraordinary paintings. Bette and Lily linked arms with Sage. Bette patted her perfectly coiffed hair. "You made me look so good, Lil."

"It wasn't hard," Lily laughed.

Next to Sage, Luke was quiet, but smiling, so maybe he didn't mind being part of her new family and future plans. She nudged his elbow. "Nice picture of you."

"Lily captured you perfectly." He turned that smile on her.

The look in his eyes was cautious, which made sense. He was a cautious businessman. But she'd swear he was happy too.

Warmth flooded her cheeks as Sage turned back to the painting. "I think she made me look sassy." At least that's what she hoped he saw too.

"Sassy is my favorite kind of woman," he said, edging closer to her shoulder.

Tingling awareness sprang up at his nearness. Now was not the time to be thinking of her near miss with Gordan.

The room went quiet. Verne cleared his throat. "The enchiladas are getting cold."

They all grabbed seats. Luke gestured for her to go first. Sage barely refrained from fanning her face. The man definitely knew how to get her pulse rushing.

With Gordan, she'd confused comfortable friendship with over-the-top passion. In comparison, the slash of intrigue that washed over her as Luke sat across from her, his gaze lingering on her face as if there was something special about her he couldn't ignore— Well, it made her feel like a woman standing on the edge of something special.

An excited buzz took over the conversation, mostly about the Amelia's Lily had captured in her paintings. By the time dinner was finished, Sage had a list of things to do. Things she could accomplish even without having the grant check in hand. Things Luke had volunteered to help her with.

~ * ~

By mid-day Wednesday, with Luke's help, except for hanging the lights and organizing her workspace, the attic was completed. She loved the blue and rust checkerboard she'd painted on the floor. Luke helped her move her grandpa's desk and her photo equipment into the space.

Luke and Amelia's Cuppa Tea. They were everything she wanted.

After they moved the desk around until she was happy with how the light from the window beamed across the top of the desk and her computer, she dusted off her hands and stood back.

"Perfect?" Luke asked, humor playing in the sparkle in his blue eyes.

"Yes." Wishing she knew what was behind the sparkle, she made a break for the door. "Charlie's friend came through with construction plans. I'm going to take them to City Hall this afternoon to apply for a permit and, while I'm there, I'll pick up an application for a business license."

"Do you want company?" Luke's question caught her before she reached the door.

She slowly spun back. That would be fun, but she owed him a big fat bear claw, probably more than one, for all his hard work. She didn't want him tagging along while she picked up his treat. "I won't be long."

And maybe when she gave Luke his pastries, she could find the courage to ask him out on a date. If he said no, then she'd know she was barking up the wrong tree, right?

With a quick wave, she went to her room to grab the plans and her bag. The faster she got her errands done, the sooner she could get back.

Her business at City Hall didn't take long. During the time it took to go to The Oak to get two of the biggest bear claws they had, and since Em wasn't there to do it for her, Sage sternly put her foot down on her foolishness. She wasn't a coward. She wouldn't start acting like one now.

The mail-lady pulled up just as Sage parked in the drive and had her sign for a certified letter. She stared at the envelope for a long time. The grant money. This was it.

Hand shaking, she used the end of her key to open the envelope and slipped out a check for enough money to fund her dream. The parade was tomorrow. The grant money had arrived. If she factored in her growing feelings for Luke, it was the best day ever.

Luke's Camaro was still parked in front of the house. Clutching the check to her chest, she raced up to the attic, stopping in her bedroom long enough to dump her shoulder bag on her bed.

She'd almost reached the attic landing when she heard Charlie and Luke arguing.

"Are you sure you want to do this? I can stop the check." *Luke.* And he didn't sound like the same flirty man she'd left earlier.

Charlie said firmly, "Of course, I do."

"At least let me take care of half of the grant." Her grant?

"Luke, we've been over this. The grant was my idea. I want to do this for Sage."

"Then you have to tell her." The sound of Luke's voice came closer. "It's a lot of money to lose if Amelia's doesn't—"

"I have faith. Sage is a remarkable woman. She'll make it work."

The sound of a freight train roaring in her ears, Sage stepped across the threshold. She and Luke spoke at the same time.

"I'm sure she will—"

"Tell me what?" Her heart sank through the floor as both men looked at her with horrified looks on their faces. "What is it you think I should know, Luke?"

Chapter Sixteen

"What is it you think I should know?"

Not since the first day they had met had Sage looked at him like he was an unwanted box of cereal she was about to toss in the garbage. He hadn't liked it then, and he sure as heck didn't want them to end up back in that same place.

"I can explain—" Luke rubbed his chest. He had to fix this before the whole situation got too far out of hand.

"This is my fault." Charlie interrupted. "I promised John and Vanessa I'd keep an eye out for you, and when you got so excited about opening Amelia's— Well, I wanted to help."

Eyes glistening, she held up the envelope. "So, instead of telling me what you were doing, you thought it was okay to go behind my back and do what? Cash in your life savings?"

"You would have said no."

"You cashed in your savings?" She squared her shoulders. "You're damned right I would have said no."

Looking miserable, his uncle shoved his hands in his pockets. "I'm not destitute, Sage. Opening your own business isn't easy, and I just wanted to make sure getting through the initial hurdles would be relatively effortless."

The scolding wasn't completely undeserved, but Luke couldn't leave his uncle hanging out there alone. He took a breath, intending to defend Charlie, but Sage didn't give him the chance.

Turning dark tear-filled eyes on him, she gave the envelope a good shake. "And you. You knew all along, didn't you?"

"Yes." All he could do was take his lumps—better him than Charlie—and lay the truth out on the table. He should have tried harder to change the old man's mind about telling Sage what he was up to.

"He's your uncle. How could you let him do something so crazy." She went very still. "That was why you were against opening Amelia's when you first came to Wally Creek."

"Yes." Her fight not to let tears fall broke his heart. "But my opposition had nothing to do with you personally." Not after he'd gotten to know her and realized she wasn't the kind of woman who was looking for a soft landing in an older man's cushy pockets. "I only wanted to make sure Charlie wasn't being taken advantage of."

"I told Luke you weren't that kind of woman," his uncle quickly tacked on, probably thinking it would help. By the way her brows shoved together, Luke would place a bet that it didn't.

Giving him a cold look, she notched her chin at Charlie.

His uncle straightened to his full height. "Don't blame the boy. I take full responsibility for my decision to keep my actions from you."

"Don't you worry, Charlie. There's plenty of blame to go around." She raised the envelope again. "Do you know how much money is in here?"

Luke looked at his uncle. Charlie nodded in answer.

"Where did it come from?" Her voice went suspiciously quiet, like a rattler's warning before it struck. "Did you rob a bank or something?"

As much trouble as he was in, Luke couldn't help but admire the way Sage took them both on. Her eyes squinted, silently suggesting their explanation had better be dang good.

Charlie shook his head. "Of course not."

Luke had a sinking feeling there was no way he could come out of this with her good opinion of him still intact. "I manage Charlie's retirement portfolio—"

She turned her growing disbelief on his uncle. "This money came out of your retirement account?"

"Yes, but—"

"I can't believe you thought I'd take that money, Charlie Brennan."

"Now, young lady. Don't you use that tone with me." Charlie crossed his arms over his chest. "You can't blame a man for wanting to do something good."

If the situation weren't so dire, Luke might have laughed at their scowling standoff. Sage pinned Luke with an uncomfortable stare as her tone took on a hard edge. "And you let me think I'd qualified for a real grant? You lied."

If it wouldn't get him in more hot water, he'd grab the woman up and kiss her until she couldn't be angry another second. He shoved his hands in his pockets. "Guilty as charged."

"Sage, please let me explain." Charlie reached out but she

would have none of the comfort his uncle offered.

Air leaked out of her anger like a deflating balloon. Luke's stomach twisted. Clearly they had issues, but if he could convince Sage he hadn't meant to be such a putz, he could have what he'd given up finding a long time ago—the love of a woman who would be the shining light of his life. He just wished he realized sooner that he had a chance at that future with Sage.

"I'm sure you had your reasons, Charlie. But, here's the deal. I don't want your retirement money. What kind of person would I be if I took it?" She shifted her tired gaze to Luke. "Do you really think I'm a woman who would rob a senior of his bank account and leave him destitute?"

Luke flushed. He had thought that in the beginning. Trusting others wasn't his top-tier strength. And truth be told, he was practically a virgin in the falling-in-love department.

Her brown eyes snapped. "You don't know me at all, do you?"

Before he could defend himself, she tucked the grant money into his uncle's shirt pocket. "Put this back into your retirement account, Charlie. I'll find another way to finance Amelia's."

"How? You're not going back to the Emerald Star, are you?" Charlie captured her hand and gently pressed it against his heart. He dropped his chin. "I'm so sorry. Do you want us to move out?"

Luke couldn't keep his mouth shut. "Charlie's heart was in the right place."

"I'm sure it was," she said, all signs of friendship and whatever more had been brewing between them gone from her gaze.

Luke had been called to the Dean's office his first year in college for a stupid freshman prank. The Dean had threatened to kick him out of the school if he didn't get his act together. This was way worse.

She turned her gaze on Charlie and said firmly. "I don't agree with what you did, but I don't want you to move out. I love you guys. And Wally Creek." Sage didn't look at Luke or include him in all the love she was giving out. "Just put your money back where it belongs as soon as you can, and I'll try to pretend this never happened."

Without looking back she left them standing, alone in the attic. The loss of her bright spirit, at least for Luke, left him feeling more lonely than the first time his parents had dropped him off at his uncle's all those years ago. The sound of her footsteps on the stairs was a drumbeat on his empty heart.

"I'm sorry, son," Charlie said, pressing his mouth into a straight line. "I should have listened to you. Now, I've gotten us both in hot water."

"We've been in hot water before," Luke said, letting out a heavy breath as he gripped Charlie's shoulder. "Remember that time we missed the train to London and made Mom and Dad miss their flight to Australia because we had their passports? They were so mad at us."

"This is much worse. I've never seen that girl so upset." Charlie's shoulders folded inward. "I didn't mean to hurt her. I just wanted her to start the remodel before I told her where the grant came from. Now, I've gotten you in trouble too."

"I'll fix this. I promise."

"How? I don't think she'll trust either one of us ever again."

Luke hoped that wasn't true. "I'll think of something." He wasn't about to give up.

But nothing came readily to mind as he watched Charlie's usual vitality disappear beneath slumped shoulders as he pulled the envelope out of his pocket. "Guess you'd better put this back in my account."

"I'll overnight it to Gabi. She'll take care of it. In the meantime, I'll see if I can catch Sage."

A car started up. Luke looked out the window. Her Sunbeam drove away.

Or not. His luck appeared to be running out. Not that he'd had much where Sage was concerned. If he was a cursing man, now would be the time to trot out all the bad ones.

Downstairs in the living room, they ran into Bette. "What did you boys do? Sage just left. She was very upset. When I asked her what was wrong, she said to ask you, Charlie."

Mouth turning down at the corners, Charlie sank onto the couch. "I made a big mistake."

"Charlie didn't make the mistake alone. I was part of it too." Luke's heart felt like it'd stopped beating.

He hated seeing his uncle hurt too and could kick himself for the sheen in the old man's eyes. He should have been more firm and insisted they tell Sage the truth sooner. Or just told her himself. Charlie would have forgiven him eventually. He wasn't so sure about Sage.

The truth was, he hadn't put his foot down more firmly because deep down inside after he'd gotten to know her better, he'd agreed with his uncle. Sage deserved the opportunity to see her vision come to life.

He hadn't wanted the old man to be the one behind the funding, which made him the guy who was too focused on business and not farsighted enough to bet on the human angle. Hadn't Gabi warned him enough times that he had to spend less time on work and more time letting folks prove how good they could be? Because he hadn't listened to his partner, and he hadn't told Sage the truth, the two most important people in his life were both in pain.

Bette sat next to his uncle. Charlie started at the beginning and didn't stop until the whole bad story was told.

Charlie downplayed Luke's part, which he couldn't allow. "It's just as much my fault. I knew all along and didn't tell Sage."

"Because I wouldn't let you."

"Well, it doesn't matter why I didn't come clean with Sage. She's hurt, and I can't blame the lady." Luke rubbed his temple. There had to be some way he could fix his mistake.

Bette eased back. "Why didn't you tell the rest of us?"

"That was not good, I know." Charlie stared at the ceiling. "I'm sorry."

"You should be ashamed of yourselves! That girl has a lot of gumption and pride, and you just told her you thought she wasn't good enough to make Amelia's happen on her own," Bette scolded.

Luke winced. A lick of panic washed over him. "Did she say where she was going?"

"Not a specific place." Bette pulled a pillow onto her lap. "Only that she was going for a ride to clear her head."

Dropping into the chair across from the couple on the couch, Luke tilted his head into his hands and closed his eyes. He'd never find her. He had no idea where she would go to sort out hurt feelings. And he didn't want to ambush her. He just wanted to hold her and tell her how sorry he was.

Suddenly, sitting straight up, he grabbed his cell from his pocket and texted, "We need to talk. Can I meet you somewhere for dinner? My treat." Luke flinched and deleted that last part. He didn't want her to think he was using money to gain her forgiveness.

If she would just let him explain, let him tell her he loved her, she'd have to believe him. Wouldn't she? It was the best he could come up with. And he'd make no excuses for his deplorable lapse in good judgment. What he wanted her to know was how much he really admired what she was doing and how he'd come to believe Amelia's had a chance of making it. Because of her belief in what she was doing. And her determination.

Verne and Lily came in from the kitchen. Lily was laughing at something Verne had said, but stopped, apparently knowing trouble when she saw it. "What's going on?"

Between Charlie and Bette, they retold the story. Luke half-listened while he drummed his fingers on the chair's arm, crossing all appendages that Sage would respond to his text.

"Not cool, man," Verne grumbled at Charlie. "You should have told her. Let her make up her own mind."

"I see that now," Charlie shot back.

Luke looked up to see Lily watching him, sympathy twisting the corners of her mouth. "You put Luke in a very awkward position. He loves Sage. She may never speak to him again."

He sat up straight. *Love her?* That was the understatement of the century. What he felt for Sage made words like 'love' seem so tiny. What he knew was that he wanted to spend the rest of his life making her happy.

"Does she want us to move back to Sunnybrook?" Verne pressed his lips together. "I wouldn't blame the poor kid."

Charlie looked down at his hands. "She said she doesn't want us to go."

"Then, we have to help her." Lily sat in the remaining chair while Verne leaned against the fireplace. "How about if we work for free?"

Luke's phone pinged an incoming message. "Finally," he muttered under his breath, but when he read the text, he didn't feel better.

"Go back to Seattle."

Nope. Not on your life lady.

He texted back. "I'll meet you wherever you want."

"Go away. I have a date tonight."

She had a date? Really? With whom? For half a second Luke believed her before he realized it wasn't possible. Not with that Gordan fella anyway. She'd been too busy with the attic, Amelia's, and the Summer Celebration parade to spare time for her personal life. He should know. He knew the signs, having spent a lot of years being too busy building his business to put much effort into anything else.

Besides, unless she'd called the guy, Gordan was back on the Emerald Star.

"I'm not going anywhere until we talk," he replied. If she wouldn't meet him tonight— "See you tomorrow at the parade."

She didn't respond. He hoped like crazy she hadn't blocked his number.

"I can help by sewing the costumes in your painting, Lil. I don't need to be paid for that. We'll call it my contribution. It'll be fun." In her enthusiasm, Bette rose to her feet.

Verne straightened away from the fireplace. "I'll cook. That way she won't have to hire someone."

With Sage on his mind, Luke wasn't sure how he could help. All he could think about was how he'd screwed up, and how right at the moment, he couldn't see a way out. He stood. "I'm going to take off."

Charlie walked him to the door. "I'm sure Sage will come around. By tomorrow everything will be better."

"I don't know, Charlie. It makes me cringe that she found out the way she did. It hurt her worse than if we'd just come right out and told her."

Charlie gripped his shoulder. "That's on me, not you, Luke. I'll tell her that."

"No." He reached for the doorknob. "I mean, yes, but only on your own behalf. I'll talk to her when I see her at the parade tomorrow."

"All right, son." Charlie huffed out a breath. "Good luck."

Luke hugged the old man. There was a new frailty in his uncle's drooping shoulders. "Same to you."

After a restless night, Luke's plan to catch Sage before she got involved in her parade duties did not pan out. He'd stopped and gotten coffee for her at The Coffee Press, but when he finally found her at the beginning of the parade route, she already had a cup in hand.

Emerson, Rickie, and Charlie were gathered around her. The ladies gave him glum looks that didn't particularly welcome him to the day's events. The posse had circled. He held out the extra coffee to Rickie anyway. A battle erupted in her eyes. His feelings weren't hurt. She was loyal to Sage. He was glad to see that. Finally, she took his offering.

"Charlie's going to drive the mayor," Sage said without looking up as she made check marks on her list. In the blocked-off area of the road, parade participants were getting in line.

He looked at his uncle and raised an eyebrow. Charlie's eyes lit up.

Coughing, then coughing again, his uncle swayed slightly. "I don't feel so good."

Handing her clipboard off to Emerson, Sage reached Charlie at the same time Luke did. She put the back of her hand on his forehead. "What's wrong?"

Luke grabbed hold of his arm.

"Headache." Charlie winced. "Dizzy."

"I'm calling 911." Sage pulled out her phone.

While she wasn't looking Charlie winked. "No need for that. If I can just sit down for a moment—"

"There's a bench right behind you." Luke barely refrained from rolling his eyes. Charlie was good. Good enough to be on stage.

He helped the old man to the bench. Stumbling just as he eased himself down, Charlie listed sideways, losing his balance.

"Don't overdo it, old man," Luke whispered close to his uncle's ear.

Charlie closed his eyes, shoulders shaking slightly. "It might take a few minutes before I'm ready to drive the mayor."

"I can drive the mayor." Luke looked over Charlie's head at Sage and saw the moment she got it. He smirked, half-daring her to object.

Staring long and hard at him, she finally nodded. He hadn't won the war, only this skirmish, but for the first time since she'd told him to go away, he began to breathe again.

After that she stayed out of his way, on purpose he guessed, as she went the opposite direction every time he started to head in her direction.

Despite the cat-and-mouse game they played, Luke found himself enjoying the bustle of merchants setting up their colorful booths along the first couple of side blocks off Birch Avenue. The sun was warm, people friendly as he traded Charlie's older model convertible Mustang for his Camaro.

Folks began to claim spots on the sidewalks. Fun, decorative flags popped up as far as he could see along the parade route. Five minutes before the parade was to start, Mayor Tupper joined him by the Camaro. She grinned. A sparkle lit her eyes. "I see you won the coin toss."

Thanks to his uncle's excellent acting. "It was touch and go there for a while."

He glanced over at the bench where he'd left Charlie. Bette sat next to his uncle. Heads together, they held hands. Luke shook his head, wishing *he* was the one holding hands with a certain special lady.

"My bet was on you the whole time," the mayor said with a laugh in her voice as her gaze followed his to Charlie and Bette.

Luke was glad for his uncle. He and Bette were a perfect fit. Charlie deserved someone amazing in his life.

He searched the growing crowd until he found Sage. She was marching toward them, chin elevated, stride long and determined. She wore a flowing summer dress, a colorful geometric print that hung to her knees, and a shirt matching the emerald green in the dress. It was a style he'd noticed she favored. And she was stunning. The sun-splashed highlights in the dark hair that was piled willy-nilly on her head. He would love to untangle the thick waves until they flowed down her back, covering his hands.

The mayor moved close to his elbow. "I've known Sage since the day her family moved to Wally Creek. She's a good girl."

That moment, watching the purpose in her walk, a woman

on a mission with her courage flying high, presumably to give him last-minute instructions, if not another piece of her mind, Luke had no doubt she would find a way to make Amelia's happen without his and Charlie's help.

And he couldn't think of anyone else he wanted to spend the rest of his life with.

Keeping his gaze glued on the impressive woman, he asked the mayor, "So, Mayor, what's with all the flags?"

"They're part of the Celebration. As the festivities wind down on Sunday, the town council will look at all the flags and choose the one that best represents the spirit of Wally Creek and its history. The winner gets a year's worth of their favorite beverage at The Oak Hotel and their flag flying at City Hall."

Surprised, he took his eyes off Sage. "That's a real thing?"

"It's a real thing," she laughed. "And Sage's brilliant idea, several years back."

Reaching them, Sage pinned him with a don't-fail-me stare. "Are you ready? The parade starts in three minutes."

She was calmly pleasant and distant at the same time. He'd expected the space she put between them, but he didn't like it at all. Opening the passenger-side door for Maggie, he stood aside while she got in.

He stopped Sage with a hand on her arm, but she dismissed him and toward the high school band lining up next. This was not the time to beat around the bush. He insisted. "We need to talk."

"I know." She straightened her shoulders. "I'll meet you at The Oak after the parade."

"I'll be there." Expression resigned, she stepped back.

His pulse raced. He could do this. He could convince Sage

they would make a great team. For the rest of their lives.

Not wanting to give her any opportunity to change her mind, he quickly circled the front of the Camaro and slid behind the wheel.

Rickie and Emerson joined Sage as he turned to Maggie and eased off the break. "Ready?"

Nodding, she rolled down her window. Sage gave the signal to start. Luke slowly rolled along, turning onto Birch as Maggie waved to the people lined up on the sidewalks.

Kicking off the Summer Celebration, he honked the horn. The crowd cheered and waved back. It was his first parade and worth every second of Charlie's performance so he could be the one driving the mayor, and while he was at it, impress the parade coordinator, which he had every intention of doing.

Rolling down his window, Luke did plenty of his own waving. Halfway through the parade, Eli, standing next to his Aunt Kendra, saw them and started jumping up and down, yelling to get Luke's attention.

Someday, if he ever had kids, this is what it would be like. His boy, or girl, leaning against their mama—Sage, he hoped— excited because dad was driving the mayor in the town's parade. They would live on Mercer Island in one of the older mid-century homes that occasionally came up for sale. He made a vow right then that spending time with his family would be his first priority.

Leaning out of the window, he gave the kid a fist pump. Eli returned the gesture with a ton of enthusiasm that warmed Luke's heart. After that, the parade was over too soon. Parking not far from the stage where Maggie would perform her mayoral duties, he helped her out of the Camaro. Feeling like a kid himself, he said, "That was a lot of fun. Thanks for letting me be your chauffeur."

"Can I buy you a lemonade or soda for being such an enthusiastic driver?" Maggie got in line at the hamburger food truck.

"Thanks, but I'm meeting Sage at The Oak. I'll grab a drink there."

A knowing smile bloomed on her face. "You'd better get going then."

Motioning him to scoot along, she advanced in line and placed her order.

It would be a while before Sage was finished with her duties, so Luke slowly wound his way to The Oak, stopping along the way to watch the fire engine, horn blaring, and then local barrel racers on their decked-out horses go by. He stopped at several booths, the last one selling flowers. He picked out a white daisy that reminded him of Sage. While he was paying, the parade finished with cowboys cleaning up after the horses and clowns handing out balloons to the kids.

Entering The Oak's dining room, he found an empty table in the corner. Watching the crowd thin, he mentally worked on his pitch to Sage. He could talk to corporate leaders like Edward Portman, and artists and their curators in the creative community like Dara, and not break a sweat. But facing Sage and the prospect that she wouldn't give him a second chance, he had nothing.

She stopped at his table before he realized she'd come in. "Hi."

"Hi yourself." He stood to pull out a chair. He hadn't felt this nervous since he was a teenager asking Tracey Rucci out to the senior prom. He gave her the daisy, wrapped in lavender paper by the seller. "This is for you."

"Thank you." She held it close to her face and breathed deeply. "It's beautiful."

So are you.

Hoping the happy flower would show her how sorry he was about the whole grant debacle, he leaned on his elbows. "I want to apologize—"

Putting the daisy aside, she held up a hand to stop him. The waitress brought the iced teas he'd pre-ordered. "You don't have to. Charlie explained everything."

Luke swallowed back the speech clamoring to get out. "So, we're good?"

"Sure." She eased back, staring at the fingers she'd laced together in her lap. Finally, her gaze met his straight on. "Look, we're friends, so I can be honest with you, right?"

Even though you weren't honest with me. Luke heard the words though they weren't spoken out loud. "Of course. I want you to be."

She nodded. "I'm going to be super busy getting Amelia's up and running. And you'll be going back to Seattle as soon as you're done visiting with Charlie. You have a life back there and shouldn't neglect it. You don't want your firm to fail from inattention."

His heart pounded. "What if I want to be more than friends?"

"Neither one of us has time for anything more." She shrugged and then lifted her chin. "Anyway, we both know that long-distance relationships don't last. When I finally find the right guy, I want it to last forever."

He was the right guy! "But—"

"I'm just not going to have the time I'd want to devote to a relationship." Sage stood. "Goodbye, Luke. Have a safe drive home."

And then she was gone, leaving behind her untouched tea, her daisy, and his splintered heart.

Chapter Seventeen

By Sunday and the end of the Summer Celebration, Sage was beginning to wonder how many more excuses she could come up with to stay out of Luke's way. Leaving the room every time he showed up wasn't what a gracious hostess should do, at least according to Grams, but honestly? She just couldn't be in the same room with the man who'd only pretended to like her to keep his secret.

She'd foolishly fallen in love, but the Luke she'd fallen for wasn't honest, was he? That man was just a figment of her imagination. The guy she'd believed him to be wouldn't have hidden important information that he knew she should know.

She rummaged through her drawers for clothes. Her walkers were under her bed.

Charlie had told her the whole story, but it hadn't changed how betrayed she felt. And Mr. Charles Brennen was still in hot water over his part in the fiasco too.

Having heard him invite Luke for breakfast last night on her way to bed, Sage planned to skip Verne's wonderful pancakes and homemade strawberry syrup before Luke got there and figured out she'd completely fallen for the villain of the story.

She slipped on walking shorts and her favorite tee shirt—the one with the moon and stars spilled across maroon fabric. Grabbing a bottle of water and an energy bar from the kitchen, she ran into Verne carrying a sack of flour and nearly knocked him over.

"Hi." She found her footing, caught her breath, and backed up. "I'm going for a walk." A long walk. "Don't hold breakfast for me."

The line between his brows deepened. "Still on the run, huh?"

"I don't know what you're talking about." There was no way she wanted to stay and talk about anything related to Charlie and Luke. It was cowardly, yes, to avoid them, but she didn't want to run into the source of her failure to see through Luke's not-sincere disguise of here-let-me-help-you. "See you later."

Verne put the bag of flower on the counter. "Uh-huh."

Escaping out the back door, not so fast as to look like she was proving Verne right, but not dragging her feet either, she crossed River Road and took the path along the river. This early on a Sunday morning, not many were out taking in nature or working out their problems to the sound of sneakers slapping against the asphalt path while birds chattered overhead.

Putting her confusing feelings for Luke on the proverbial back shelf was the only way to move forward and focus on finding a way to fund Amelia's. *And* it was the only way to prove to herself—and anyone else paying attention, like Luke—that she *could* open Amelia's Cuppa Tea and make it a success.

She blinked away tears. Then why did she hurt so much? Much more than it should to walk away from the man who, aside from his omission of the truth, was everything she wanted in a lifetime partner?

Luke unsettled her and made her question everything. Especially what she wanted her best life to look like. Ironically, he inspired her to not give up on her dream. And now, unknowingly, he was challenging her to move forward, to make a future that unfortunately couldn't include Luke.

Breathless, she suddenly realized she'd stopped walking. She was standing on the sidewalk just around the corner from The Oak. The place where this whole crazy situation with Luke had begun. Em was just the person she needed to talk to.

Luckily, her friend was behind the check-in counter with Allie when Sage walked into the reception area. "Hi, Allie. Do you mind if I steal your sister for a little bit?"

The teenager looked up from the computer screen and smiled. "Of course not."

Sage went behind the counter, and winding her arm through Em's, tugged her friend toward the office. "I need to talk to you. Privately."

Em closed the door behind them. Sage flopped into one of the cushy chairs in front of her desk. The room was simplicity itself in shades of teal and white, but cozy too, with several of Sage's photographs on the walls. Aside from her grandparents, Em had been her first real fan.

The photos captured the restoration of the rundown building Em had bought and turned into a popular boutique hotel. The Oak was usually booked up six months in advance. Which was exactly what Sage wanted for Amelia's. Her vision was for the tea room to be everyone's—residents and visitors alike—favorite destination.

Em dropped gracefully into the matching chair across from Sage. "So, what's the emergency?"

"Me!" She practically wailed. Pushing the tendrils of hair that had escaped from her braid during her walk off her forehead, Sage told her friend the whole sorry story. From start to finish. Except for the part where she'd fallen madly in love with one of the perpetrators of the mad scheme.

"That rat!" Em said, her lips twitching. "It's a good thing he's leaving town—you did say he was leaving, right?—otherwise, we'd have to hogtie him and send him out of town on a mule train just like they used to do when Wally Creek was first founded."

According to the Wally Creek Historical Society, that happened more than once when miners came to town with their gold and silver and got rowdy after getting drunk at the saloon.

Em was a woman after her own heart and probably why they'd been besties for so long. Running Luke out of town on a mule train didn't sound like a bad idea. The mental visual made Sage feel marginally better. "What am I going to do, Em?

"About Luke or Amelia's?"

Covering her eyes, Sage leaned forward with her elbows on her knees. Almost immediately she lowered her hands. "The bank. Would they give me a loan?"

"Do you have collateral?"

"The house. Grams and Grandpa put the title in my name. They said I could do whatever I want with it." Her mind racing with the possibilities, she eased back in the chair and wondered why she hadn't thought of this solution before. Chalk that up to her inexperience. "I'll see what the bank has to say tomorrow."

"Ask for Sullivan Higgins. He did my loan for The Oak." Tenting her hands just below her chin, Em grinned. "Now, tell me what's going on between you and Luke."

Sage groaned. She'd hoped Em wouldn't catch on to that part of the story. "Nothing's going on. His life is in Seattle. Mine's here. And like I told him, we're both very busy people who don't have time for a long-distance relationship."

Em's brows shot up. "You told him that? What did he say?"

What if I want to be more than friends?

What did that mean exactly? Did he want to be friends with benefits? More than friends, like boyfriend-girlfriend who dated on the rare occasion when they were both in the same town? Maybe become a couple who would talk about spending the rest of their lives together?

It didn't matter. She wasn't going to tell Em what he'd said. Her friend, who saw romance in everything, would want to talk about his intentions to death. "All I'm saying is I'm trying to be realistic and not get in over my head. Like you said, opening Amelia's will keep me busy enough."

"Don't blame your decision on me." Em leaned forward and took both of Sage's hands. She said softly, "My friend, despite what I said, I've seen the way Luke looks at you. Don't be scared."

Sage pulled her hands free. She jumped up and circled the room until she'd put the empty chair between her and her best friend. "First off, I'm not scared." Not so much that she would be silly and let a mere two hundred miles come between her and a serious rival for her heart. "Secondly, Luke's not shy. If he loved me, he would say so straight out." Not beat around the bush.

What if I want to be more than friends?

"Anyway, he's leaving so that's your answer."

"You told him to go. What's the guy supposed to do?"

Stand his ground? Fight for her? Sage frowned. *Don't be an idiot.*

"Can you give me the name of a good general contractor?"

Em sat down at her desk. "I can. And a good electrician and plumber." She pulled up a file on her computer and wrote down names and phone numbers. She handed the slip of paper to Sage. "Can I give you some advice too?"

Pretty sure she knew what that advice would be, Sage pushed the paper into her pocket. She nodded.

"For what it's worth," Em came around her desk. She pulled Sage close with an arm around her shoulders as they walked into the hallway that led to the reception area. "Long-distance relationships might be challenging, but they can work. Don't give up on Luke. From what I can see, you're crazy about him, and I think if you give him a chance, you'll find out he's crazy about you too."

Avoiding the door as it swung open to let in new guests, Sage hugged Em. "So says the woman who doesn't have a steady guy in her life."

A momentary sad look passed through Em's eyes, but then it was gone so fast Sage couldn't be sure she'd seen anything but the hint of laughter reaching out to embrace her. "That's because I have to find the perfect guy first.

"Okay, Miss I-don't-need-a-man-but-I'm-happy-to-give-my-best-friend-advice-on-the-subject."

That made Em laugh. "Now, I wouldn't go quite that far."

"I'll let you know how it goes at the bank." Sage gave Em another quick hug before walking out into the sunshine.

Em had given her a lot to think about. Was she giving up on Luke? While he'd had his secrets, he'd kept them to protect Charlie. She was doing the same, wasn't she, by not taking his money? And he wasn't even her blood relative.

By the time she made it back to the house, she was second-guessing everything. What he meant by telling her he wanted something more. Insisting the man leave Wally Creek and go back to Seattle—

When she walked into the house, it sounded like the gang was gathered in the kitchen. Maybe this was her chance to recant her demands and find out if they had a chance. They'd still have the distance thing to work out, but if Em was right—Sage hoped she was—how far apart they lived wasn't a problem they couldn't fix.

"We have to make this up to Sage." That was Lily.

Sage stepped into the kitchen. "Make what up?"

Charlie motioned her to sit by him at the breakfast bar. "The whole grant thing."

"You guys don't have to worry about that," she reassured him as she pulled the slip of paper from her pocket and sat next to him. "Em gave me a list of tradespeople we can trust, and tomorrow I'm going to the bank to see if I can get a loan against the house."

Charlie put a gentle hand on her arm. "Are you sure? I can still—"

"I'm sure, Charlie." She patted his arm. He was a sweet man and a true friend. No way would she take advantage of his kind nature. "Um, did Luke come for breakfast?"

Bette brought her a cup of her favorite tea. "He did, but he didn't stay long. Said he had to get on the road."

Back to Seattle. "I see."

Not really, She'd told him to leave and he had. So why was she so disappointed?

~ * ~

Luke had been back in Seattle for three days when he finally gave up trying to put Sage out of his mind. He couldn't forget the woman, and he wasn't going to move on without her in his life. It just wasn't going to happen. Even though she didn't want to have anything to do with him, all he could think about was the way her dark eyes sparkled when she laughed. The way she was all in when she got her sights set on an outcome. How she couldn't say no to the book club members who'd become more like family than people she enjoyed reading books with.

That was his problem. He wanted to be part of her tribe too. He wanted to be the one who helped things go smoothly and who always had her back. He wanted to grow old with her. But how could he do all these things if she wouldn't give him a chance?

"Are you ready for the meeting with Edward?"

Luke stopped tapping his pen on the pad where he'd jotted down his thoughts for the meeting. He looked at Gabi. She hadn't questioned him when he'd returned suddenly without notice. Apparently, she wasn't going to wait any longer. The look in her eyes that she got when she went into interrogation mode was not a good sign.

"As ready as I'll ever be, I guess." He looked at his notes and all around the margins he'd scribbled *Sage* over and over. What was wrong with him? Huffing out a fed-up breath, he tore off the top sheet, wadded it into a ball, and tossed it into the trash bin.

Gabi dropped into the chair in front of his desk and wove her fingers together in her lap. "Okay, mister. That's it. I've left you alone long enough. Tell me what's going on."

He rose from his chair and stalked toward the window. Usually, the view soothed him. Not tonight.

"Does your bad mood have anything to do with Sage Dawson?"

Shoving his hands in his pockets, he spun to face her, giving in to the sympathy pulling at the corners of her mouth. "I thought coming back here would help me forget Sage."

"Of course, you can't forget her. Love doesn't work like that." Gabi joined him by the window. Streetlights across the skyline began to pop on. "From where I'm standing, you're crazy about her."

"What makes you think that?"

She bumped his shoulder. "Because I'm crazy about Dara. I know that feeling of not wanting to be away from her and how miserable I get when I am."

"Well. You guessed right. I'm more than crazy about Sage. I love her more than anything in this world. She, however, doesn't want to have anything to do with me after the grant fiasco."

"Yeah, that was unfortunate. Have you talked to your uncle?"

"Not yet. I thought I'd let the dust settle first."

"Your meeting with Edward is tomorrow afternoon. You'll have to set this little bump in the road aside for the moment. If you can." she said. She'd called it right from the beginning. Less work and more play would make Luke Marshell a happy puppy. It had if he didn't count the fact that Sage had kicked him out of her life.

Gabi turned completely serious. "There's something else I want to talk to you about."

He went back to his desk and sat down. "Should I order Thai food first?"

"None for me." She sat across from him. "I want to talk to you about our plan to open an office in London."

If Sage thought Seattle was too far from Wally Creek to sustain a relationship, she would undoubtedly nix the idea of London. And with Charlie throwing his lot in with Sage and Amelia's—there was also his uncle's feelings for Bette to consider—no way would he be able to talk the old man into joining him in Europe.

He couldn't blame Charlie. He felt the same way about Sage. London was not his next move. Not right now anyway.

"What are you thinking?" he asked Gabi.

"Dara and I have been talking, and well, if this deal with Edward goes through, we'd really like to live in England. While you were in Wally Creek, a gallery in London offered to exhibit Dara's sculptures. She's so excited, she already accepted the offer. I want to be the one to open the London office."

"Are you serious?" Luke sat up straight. "That's wonderful!"

"It's the opportunity of a lifetime." Gabi grinned, jumping up to pace in front of his desk. "We could keep our head office here in Seattle, but, with today's technology, it won't be hard to do my part from London. You could have a satellite office anywhere you wanted as well. And we could hire a manager to coordinate the offices and the staff we'd need here and in London."

She stopped long enough to give him a calculating look before continuing. "If you're serious about Sage, you need to be here, or better yet, in Wally Creek. You are serious about her, aren't you?"

The tension dropped from his shoulders. He matched Gabi's grin. "Oh, yeah."

"So what's our plan?"

"Our?"

She sat on the edge of his desk. "Of course our plan. You're not so good at the romance stuff."

"Haha. I'll come up with my own plan." Circling his desk, he pulled Gabi to her feet. "You go home and tell Dara you're all moving to London. I'm guessing you'll want to take Fran with you?"

"Absolutely. There is no way my grandmother will stay behind. She spent a summer in London when she was a young woman. She loves it there."

He walked her to the door. "I figured as much."

Shooing her off, he went back to the window, but it wasn't Mercer Island he saw fading into the sunset. It was Wally Creek, with its charming main street and friendly community. It was Sage, standing in Amelia's brimming with customers coming and going. The Oak, with its striped awning. And Luna's Books, where in the future he hoped to buy all the books he could read.

Gabi wasn't far off the mark. He wasn't good at romancing the ladies, so whatever he came up with, it had to show Sage he wasn't a fly-by-night kind of guy and that he intended to stay by her side until they were both so old, the only energy they had left was holding hands as they strolled down Birch Street.

He didn't have to run MR Investments from Mercer Island. He could keep the building for the majority of his staff. Make the adjustments he needed to coordinate additional offices. And in the beginning, run the business from Charlie's cottage instead of putting the house on the vacation rental market. At least until he found a place more suitable.

He'd have to discuss rent with his uncle. That would be a fun conversation. Luke snickered as he sat at his desk. Time to come up with a new plan. He had to come up with something really good to convince his lady she wasn't getting rid of him just because she'd ordered him to leave town.

Chapter Eighteen

The next day, hoping she was feeling a little more charitable toward him than when she'd closed him out, Luke texted Sage. The funny thing about her brushoff—not ha-ha, but more like this can't be happening right now—was that Mercer Island didn't feel like home anymore.

By noon, when she hadn't responded, he called his uncle. It was a relief to know someone who knew someone.

"Hello." Charlie's voice sounded chipper, a far cry better than the last time Luke had talked to him.

"Hi, Uncle Charlie."

"Luke! So glad you called. I was going to ring you up today. I've got news."

He glanced at the time on his monitor. He had an hour before he was due to head to the conference room for his meeting with Portman, which gave him plenty of time to quiz Charlie.

He rocked back in his chair. A creak broke the silence. Checking on the old man was his primary motive, of course, but there was no reason why he couldn't see how Sage was doing while he was at it. "News? Are you doing okay? How about Sage?"

"I have other news too, but she's doing good. Full steam ahead after the bank gave her the thumbs up on the loan. She found a general contractor with great references. They're almost ready to start the downstairs remodel."

Luke rocked back and forth. "So she's cut you a break on the whole grant thing?"

"Yeah, we're good." Luke didn't miss the relief in his uncle's voice. "You haven't talked to her?"

"I've tried, but I'm still in the dog house." Which he intended to remedy as soon as possible—if he was ever able to get her into a conversation that didn't include silence on her part.

When he was a kid he'd longed for a solid, dependable life at home. It wasn't that his parents hadn't tried to give him a reliable home life. It was more that things were always up in the air—their jobs, where they would live after another move, different schools every year—

So, after he left home and finished college, he'd built a substantial business with the most dependable partner he could get, in a city he loved and never thought he'd want to leave. He'd had enough of moving around in his younger life.

Then he met Sage, a woman who was his exact opposite, a total risk-taker. His need for control and stability was why he'd been against her opening a business that was so fragile. Yes, using Charlie's money was also not right in his book, but the possibility of watching her dream fail made him uneasy because he couldn't offer his uncle or Sage any guarantees. His thought back then was that Amelia's couldn't possibly offer anything remotely resembling longevity or a stable, steady income. He'd meant well, but it wasn't his finest moment, for sure.

Charlie, of course, had been all in from the beginning. But his uncle deserved to have a rock-solid retirement with no financial worries. That's where they'd both gone off the rails. And it'd taken him a while to figure out Sage didn't want predictable. She wanted the adventure of building something from scratch that would last.

Now it was his turn to take a risk, as uncomfortable as that might be, and convince the sweet woman that he was worth her taking the leap. *They* could be her adventure that would last a lifetime.

"Luke?"

"Sorry." Luke cleared his throat. "You were saying?"

"I think Sage is coming around. It could be the right time to come back and offer to help with the construction on the house. It would give you the opportunity you need to sweep the lady off her feet."

Subtlety wasn't his uncle's middle name.

"Not yet, Uncle Charlie." The heavy sigh on the other end of the line warmed his heart. No one could say his uncle didn't care. "You were saying you had news?"

There was a momentary silence before Charlie said softly, almost as if he couldn't believe what he was about to say, "Bette and I are getting married."

Luke practically catapulted out of his chair. A thunk sounded behind him as the chair abruptly righted itself. "That's wonderful! Congratulations! You old coot. How did you manage to talk her into marriage?"

He remembered a conversation on the riverbank while he and Charlie were fishing the last time. Bette never talked about it, his uncle had said, but she was a war widow who was more comfortable keeping her distance than inviting folks in. Charlie had been pleased they were friends, and though he didn't say more than that, it'd been clear his uncle was smitten.

So he'd gotten what he wanted. Not surprising since Charles Brennan could be like water against stone when he wanted something bad enough. Drip, drip, drip until he wore the other person down. Look at the situation with Sage.

"Well, for one thing, I asked her," Charlie said dryly.

"Would you look at that? It's been fun talking to you, Uncle, but it's time for my meeting with Portman." Not a complete fabrication.

"Okay, Luke. I know this isn't what you want to hear, but don't wait too long. Sage won't be single forever." With that unnecessary reminder, Charlie hung up.

Luke let go of his breath as he went to his favorite thinking spot. Despite the clouds scattered across the sky, summer warmed his view of the neighborhood. It was one thing to make plans for a date at the altar, and quite another to get shoved in that direction. Luke laughed. Truth was, he didn't mind the shove.

He would love to return to Wally Creek and the woman who made his heart race faster than a horse heading for the finish line. He could see himself living in the small town with Sage, ultimately running MR Investments from there, raising a family in the close community. A boy and girl, maybe two girls who were just like their mother.

Sage would be the best mom ever. Their children would never feel left out. Together they could give them all the stability and love they could want, mixed with a large dose of adventure too.

But he had things to do first. Groundwork to lay. He didn't want to return to Wally Creek and Sage until he was certain he could win her heart for the long haul. Luke had never been anyone's knight. He'd like to be hers. But first, he needed a better plan than showing up out of the blue without the most compelling offer.

Gabi walked in. "What's so funny?"

"Something Uncle Charlie said. Sometimes he's impossible."

"But you love him."

"That I do." He picked up the folder he'd prepared for the meeting. "Is the contract ready?"

Gabi patted the large, heavy envelope she held close to her chest. "Got it right here."

"Let's do this, then." Standing aside, he let her precede him out of his office.

She glanced at him over her shoulder. "How's it going with Sage?"

"I'm working on a plan." At least he would be as soon as he came up with the plan.

Gabi spun to face him. "You haven't talked to her, have you?"

He shoved his free hand in his pocket. "How do you suggest I do that when she won't answer my texts or return my calls?"

Gabi's sharp, astute gaze softened. "You'll think of something. You always do." Squeezing his wrist, she turned back toward the boardroom. "Just don't take forever. That girl's a great catch."

"Have you been talking to Uncle Charlie?" he asked dryly.

She laughed as they entered the meeting room. "No."

They'd just finished setting up the table when Gabi's phone

pinged. "That's Edward. He's almost here. I'll meet him in the lobby and bring him up."

He nodded, but Luke's mind would not settle down. It was ridiculous. There had to be some strategy he could come up with that would change Sage's mind. Even as he paced in the boardroom, nothing came. Nada.

How was it possible that he knew exactly what to do and say to convince Edward Portman that MR Investments was everything Portman Technologies needed in an investment firm, that MR, and he in particular, brought something special to the table, but he couldn't come up with a single idea or actionable strategy that would convince Sage to see that together, they were a perfect partnership?

Gabi arrived with Edward. As much as he could, Luke put his dilemma on the back burner. Determined to make his potential new client feel at home, he motioned for Edward to have a seat. "How was your flight to Seattle?"

"Good. I'm only here for three days, then I fly to Georgia to check up on a plant we're opening there."

"I appreciate you fitting us in."

As soon as Gabi sat across from Edward, Luke got down to business. Edward was a tough negotiator, not a surprise. It took some time, but he convinced the CEO that MR Investments was just what he needed as his company grew into its next phase. They came to terms they could both agree on. Their meeting concluded, they stood and shook hands on the new deal.

Before his recent trip to Wally Creek and meeting Sage, Luke would have been thrilled to have brought Portman on board and double thrilled that the acquisition would take MR international. Instead, all he could think about was how to get back to Sage and change her mind.

Not wanting to go home to his empty house where there was nothing to stop him from spinning in circles, he asked, "Can I buy you both dinner to celebrate our new partnership? There's a nice little home-style restaurant just down the street."

"Not me." Gabi grabbed her notes. "I need to finish up this contract, and I have a date with Dara I don't want to be late for."

Edward put his glasses in the inside pocket of his suit jacket. "I'm staying with Eliza and her family. I promised to be home for dinner, but I wouldn't mind stretching my legs before I grab a taxi."

"There's a park nearby with a walking path." Luke led the way out of the boardroom.

They were on the sidewalk before the older man spoke again. "How's your uncle?"

Luke glanced his way. "Charlie? He's fine."

"When we were setting up this meeting, Ms. Rendal mentioned there was a situation that needed your attention. Wally Creek, I think she said?"

Luke got them both coffees at a kiosk on the next block. "Wally Creek is where my uncle lives. He and his friends are temporarily staying with a friend who's opening a new business."

"It's none of my business, but I got the impression from Ms. Rendal— Is this friend someone special?"

So special. "I'd like her to be, but I was a putz."

They found a bench off to the side of the path and before Luke could stop himself, he was telling Edward all about Sage, including the part where she was not happy with him, but not why. It felt good to get it off his chest and talk to someone with an outside perspective.

"You know, my wife loved flowers. Until the day she passed, when I did something stupid, I could always get her to forgive my ineptness by giving her flowers. Her favorites were white lilies." Edward patted Luke's shoulder, then stood. "It's time I got that taxi." He winked and held out his hand. "Good luck, Luke."

Luke sat back down and watched Edward stroll away. Suddenly, he knew exactly how he could convince Sage that together they were the real deal.

Leaning back, he put his hands behind his head and stretched out his legs, ankles crossed. He closed his eyes, lifting his face to the late afternoon summer sun. For the first time since she'd told him to go home, the smile he let spread across his face reached his heart.

This could work.

No one was more surprised than he that love was actually worth it. He had a couple of things to do to put together his brilliant plan. And it began with a quick phone call to Charlie.

~ * ~

Sage couldn't get Luke Marshell out of her mind. Of course, she couldn't. But why? They were so different. Despite her best efforts, his coolly analytical outlook sidetracked Sage every time she had to make a decision about Amelia's. How irritating was that? He liked to think he had all the answers. Let her be the first to tell him he didn't, except she wasn't talking to him, was she?

And he was uber-logical. Another thing they didn't have in common. She much preferred flying by the seat of her pants. At least she used to.

To be fair, and Sage had to be, he also wasn't rash like she could be. He was genuine. She never had to guess what he was thinking. That was refreshing. He was unexpectedly kind and handy to have around. Look how the big city businessman had jumped right in to play carpenter and help update the small-town girl's attic.

He never once complained. And though he hadn't come right out and said so, she could tell he loved Wally Creek as much as she did. He was sweet with Rickie and her son. Without prompting, he'd quickly stepped up for the parade committee. Even pulled some shenanigans with his uncle so he could drive the mayor in the parade. He was persistent and reliable, both big hits on her list of what she liked in a man.

How could she not love all of that about Luke? Was he the guy she'd been looking for all along? They disagreed on the future of Amelia's because they came at problems from opposite sides of the room. Was that a bad thing? It hadn't felt good at the time, but she was beginning to wonder.

Flinging the covers back, she staggered to the bathroom and stared at her face in the mirror. Her hair was a mess. Tired eyes looked back. Lips drooped at the corners.

Luke wasn't perfect but then, neither was she. Sage smirked. Turning on the faucets until warm water poured out, she splashed her face. Blotting the water with a towel, she met the tired gaze in the mirror.

"You could fight for your guy just like you're fighting for Amelia's." If she would just admit, Luke *was* her guy.

It'd been a week since he'd gone home to Mercer Island. His absence had left her unexpectedly unsettled. And just a little bit lonely. Kind of like she didn't fit in her own skin.

Why was it only now that she realized he'd taken her heart with him?

She hung the towel over the shower curtain railing. So what? The general contractor was coming first thing to take a look at the changes she wanted to make. She would have no time to be lonely or to yearn for a guy she'd sent on his way.

Back in her room, Sage changed into jeans and a rose-colored tee shirt with a field of wildflowers growing at the base of a snow-capped mountain painted across the front. She pulled her hair into a ponytail. When she got down to the kitchen, Verne and Lily were already there. Charlie and Bette came in moments later.

"We have a surprise announcement to make." Charlie was holding Bette's hand. "We're getting married!"

"Congratulations!" Lily squealed, hugging Bette.

"That's no surprise," Verne grumbled, wiping his hands on the towel slung over his shoulder. "What took you so long to pop the question?" He targeted the question at Charlie. "You two have been mooning over each other for the better part of six months."

Echoing Lily's sentiment, Sage wrapped her arms around both women. "I'm so happy for you."

"Your turn next," Bette whispered in her ear.

Lily followed up with. "If you play your cards right,"

Sage pulled back. "I don't know what you mean."

"Yes, you do." Lily took both her hands. "Luke is crazy about you. Surely you're not going to let him get away? You'll never find another man who fits you as well as he does."

"She's right." Bette grabbed a bottle of bubbly from the pantry.

Stunned into silence, Sage searched the cupboards until she found five champagne flutes and put them on the counter. Lily *was* right. She'd been in such a rush to protect her heart, she'd been rash to drive him away. All because, for the first time in her life she'd been afraid to dive into the unknown.

She'd always thought the kind of love her grandparents had would come easy, like the gentle waters of the slowly moving Wally River. Not that it would be like the raging rush of rolling white water as it plunged over a cliff.

Sympathy shined from Lily's eyes. Sage shrugged. Before she could come up with something that didn't sound like a woman who was wandering, lost in love's dessert, the doorbell rang.

"I'll get that. It's probably the general contractor." Anything to get out of the present conversation. When she opened the front door it wasn't Hank Stevens but a gangly, teenage boy holding a beautiful, potted hydrangea. "Hello. Can I help you?"

He pushed the plant into her hands. "These are for Sage Dawson."

"That's me. Who are they from?"

"Couldn't say, ma'am." *Ma'am?* "I'm just delivering flowers."

The kid headed back down the drive to a white van parked at the curb. There was a mural of flowers painted on its side. Closing the door, she carried the plant into the kitchen.

"Those are pretty." Bette poured the bubbly, then touched a finger to the pink flower ball fading to lavender. "Who are they for?"

"Me." Confused, Sage looked up to find four sets of eyes on her.

Bacon sizzled on the stove. Verne was mid-flip in a batch of pancakes.

Lily gestured toward the white envelope peeking from between two large blooms. "Are you going to read the card?"

As she pulled the envelope free, Verne turned off the griddle and they all gathered around.

"They're probably from Grandpa and Grams," Sage slipped the small card from the envelope. "I talked to them last night and told them about applying for the bank loan—" Her eyes caught on the message. *Sage, I love you because . . .* and signed by— "I'll, um, be right back. I forgot something upstairs."

Quickly shoving the card back in its envelope and then into her pocket, she spun away from her friend's curious gazes and dashed up to her new office where she pulled the envelope free before sinking into the chair.

Leaning on both elbows, she turned the white square over and over. Why would Luke send her flowers?

Because you won't answer his texts?

How couldn't he possibly love a girl he didn't really know?

Placing the envelope in the middle of the desk, the scribbled Sage Dawson side up, she rose from the chair and circled the room. Everywhere she looked she saw Luke in the work he'd done to make the old space into something fresh and fun and usable. For her.

After he left, Charlie and Verne had brought up Grandpa's old desk and chair, and a matching wooden table. She and the ladies had carried up her photography equipment. She'd already started to gather pictures for a collage of the book club friends that she wanted to hang in the tea room.

Why in the world did he love her?

When she'd pulled out the photos of Charlie and Bette, sorting them in the order she'd taken them, it was so easy to see the progression of their love. Heads close together as if Charlie was whispering a secret in Bette's ear. Arms linked as they sat on a bench watching the parade. Fingers woven together, a promise to stay together for the rest of their lives. Now, that was love.

Her own love story was less obvious. A breakup. Coming home to Wally Creek to mend her broken heart, which it turned out wasn't all that broken. Meeting a stranger who wasn't the enemy she'd thought he was at the beginning and the secret he kept to himself. Luke sending text after unstoppable text. Now make-up flowers.

She went back to the desk and took the card out of its envelope.

Sage, I love you because you know what you want and don't hesitate to go after it. Luke.

He loved her for that, even though she'd pushed him away.

Leaving the card in the middle of her desk, she went downstairs and found Charlie talking to Hank. They were going over the structural changes she wanted. Determined to stop thinking about Luke and his beautiful hydrangeas— how did he know they were her favorite?—after grabbing the potted plant from the breakfast bar and putting it on the coffee table, she joined Verne and Hank's conversation.

Bette and Lily watched her from the entry to the dining room, arms crossed, brows raised, smiles playing at the corners of their mouths.

Sage gave in. "They're from Luke, but don't read too much into it."

"See, I told you," Lily said to Bette, excitedly smacking Bette's arm with the back of her hand.

Rolling her eyes, Sage went back to finishing her planning session with Charlie and Hank. By the time she went to bed that night, she was exhausted. And had only gone up to her desk to run a finger over the card, oh, three or four times.

The next morning, she'd barely finished her coffee and french toast when the doorbell rang. Deliberately not racing to answer the summons, she finally opened the door to find her flower-bearing messenger holding another potted hydrangea, this one pale green blooms edged in dark cherry-red.

This morning the teenager didn't look so bored. "Sage Dawson?"

"Yes," she said, eyeing the plant with suspicion even as sudden excitement rippled up her spine.

He handed her the plant. "These are for you."

"Thanks." A white envelope winked at her from between two blooms just beginning to open. Closing the door, she grabbed the envelope and slid out the card.

"More flowers from Luke?" Lily asked. They'd all followed her from the kitchen.

Sage, I love you because you inspire me. Luke.

Lily shifted from one foot to the other. "What does he say?"

Pressing the card against her racing heart, she wagged her finger at her audience. Without missing a beat, she put the plant on the coffee table before dashing up the stairs to place the new card next to the one from the day before.

She sank into the chair. Did she dare believe Luke? Did she want to believe him? Should she thank him? For the flowers? Text him or something?

Her phone rang. Her heart skipped for a second until a voice that wasn't Luke spoke.

"Sage? It's Sullivan Higgins." The banker handling her loan. "Your loan has been approved. Can you come in today to sign the papers?"

For the first time, Amelia's Cuppa Tea paled in comparison to the fact that Luke was going to a lot of trouble to convince her he loved her. It was a good thing she had a long list of things to keep her busy. "Of course."

The next day, Sage couldn't help it. She woke up early and was waiting over bacon and eggs, and a cup of Verne's strong coffee, hoping the hydrangeas weren't a fluke. Verne, Charlie, Bette, and Lily waited with her, chatting quietly.

"Charlie and I want to get married here. In the backyard."

Everyone agreed that a garden wedding would be perfect. Right on schedule, the doorbell rang.

Sage jumped up and bolted for the door. Her teenage delivery boy was there holding out a stunning white hydrangea. When he saw her, a grin splashed across his young face. "This dude really likes you."

I hope so. "Thanks." Taking the plant, she laughed and put the plant next to the other two. With shaking hands, she opened the card as her roomies made themselves comfortable on the sofa and chairs.

Sage, I love you because you make me want to be a better man. Luke.

You make me want to be a better person too, Luke.

"So, what's on the agenda today?" Charlie asked, his eyes twinkling.

Straightening her back, she made one last effort not to fall harder than she'd ever fallen for a guy. "Sign the loan papers, then move everything except the kitchen into the garage for the time being. Hank wants to get started on demolition tomorrow."

"Where should we put the hydrangeas?" Lily asked, as innocent as a whole chocolate cream pie begging to be eaten in one sitting.

Grabbing all three, Sage held them tight so she didn't drop

the surprising gifts. "Back porch for now."

Lunchtime wasn't even close when she gave up pretending she had anything else but Luke on her mind. There was no question about it. She was crazy in love with the man. He was her grand passion after all. Luke was the one.

He'd finished the job of capturing her heart with his first *I love you* note. It was time to tell him, he was the light of her life, and she loved him because he was strong, and caring and because he didn't give up easily. He was the only guy she could imagine spending the rest of her life with.

In the living room, they were all still packing up the bookshelves when she said, "Can you guys finish up here? I have to go to Seattle."

Lily bounced up onto her toes and clapped her hands. "You go, girl."

Charlie pulled her into a big hug. "Welcome to the family. Go pack your bags. We'll sort the rest of this and keep an eye on things while you're gone."

"Thanks, Charlie." She pulled away and faced the others. "Thanks, all of you."

Not wasting any time, she was back down pulling her suitcase behind her in less than fifteen minutes. Stomach full of jitters, she hugged and kissed each dear member of the book club who'd become a part of her family.

When the doorbell rang, she laughed. Leaving her bag where it stood, she opened the door. Her breath caught. It wasn't her flower delivery boy. Luke stood there with the biggest, stunning blue hydrangea in his arms and a goofy grin on his face. His dark hair was windblown. Blue eyes drank her in, sending her heart rocking, even as the nerves in her stomach kicked up like a small twirl of wind.

"You're here." She couldn't believe it.

He glanced behind her and saw her suitcase. "Going somewhere?"

"Are those for me?" she asked at the same time. "I was coming to Seattle to tell you thank you for the flowers. I love them."

He stepped into the house edging her backwards. "Is that the only thing you love?"

It was now or never. "I love *you*, Luke. With my whole heart."

He handed the hydrangea to Charlie. Taking her face in gentle hands, he said, his voice deep with emotion, "Marry me, Sage."

Before she could say, oh my God, yes! he drew close for a kiss. "I love you because you are the best adventure I could ever go on. Marry me and I promise all our adventures will start right here at home in Wally Creek."

Pulling on his forearms, she tugged him close so their breath mingled. "Yes, I'll marry you, Luke Marshell. I love you because you help me bloom where I'm planted. I promise to be yours forever."

Fireworks went off his eyes. Their lips met. Love short-circuited her racing heartbeat.

Wild cheers erupted behind Sage. Reluctantly breaking free, she curled into Luke's chest. Together they faced the best family a girl could ever have. She was home.

All that was left to do was say, *I do.*

About the Author

Susan is an award-winning author of bold, brave, heartwarming romance and women's fiction. Like all children of military families, she spent much of her childhood moving from one duty station to the next. Did it turn her into a nomad? Heck yes! Along the way, she acquired a love of ancient history and myth, and admits to collecting way too much useless information. She writes whenever she can. Her favorite things are that first cup of coffee in the morning, spending time with her family and friends, reading, watching movies, gardening, taking pictures of nature and architectural marvels, traveling, and remodeling the house that after thirty years, is finally starting to feel like home.

You can connect with me on:

- https://www.susanlute.com
- https://www.facebook.com/SusanLuteBooks
- https://www.pinterest.com/sidella
- https://www.instagram.com/authorsusanlute
- https://www.bookbub.com/authors/susan-lute

Subscribe to my newsletter:

- https://www.susanlute.com/new-release-alert

Also by Susan Lute

Other Books by Susan Lute

Angel Point Series
The Sheriff's Baby Bargain
Wanted by the Marshal
The Christmas Makeover
The Valentine Project
The Fake Marriage Proposal

Sellwood Series
A Fool For Love
A Merry Little Sellwood Christmas, A Sellwood Short
Sealed With A Kiss
Love Lessons

Falling For a Hero Series
A Girl Named Jane
Jane's Long March Home
A Marine's Christmas Proposal, A Short Story

Rosewood Series
The Return of Benjamin Quincy
Be My Valentine? A Rosewood Short

The London Affair

The Broken Road

The Girl Most Likely To: An Anthology
    The Gift Of Christmas: An Anthology
    Gifts From The Heart: An Anthology

Oops…We're Married? A Silhouette Romance Classic